First Stone

By L. D. Bergsgaard

First published by Dog Ear Publishing
4010 W. 86th Street, Ste H
Indianapolis, IN 46268
www.dogearpublishing.net

ISBN: 978-1-4575-3241-2

Library of Congress Control Number: has been applied for

This book is printed on acid-free paper.

This book is a work of fiction. Places, events, and situations in this book are purely fictional and any resemblance to actual persons, living or dead, is coincidental.

Printed in the United States of America

Acknowledgements:

A special thanks to Donna for her outstanding editorial contributions and to Diana Stanley for her thorough review before going to press!

Monte Gruhlke, you've once again made a magnificent cover.

Thanks to all.

CHAPTER ONE

(Wednesday)

*M*y nipples nearly burst through my cashmere sweater. My skin blushed from my chest right up to my ears which had turned the color of ripe tomatoes. Other than my ex-husband, only one man, Clayton Johansson, could make my body react this way.

The cause of my stimulated condition which I viewed in the mirror over Clayton's shoulder was not what you might assume. My intercourse with Clayton Johansson was anything but romantic. Anger, not sexual desire, is what caused this most embarrassing effect. I wanted to flee. Run out of my own office to escape this tyrant — this little dictator. I had an unobstructed view of myself in the full length mirror hanging on the closed office door. The more attention I paid to my physical response the more pronounced the unwanted reaction.

"Kathy, I just don't understand why you can't change the wedding schedule. It's not such a big deal." Clayton leaned forward towards my desk, moved my inbox aside and raised his voice even though he was only inches away — like a rapist closing in on his victim.

"Clayton, you have no idea what you are asking. There is the caterer, photographer, florist, pianist, vocalist, and a dozen other players all of whom will be ready on Saturday at one o'clock." I leaned back in my chair thankful I could be afforded some shelter from behind my desk.

"So they wait a few hours. What's the … big deal?" Clayton gawked at my breasts as he dragged the 'big deal' out of his curled lips like a wolf making the final lunge at the cornered rabbit.

"What's the 'big deal' about making your cousin, Ron, wait until Saturday evening or Monday morning? It's not like he's going anywhere." I was ashamed of my sarcasm.

"There is your attitude I've been talking about for months. You don't stiff your best paying customers when they need special attention."

He prodded the air with his finger. If I had been two feet closer, he would have hit my chest.

I glanced at my watch, the one with the inlaid diamonds my ex-husband had inscribed, "Forever, my love" on the back. It was twenty-to-three and behind a closed door we'd been at this for a half-hour. We had made no progress and never would until I submitted to Clayton Johansson. Such was the last comment my predecessor made to me, "Kathy, you can't win a battle of wills with Clayton." Clayton, I later learned had literally driven my predecessor out of town.

"Kathy, today's Wednesday. Ron can't wait until Monday. I can't wait until Monday. I'm traveling to Minneapolis on Monday."

"Friday, will Ron be ready on Friday?" I asked. I could put a rush on the matter and have it together in a day. There wasn't much to get ready for Ron.

Clayton ran his fingers through the close-cut curly black hair. He crunched his forehead creating rough ridges. Like my ears, his face had turned red. Beneath his bushy mustache, his lower lip quivered. I thought he might stroke out. I hoped he might stroke out. "No, this just happened yesterday. You can't rush things like this. By god, you of all people should know better ..." His fist hit my desk with a bang that made me jump.

I held my trembling hand up to stop the onslaught of insults and reprimands I knew was forthcoming. I surrendered to his will. Clayton Johansson had a short fuse and no filter on what spewed forth when he had been challenged. Today, I'd poked him one too many times. Fleeting thoughts of shoving Clayton off the Pelican River Bridge raced through my mind. It had become a recurring fantasy.

"I told the council you'd be difficult to handle..." This had become Clayton's favorite remark. I supposed to put me in my place and make me feel grateful I even had a job.

"Clayton! Enough! Ron will be buried Saturday after the wedding. Tell the undertaker, Saturday at four." I left my office with Clayton still parked and fuming in front of my old oak desk. If he stroked out, at least I wouldn't be faced with the dilemma of providing CPR.

CHAPTER TWO

(Wednesday)

*T*he *two-story brick rectory Father Gallo calls home* is only three blocks from my office. Headed towards the lovely house, I slowed my escape from Clayton to a stroll as I passed St. Mary's Church. It is the largest of the five churches in Pelican Falls. It is also the only one built of brick in a style similar to those of the Black Forest area in Germany. St. Mary's was constructed to be the most important structure in town and for sure it will be standing long after the simple wooden structures of the Protestants see the wrecking ball. When St. Mary's bells toll everyone in town takes notice. After the second block was behind me, I forgave myself for being so abrupt with Clayton and asked forgiveness from above for the pleasure of imagining Clayton screaming and tumbling off the covered bridge towards the rushing river. I felt guilty such a vision gave me so much pleasure.

The walk was refreshing in the cool autumn air and I began to regain some composure. Somewhere a Pelican Falls resident or two had lit fires to the leaves they'd raked into piles the size of a VW Beetle. Burning leaves are my favorite smell on earth, leaves and baking chocolate chip cookies and baking bread, and horses' noses. Turns out I've many favorite smells. I breathed in deeply and recalled the days of my youth when fall meant rolling in piles of crackling leaves my grandfather had spent hours raking and I spent minutes scattering. Autumn is the most pleasant time of year, especially in Northern Minnesota. The blood-sucking insects and suffocating humidity gave way to sunshine and cool nights before campfires. A half-block away, the school bell sounded signaling the end of recess for the children whose banter carried across town like a sweet melody.

"Kathy, wait up!" It was Tammy's husky voice which sounded so pleasant to my ears. Exceptionally pleasing after the bitter tongue lashing I'd just experienced from Clayton.

I turned and watched her approaching at a slow jog. Like one of those fancy models in the shampoo commercials, her long auburn hair bounced with each step. Tammy and I first met a little over a year ago when I picked her up at the bus depot in Fargo. She was traveling from San Francisco to take her first post as a minister in Pelican Falls. I liked her immediately. She was the sister I never had. Outwardly, we couldn't be more different. I've always favored the tomboy look, clad in jeans and a sweater as my typical work attire. I have blonde hair, cut short, eschew makeup, and earned the nickname 'Kat' in my younger days. Tammy mirrored the Julia Roberts look but with freckles. She was never without her makeup and by her own description was 'top-heavy.' Inwardly, we were soul sisters.

We embraced each other with the excitement of Wheel of Fortune winners. "Thanks, I needed the support."

"Clayton Johansson?"

"He makes my life miserable and now his cousin, Ron, got drunk and rolled his pickup into Bullhead Lake. He's had at least six other accidents and four DUIs. This time Ron wasn't so lucky. This time he drowned."

"There is a funeral sermon Spurgeon, himself, would find challenging. What would you even say?"

I replied in my best Sunday morning voice which was an octave lower than normal, "'If St. Peter needs a good bartender, the bells will be ringing to welcome Ron Johansson.'"

"What was the problem with Clayton?" Tammy asked.

"The Olsons have a wedding this Saturday and Clayton demanded the funeral precede the wedding," I explained.

"Oh, that would add cheer to the nuptial vows. I can see it now. The newlywed's limo pulls up behind the hearse."

"Clayton even offered to leave the funeral flowers to decorate the chancel."

"What class!"

"Life without Clayton, it is what I dream about," I offered.

"I know what you mean. My tormentor has struck again, too," Tammy said. Tammy's face saddened.

We paused under the wooden eave of the front entrance to the priest's home. Tammy dug into the side pocket of her Coach purse. Her slim hands pulled out an orange-colored paper, folded several times. She handed it to me. Her hand was shaking. I unfolded it and read to myself, 'I know what you are and so will the rest of Pelican Falls!' I handed it back to Tammy. She was wiping a tear from her eye. Soon the mascara would smudge. I gave her a Kleenex and she dabbed her cheek with the tissue and took a couple of deep breaths.

"Do you have any idea who sent this?" I pulled her close wishing I could heal the hurt written all over her face. She shook her head.

"Am I interrupting something?"

I didn't have to turn to know the speaker was Pastor Randy Peterson. I didn't have to look at him to know there would be a scowl on Randy's face, there always was. The scowl was plastic surgery gone bad, Tammy once teased. I believe it was more likely a reflection of Randy's inner soul.

I released Tammy and greeted Randy with more enthusiasm than he knew how to handle. Pumping his hand with two hands and slapping him on the back. Tammy followed my lead and we both watched Randy harrumph and brush past letting himself into the rectory. We giggled. It is ironic an old grump like Randy could bring cheer in the face of heartache.

Tammy and I took secret delight in tweaking Randy's nose. He was a bit too pious, too righteous to ever feel close to. I suspect Randy never wanted to be friends with Tammy or me. He would have had to drop his suspicion we were trying to 'steal his people' from him. It would be an understatement to assert Randy was insecure. You'd never guess from his appearance or demeanor. Randy was tall and sturdy. Some said he looked 'Presidential.' Twice he'd run for a seat in the state house and twice he had been soundly defeated. Evidently, the 'Presidential' look couldn't trump the scowl or his pious nature which he wore like a bad suit. He certainly was as vain as any politician I'd ever met. Lately, Randy had taken to shaving his head rather than allow his receding hairline to be seen. He sported a grey goatee and was never without a suit, always black, and always accompanied by a red tie and an American flag on the lapel.

I trailed a now composed Tammy as she followed on Randy's heels – his wingtip shoes with the plastic cleats clicking on the maple floor like a tap dancer on the Lawrence Welk Show. Randy brushed by the housekeeper and into the library. We stopped and handed our lightweight coats to Maria, a tiny dark-skinned woman with waist length hair who never spoke. She maintained eye contact with the hardwood floor. Maria shuffled away with our coats in her arms. Tammy put her hand on my shoulder.

She pointed to my chest. "Girl, you've got to do something to cover them up."

I looked down at my ivory colored sweater. I had not recovered from 'my condition.' I suppose the chilly wind I faced during my walk didn't help the matter. I chased the little housekeeper down and recovered my windbreaker. My day was going badly enough without having Randy staring at my breasts.

Tammy was smiling when I returned. She had a twinkle in her clear green eyes. At least my misfortune had cheered her up. It has always amazed me how others can find amusement in a fellow human's sad predicament. But then I am no better.

Father Gallo was seated in one of five cozy leather chairs form- ing a circle in the middle of the library. Aldo Gallo was old enough to be my father and at times I thought of him as such. He was the father I never had.

Aldo was a tad pudgy. At five-six, even a couple of pounds exac- erbated his appearance of being overweight. Aldo's snow-white hair and rosy complexion gave me confidence in the words he so carefully weighed and spoke in a deep bass voice. When I was down in the dumps, perplexed, or just needed to vent, it was Father Aldo Gallo who was always willing to spend an afternoon in front of the library fireplace. Sometimes, when Randy wasn't present, we'd even enjoy a glass of brandy or the high-octane chokecherry wine Aldo brewed in the basement.

Randy was already seated and checking his faux Tag Heuer wristwatch as Tammy and I settled into oversized chairs next to each other. In the far corner, the ornate Bavarian grandfather clock struck three and three carved bears chased a *fraulein* in and out of the *haus* carved in the clock face. Father Gallo cleared his throat and suggested we get started with the third meeting of the ad hoc committee of the five ministers representing the churches of Pelican Falls to share in the planning of the community celebration of the Thanksgiving Festival. It was, after all, only a few weeks away.

CHAPTER THREE

(Wednesday)

*T*he antique clock pealed announcing half-past three when Morgan Wentworth blew in breathlessly. The fifth member of the committee arrived wiping his face of sweat with a small green towel embroidered with the Pelican Falls Country Club logo.

"So, you started without me?" Morgan enjoyed initiating a conversation with a potent offense, especially when he was in the wrong. "I ran over from the church, a ten mile route ... down to the Old Mill, up to the dam, and back by the game refuge. Full of geese headed south." He stripped his silver nylon jacket off and tossed it on the floor next to the fireplace. He plopped into the chair like a recalcitrant teenager. "What'd I miss?" he asked and then added sarcastically, "... if anything?"

"Oddly enough, we made progress without you," Tammy said with an equal dose of sarcasm. She didn't suffer boorish behavior at which Morgan excelled. I remember when Tammy first saw Morgan at Connie's Pelican Inn. He was introducing himself to everyone in the café. "Look, Kathy, it's John Edwards," she whispered in my ear. Morgan did indeed resemble Edwards, the forlorn politician. Perfect hair, a leading man's face, and what is more important he had the presence of a rock star. When he entered a room, his charisma filled the air causing folks to turn their heads and stop conversations. There was no doubt, Morgan, like John Edwards, had the entire package. Well, he was missing the gorgeous blonde at his side and substance. Someday, he'll find the blonde but I doubted he'd add substance to his character. Sometimes I can be too critical ... I'm working on changing.

Father Gallo lowered his reading glasses and picked up handwritten notes from his lap. "So far, these are the suggestions we four clergy have for our ecumenical contribution to the proposed community celebration ..."

"I have some ideas of my own. We're going to have a 5K run with medals for the top finishers. I'm organizing a coed flag football game for Saturday. I have the high school field reserved. Additionally, our church bowling team has issued a challenge for a tournament ..."

Father Gallo interrupted, "I can add your suggestions although they will have to join the others we already have to be voted on by this committee."

Morgan looked like he'd just been sent to the corner with a dunce cap. In typical Morgan fashion he recovered quickly and continued, "Of course ..." not meaning a word of it, "and the church ladies will have a bouya and everyone is welcomed to contribute ..."

"What's a bouya?" Randy surprised us with his question. I thought he had dozed off ten minutes earlier. Tammy giggled. I hoped Morgan didn't mean Bouya in street parlance as defined by the Urban Dictionary. I believe Tammy had the same concern. We often did share a single mind or so it seemed.

"It's like soup or stew. One of my parishioners brought his grandfather's bouya kettle up from St. Paul. They used it for years at St. Luke's and made enough to pay for the Luther Leaguers to go to New York each year. It'll cook enough to feed a multitude ... just like the fishes and loaves. We'll charge five bucks for a pint of bouya thereby paying for the flag football officials and the 5K race T-shirts, and ..."

Morgan's ego and plans always exceeded the size of Pelican Falls. Our community was like most of those in Minnesota's lake country. We have a high school and a small business community on Main Street. The big box stores in Fergus Falls, Detroit Lakes, and Brainerd robbed the community of any hope for growth. Most residents made their major purchases fifty miles away. Morgan had been the pastor of the Community Church for the last six years. While the other four churches were losing members or holding steady, the Community Church was growing. I know this because the growth chart prominently displayed in his mahogany paneled office looked like Bernie Madoff's profit projection – before he went to jail. Tammy and I sometimes speculated on how much longer

Morgan would be satisfied with our simple town. Tammy predicted it would be Morgan's search for a suitable mate which would cause his migration to The Cities. I suggested Morgan's ego was simply too large to be contained in our small town.

"Morgan, let me just read the other suggestions, then we can take a few days to consider the options and meet here next week, if our schedules permit."

"Of course, I was just trying to be helpful. I didn't know you had so many other ideas," Morgan said in a voice lacking any sincerity.

I looked at Tammy. She was thinking the same as me. If Morgan had been on time, he would have known what we had already presented. It was just last week when we met and agreed to return today to present each of our suggestions and finalize the plans. I penned a note to myself, 'PATIENCE!!!!'

Father Gallo brought the scribbled list close to his face. He misplaced his cheaters again. I didn't want to embarrass him by pointing out they were on top of his head. "Here's what we have:

"1. A community garage sale.

"2. A bake sale. Last sale we made nearly three hundred and had no reported illness.

"3. A bonfire with music and marshmallow roast. The Buddy Holly imitator will come down from Lake Park to sing.

"4. Bingo, Beer, and Brats. My idea and/or a contest to break the Guinness record for most turkey legs cooked in a single day.

"5. A costume contest with a prize for the best dressed turkey.

"6. A hay ride. Arnesson over by the state park has two Clydesdales and a large wagon. He comes darn cheap, too.

"7. A pet costume party followed by a blessing of the pets. I'll do the honors.

"8. A maze made of straw bales and pumpkins at the end for prizes.

"9. A raffle. Jerry the butcher will do up a special batch of bacon and sausage. The Lions Club made over five hundred on their raffle and you can make a lot more if you add beer and strong drink.

"10. Races: a sack race, a turkey catching contest, a greased pig catching contest. And finally,

"11. A reading of the Legend of Sleepy Hollow by Tammy Chang, Pelican Falls' finest actress."

Morgan wore a pained looked on his face. Randy scowled, he always did. Tammy shrugged. I have to admit Morgan's suggestions were grander although if we held a carnival and had items 1 through 11, it would be acceptable and more appealing than Morgan's money making bouya. I said so.

Randy frowned. Morgan grabbed his jacket from the floor and stood, "I have to go. We have a racket ball tournament tonight and I have to drive to Fergus to get the trophies. Consider my ideas as still being on the table." He finished his sentence in the hallway.

Randy was on his heels. "I have to get to the nursing home before supper is served. I need to give the sacraments to Mrs. Hokenson. Her daughter said I best get there before the meal. She gets such bad gas, you know. It's the pills, you know. She takes a handful with her dinner and bloats from the pills." After providing too much information, Randy left.

CHAPTER FOUR

(Wednesday)

*W*e stared at the crackling fire framed by the fireplace stone facade. It was peaceful in the room as the flames flickered on the stained glass chandelier. The housekeeper arrived and lit several candles, all without uttering a word. I sometimes wonder if she spoke English. I never asked, however, I believe Aldo brought her up from Mexico and perhaps without the benefit of a visa.

The room held the aroma of old leather and burning oak logs. I processed what I'd seen and heard over the last few hours. I asked for forgiveness of the malicious thoughts which had occupied my mind. I asked for guidance to still my critical tongue. Pastors were supposed to be immune from such sinful ways. So I bounced back and forth between harboring those spiteful thoughts and bearing a crushing guilt for doing so. Father Gallo interrupted a guilt phase.

"Brandy?" He rose from his chair and headed for the hidden decanter he kept behind the rosewood panels. The bottles clinked as he spun the Lazy Susan shelves filled with bottles and crystal glasses, a gift from Mrs. LeBlanc, the widow lady who resided in Pelican Falls' grand home on the steep hill overlooking the town.

He returned with three crystal goblets filled with a lovely amber colored liquid, "Hennessy V.S.," Aldo told us and with a slight bow. He served Tammy and then me before taking his seat. I sniffed the bouquet. It was indeed "the good stuff" my unsophisticated nose affirmed. I took a sip. It burned nicely going down. I pushed back into my chair and watched the flames dance to an unheard melody on my glass. Twirling it slowly, I envisioned Clayton's face burning amongst the logs. I chased the thought from my mind.

"Brandy, come here boy!" Father Gallo sang out in a chant-like cadence breaking the silence I'd so enjoyed. A basset hound, ears dragging on the rich burgundy-colored carpet, waddled past my chair.

communion or whose turn it is to mow the lawn. I posted those matters in enormous hand printed letters on a chart in front of Olive's desk. All in all, the office and the church ran smoothly.

My modest-sized office with its freshly painted burnt orange walls smelled of a lovely lavender and sage candle which Olive kept burning. I turned on the green accountant's lamp and looked at the scribbled messages piled neatly in my inbox. I sat only long enough to call the group home where Benny lived and inquire whether he had pants on when he departed this morning. The director wasn't certain as she didn't see him leave. She did assure me a pants check would be instituted before allowing Benny to depart on the handicap bus. I considered calling the bus company but thought better of it. The tub-of-lard driver was likely down at Connie's café recounting the story of delivering a half-naked Benny to the church steps. Perhaps I would run into him later.

As I walked briskly towards Main Street, I couldn't help but look back at my church home, Grace Lutheran. The building was not nearly as spectacular as St. Mary's, however it did reflect the character of those largely Norwegian immigrants who built her. She was humble in character and modest and practical in style and size, like the first parishioners. Even if they'd had a fortune, it would not have been spent on something frivolous. Last year, I found and read the handwritten journal of the first pastor, Ole Knutson. Pastor Knutson wrote of a faction who thought the steeple was unnecessary. What would they use such a big structure for? You couldn't sit in it or even store the nativity crèche in the narrow appendage. However, the steeple crowd must have won the debate because Grace Lutheran had the tallest steeple in Pelican Falls. I stood for a moment and admired the pristine white clapboard and her fine clean lines. She reminded me of an ancient Viking boat, small and sturdy, and I was proud to be her captain. I turned back and picked up my pace to get to lunch. My stomach was growling.

Father Gallo perched on a chair in the window of Connie's Pelican Inn. He tapped on the glass as I walked past. Brandy, his faithful dog, was parked outside on a piece of green shag carpet which

Connie put there for the dogs, along with a water bowl and a treat hand-delivered by Connie. She loved dogs even though she was allergic to all four-legged creatures.

Connie, with her bottle-blonde hair worn up in a style favored by homecoming queens and bridesmaids, waved to me when I entered. Dressed in a too-tight pink waitress get up and a white apron she looked like she'd bought the last French Maid costume at K-Mart. She stood behind the framed-in grill slinging pancakes and eggs, the last of the morning senior special – two eggs and a cake or toast for a buck ninety-nine. The place was warm and smelled of sizzling bacon and flapjacks.

"Good morning, my dear. You look none the worse for wear from our ad hoc party sans the party poopers." I patted the priest on his back and he returned a broad smile. He had perfect teeth or false teeth. I haven't the courage to ask or the eye to tell.

"Yes, we had fun … fun indeed. We should make it a habit. Every Wednesday we could have a counseling session with Tammy. I love that girl, so witty yet insightful." He sipped his coffee with a noticeable slurp ending in a whistle.

"We should. We can help each other," I said as I poured my sixth cup of the day.

"Along those lines, I have something to tell you although it's best done in private. Let's eat and then take a stroll."

Within a half-hour, I'd polished off the blue plate special or as Connie called it "the commercial," about a pound of mashed potatoes smothered in thinly sliced beef and dark gravy with a side of cold green peas in cream sauce. Father Gallo put down a bowl of knefla soup and a short loaf of Connie's homemade rye bread topped with fresh honey butter.

"I'm afraid I've put on a few pounds since my slender days in Mexico," the priest said out of the blue perhaps triggered by guilt as he buttered his fourth slice of bread.

"You're just right. A fellow needs to have a little stored away as the winter approaches." I looked past Aldo at the mirror which ran the length of the café. I looked better than I felt. Too little sleep, too much worry I told myself. I fussed with the bangs of my short blonde hair. I checked my makeup. It was minimal and acceptable. I have always been critical of myself when confronting a mirror … ears too small and pinned back like an annoyed mare, eyes too large like a fawn, thin lips, and a nose my cousins called equine-like. Perhaps that explains my attraction to horses.

"Are you listening to me?" Aldo asked impatiently and rightly so.

"Yes, of course," I replied even though I wasn't as my attention had been drawn to performing a critique of my appearance. It was a nasty habit I vowed to work on.

"When I was in Mexico, I smoked three packs a day and was so nervous I didn't have an appetite."

"You were lucky to get out of there with your head still attached," I said recalling his stories of harrowing escapes and assassination attempts.

"Indeed. Smoking didn't seem to matter so much when I estimated my life expectancy in days. Never take on the drug lords or corrupt politicians, I learned. Perhaps that's why the problems which I come across here in Pelican Falls seem so petty – at least I'm not staring down the muzzle of an AK47."

"I know what you mean. The five years I spent with the convicts at the New Life Ministries were like getting a PH.D. in interpersonal problem solving," I offered.

"I imagined they had almost insurmountable problems."

"They did. Although, if we gathered everyone in Pelican Falls together, we'd find the same problems. It is just the inmates had so many at one time. Unemployed, chemically dependent, three women with five children all wanting child support, products of abusive broken homes, and bankrupt. That would be typical on day one and day two, after they rob the local liquor store, it gets worse and the list grows until they give up."

We grew quiet, each lost in our own recollections of earlier lives.

We were about to leave when Lard Ass, (that's what all of his friends and enemies called him and the tattoo on his shoulder affirmed: 'Lard Ass' inside a bleeding red heart) the bus driver for the disabled and handicapped strolled past with three of his halfwit cronies. His smirk as he looked at me drew the sharp remark I'll never regret. "Hey Lard Ass, you think it's funny to send Benny to work without his pants? Watch your back pal, payback is a bitch." His smirk fell to his knees as he dragged his heavy posterior out the door.

"My, must be some story there," Father Gallo said in a hushed tone.

"I'll tell you later." I dropped a ten for both of us and slid out of the booth. I left the money on the table because Connie always refused to accept payment from Tammy, Father Gallo, or me. "God wouldn't want me to take your money, honey," she often said like a little poem.

Thunder clapped as we left the café and rousted the basset hound. He needed no leash as he was loyal to the priest and too slow and unmotivated to go anywhere unattended. Not that he wouldn't follow a total stranger with a T-bone in his pocket, it's just such strangers are a rare sight in Pelican Falls. The maple leaves waved in the imperceptible breeze and some fell like flitting butterflies to the ground. A single golden leaf landed on Brandy's head and balanced for the entire block ending at the mill pond. We three shuffled through the red and yellow piles of leaves without exchanging words, just enjoying the grandeur the Creator provided and the warmth of friendship which remains unspoken.

A few drops of rain rushed us to address the matter my lunch partner hadn't wanted to discuss in the café. "This must go no further. Well, you may share it with Tammy but no one else. Are we clear?"

I'd never heard him sound so stern, so somber. "This sounds serious." I stopped by the pond where a dozen or so mallards unleashed a cacophony of quacks and squawks while they swam to the other side of the pond leaving a wake among expanding ripples created by the rain drops.

Father Gallo watched the ducks. "I know who Clayton Johansson's mistress is!" He said without looking at me.

"What?"

"Clayton Johansson's mistress is Gabrielle Durand, the owner of the Curl Up and Dye hair salon."

"I know who Gabrielle is, but how do you know this?"

"This is the difficult part of our conversation. I can't disclose the details of how I learned about this relationship." He continued to gaze at the mallards.

"I must admit, I'm not surprised," I finally said. "She's such an attractive woman, I don't see what she would find attractive about him," I said making my own assessment from a woman's point of view.

"Alpha Dog. Lefty is an Alpha Dog. Women, some women, find it to be an attraction," Aldo offered.

"Very true. Look on the back of any motorcycle ridden by an outlaw bandit and there will be a drop dead gorgeous gal hanging on to the slob for dear life." I spent way too much time working with the convicts and know that experience has tainted my outlook on life, although maybe I've just become "street wise."

"My brother, he's ridden with the Bandito's motorcycle gang since he was twenty. These last few years he's slowed down, nonetheless, each Christmas I receive a photo with a new babe riding behind him on the back of a new Harley. Well, except the five years he spent in Leavenworth. Those five years, I got the cards made by the prisoners in the craft shop, quite nice I might add," Aldo said.

"Getting back to Clayton and Gabrielle. Why do you tell me this? I know you're not given to gossip."

"Gossip, oh no, no indeed not for purpose of gossip. I was just thinking about what Tammy said last night," Father Gallo answered.

"You mean about helping each other with our problem parishioners?"

"Yes, exactly. There is nothing in scripture which would prohibit us from doing this. I'd submit helping our neighbors with a problem is in line with scripture's intent."

"So, how would I use this information to get my problem with Clayton under control? You're not suggesting blackmail?" I asked.

"No, of course not. As I pondered this question last night, it occurred to me that two fine female minds could be counted on to …"

"What you mean is two women could use their cunning ways to conjure up a recipe to cook Mr. Johansson's goose."

"Exactly!"

"As I was driving home last night I had several thoughts about our discussions as we sipped your fine brandy," I said.

"Such as?"

"Specifically, Tammy, you, and I should join hands to get rid of our problem parishioners," I replied.

"Oh, good lord no, I'll not be a party to murder," Father Gallo exclaimed too loudly considering three of the town's most prolific gossips were walking nearby.

"Shhh," I said putting a finger to my lips. "I'm not talking murder. I'm just saying we could help each other. Who else can we even turn to? Tammy and I will help you by persuading Mrs. LeBlanc to stop her protest of your sabbatical to the Vatican. You and I will help Tammy by finding the malicious note writer. And Tammy and you will help me get control over Clayton."

"But how …"

"Anything short of murder," I said, although I might make an exception for Clayton.

CHAPTER SIX

(Thursday)

*T*he horses, cats, and dog had been fed as the rain trickled to an end and the sun set amidst a brilliant pink hue on the last of the thunder clouds. I stood at the threshold of double doors of the red barn, decked-out in a faded yellow rain slicker and red barn boots decorated with painted daisies and caked with manure. I breathed deeply relishing the rain-cleansed air. Across the yard stood my home, 'small but cozy' I'd taken to calling it. The home had been built by immigrants who struggled to farm land that held more trees and rocks than promise. When I bought it, the realtor called it a 'fixer-upper' and I hired a local man, also a fixer-upper, to remodel the home and barn. He was a superb craftsman who produced a masterpiece from little more than a wooden rectangular box. Of course he stayed long enough to be named as a dependent on my tax return. In hindsight, I shouldn't have fed him so well. In the end, he created a superb cottage with the wraparound porch I'd always dreamed of owning.

In the distance, Tammy's red and black Mini Cooper bounced down the potholes of the half-mile driveway to my turn-of-the-century farmstead I called home. I waited with anticipation.

"I'm over here, in the barn," I called when she dragged herself from the little coupe. She waved and pulled a cardboard box from the backseat. Dodging puddles, she waltzed towards me wearing a broad smile and carrying the box. My golden retriever, Max, sprinted to meet her, nearly knocking her down with his exuberant greeting. I'd been working with him, since he was a pup, five years ago, to manage his style of welcoming visitors. It seemed he'd only gotten worse, or perhaps better from his point of view. After all, he was a Golden and had a reputation to live up to.

"I brought enough to get started!" she said.

"Come into the barn. Set the box on the table."

We both moved to the rustic wooden table that served a multitude of purposes around the barn. Most recently I used it to apply leather conditioner to the tack. I cleared the saddles away and Tammy set the box on the rough and stained surface.

"All right, after our discussion this afternoon I did some shopping at Second Life Thrift store and some closet diving into my own wardrobe. I think we have enough to get you started." She unfolded the box flaps and spread out her treasures. I watched like a kid at Christmas while she laid each item on the table. Soon the box was empty and the table was full.

"Okay, first the shoes. She always wears spikes. What size do you wear?" She held up a pair of red shiny heels.

"Nines, sometimes, nine and a half," I answered looking skeptical at the pair she'd brought.

"These are ten and a half. Try them on." She handed the flimsy shoes to me.

I kicked off my soiled rubber boots and easily slipped into the shoes. Not since my senior prom had I ventured into such footwear. There was an inch gap at my heel. "Too big," I pronounced.

"No, they'll do. We'll stuff toilet paper into the toes. They are closed toes and no one will ever notice. You just have to wear them for what, maybe an hour?"

"What else did you bring?" I began to paw through the merchandise. I selected a turquoise ring and matching bracelet. "She doesn't wear these, does she?"

"Every year she makes a trip to Tucson and loads up on turquoise at the Gem Show."

I put them on and instantly felt like a cowgirl, despite the spiked heels. I selected a slender silver bottle of Charlie perfume. I sprayed an exorbitant amount in the air and walked into the cloud. Max retreated towards the door and Smokey, the grey cat, jumped from his perch in the hay loft and scrambled outside.

"Now I understand why Gabrielle is so irresistible to Clayton. It's this alluring perfume. It works like magic. How will I ever keep Clayton from attacking me?" I feigned a swoon.

"That's the point, my dear. Clayton gets one whiff of the potion and he'll lose control. He will be like putty in your hand," Tammy said as she rolled the pretend Clayton in her finely manicured hands.

I plopped into the director's chair bearing my name. "Tammy, do you think this will really work?" It had seemed like such a possibility when we hatched this plan behind the closed door of her tiny office at her church earlier this afternoon. Ideas rolled off our tongues when armed with Father Gallo's revelation, we imagined laying siege on Clayton. Now, with the props of our theater laid out on this humble table in the barn, I was not so confident and felt more than a little silly, if not petty.

"Look, we agreed, you can't just confront Clayton. You can't just brace him with the allegation, 'Clayton, I know you're an adulterer and I'll take no more of your guff.'"

"I know that would too bombastic. It would incite him to who knows what end," I said.

"Trust me, all my years of studying human behavior tells me this will work. It's psychological warfare at its best. We'll do it slow. It will be more painful and more effective, trust me."

"Okay, show me the rest of your prizes."

I spent the next thirty minutes or so trying on the dresses, the blouses, the scarves, the sunglasses, and a padded bra that Tammy didn't explain how she'd acquired. I had hoped she hadn't swiped it from a neighbor's clothes line. When we were done, Max cocked his head and let out a small groan.

"That's enough for today," I declared. "Let's go inside. I'll put water on for tea. It should take the chill out of our bones." The temperature had dropped into the mid-forties as a north wind introduced a fast moving cold front.

I took the heels off and hopped into my muck boots. Tammy laughed as I traipsed towards the house, wearing a Gabrielle inspired short skirt accented by the bright red rubber boots. The kitchen was warm and smelled of burning candles I couldn't resist at the last church craft sale – lavender and sage. The new propane gas stove fired up nicely since the fuel truck finally made a delivery. I darn near burned out the microwave waiting a week for the delivery man to visit so I could resume cooking on the range. Tammy disappeared into the hallway and down to the modest bathroom, a stool, shower and a sink was all I'd gotten around to installing after tearing out the old cast iron fixtures. Someday, when the budget allowed, I planned to put in a claw-footed tub. I dreamed of the long luxurious baths I would take surrounded by candles and rose petals and through the window an unobstructed view of my three horses loping across the pasture.

"Tea's on," I announced. I removed a bag of Mrs. Peterson's peanut butter cookies from the freezer – another treat from the craft and bake sale. Joined by Max, then Smokey and Tammy, I sipped the brewed oolong tea and passed bits of cookies to my pets.

Tammy's face seemed strained and worried.

"What's troubling you?" I asked.

She reached into her purse, a Gucci, she changed purses like most folks change underwear, and pulled out a folded piece of paper. "I got another note today. She pushed it across the table. I picked it up and read out loud:

"I'm tired of waiting for you to leave. You have until Halloween to fly on your broom away from Pelican Falls to join the rest of the evil witches. UNTIL HALLOWEEN!!!!!"

I read it twice and was repulsed with the vitriolic words. Who could be so vicious and evil within our Christian Community?

"I swear on all that is holy, we – you and I – will find the person and put an end to this hateful speech. You have my word." I reached across the table and pressed her hand into mine. A tear fell from her check and onto my hand. I cried and we embraced.

CHAPTER SEVEN

(Friday)

Clayton Johansson was in rare form even by his own loathsome standards. I'd arrived early at my office, skipping a morning ride on my favorite buckskin mare. I had a wedding, a funeral, two Sunday services, and a noon potluck to prepare for and all in the next three days. I decided to take them on in that order when Clayton breezed past Olive as she was mid-verse of the *Old Rugged Cross.*

He tossed several pages of paper on top of my already cluttered desk. "That's what I want you to say at Ron's funeral. I wrote it last night." He stood leaning over the desk into my personal space. His nose flared and eyebrows crunched. Both badly needed trimming. Funny what a gal notices even in stressful times like this.

I picked up the handwritten eulogy and read:

"Ron Johansson was a saint of a man, godly, good and generous ..."

Then it got worse, more outrageous glorification of a man who by most accounts was a moral degenerate bent upon drinking himself to death.

I rose slowly and seductively moved around the desk. I went ever so slow, trying my best not to sprain an ankle in the red spiked heels yet still get a couple of hip swings into play. I moved in close to Clayton. He didn't give an inch. Nor did I, instead sauntered closer and thrust the fictional account of Ron's life back into Clayton's puffed-up chest.

"New perfume?" He ogled my breasts padded by the uplifting bra. I had left open the top button of the sheer blouse. He raised an eyebrow like the lechers I knew from my college bartending days. I bent at the waist, hips jutted out and sinfully close to Clayton.

"Now Clayton, is that anything to ask? As for these words you've penned, I'll write my own. I've got some special phrases I use for the likes of Ron."

He held his hands up close to my body in defiance. "What do you mean the likes of Ron? He was my cousin and as good a man as ever entered this church."

"Well, for starters Clayton, I have no recollection of ever watching Ron enter our humble little church. Perhaps he was a regular with Pastor Randy or …"

"That's not the only measure of a man's worth. Ron was …"

This time I held my palms up to stop Clayton. His eyes riveted on the oversized turquoise bracelet and ring. It was like magic. The heels, the short tight fitting skirt Clayton had fixated on when I came around my desk, the jewelry, and the perfume worked a spell on Clayton. He sat back clutching the arms of the chair. His eyes bulged with interest.

Not wanting to retreat from certain victory, I pressed on. "Clayton, you and the family don't have to worry. I'll put some special words together which will give Ron an honorable sendoff. Let's not dishonor his memory with anything like that." I pointed to the papers which now rested in his lap.

Clayton's expression changed from the hard charging aggressor to the little boy look men get when they are perplexed by a female. The thickskulled bully had been overloaded by Tammy's magic, just as she promised.

I decided to close the deal. "Now, Clayton, please let me get back to my business. I have three busy days ahead and I want to do my very best for you, your family, and the congregation." I put my jewelry burdened hand on his shoulder and squeezed, too hard perhaps. His blue eyes fixed on the bracelet. I held a stalwart grip until his shoulder relaxed then spun on my tissue wrapped toes without tripping, threw a couple of hip bumps for good measure, and returned to my still warm seat and my work. When I looked up again he was gone. I grabbed the phone and pressed in Tammy's office number.

"It worked! You did it. I love you!"

"My mother would be so proud … all those years in graduate school and at last a successful outcome."

"I'm buying you lunch at Connie's. I have to finish a few things here. Can you meet me at eleven?"

"Yes, of course. I have to stop by Gabrielle's and get my nails done at ten then I'll be there."

"You just had your nails done three days ago," I said.

"I know, but I want to get a few more ideas. I've got to study her further. This little spell won't last long without some more material. That was just the opening salvo, my dear, just the shot across Clayton's bow."

"Lunch at eleven. I'm eager to hear your latest observations."

By ten-thirty I worked my way to the bottom of the morning To Do list. The last item on the list was to address Mrs. Olson's, Marlene Olson's, allegation that someone was stealing canned goods from the donation box next to the kitchen. Marlene was getting up there in years and according to her middle-aged son, she was accusing family members of stealing her cash and the youngsters of stealing her sherry and cigarettes. Marlene was a faithful member and I did not like ignoring her concern. I called her and told her so. "What would you like me to do?" I asked.

"Catch the thief and put him in jail. That's what you should do." I could tell she was already into the sherry as she spoke with a bit of an alcohol induced slur.

"Do you know who is taking the groceries?"

"Yeah sure, I have my suspicions then, but I'll not be saying without proof that the O'Malley boy, Jack, filches the canned goods."

"I agree. We'll not be pointing any long fingers of accusations without proof. Marlene, here's what I am going to do. I'm moving the box into Olive's office. She'll keep a watchful eye on the groceries. Is that an acceptable solution to you?"

"Well, I guess so. I just don't want those who have enough to be stealing from those who don't."

"Nor do I, Mrs. Olson, nor do I, good-by."

I would be a happy pastor if all my problems were so easily solved.

I wore a smile over my morning victories as I pranced past Olive. I felt like when I was ten and paraded down the boulevard in my grandmother's high-heeled shoes and the pretend clothes I'd purchased from my neighbors rummage sale. Olive noticed.

"My, Pastor Kathy you're all spiffed-up today. Is there a man in your life?" She winked an eye plastered with pink shadow and a new set of false lashes.

"No, Olive, no man – I thought I'd give myself a new look. Some folks have commented in the suggestion box I should update my wardrobe." That was no fib. Actually, the anonymous note said I dress like a scrubwoman. I hadn't heard that term since Grandma told me I'd never amount to anything more than a scrubwoman if I continued to ignore my studies.

I performed an awkward pirouette in front of Olive's desk. "What do you think?"

"You'd fit in nicely at a pole on the strip in Vegas." She returned to her crossword puzzle.

"Why thank you, Olive. I'm going to lunch with Pastor Tammy. I'll be back around two."

"Are you wearing those clothes?"

"Why of course," I said and winked. With my heels clicking, I made for the women's bathroom where I'd stashed my jeans, blouse, and sneakers, the new orange and black ones which reminded me of Halloween.

"Pastor Kathy, you must come look at this!" It was Mrs. Bertelsen and she looked upset, which was fairly normal for her. She grasped my hand and dragged me to the steps leading to the church basement. She led me to a table festively decorated for the potluck.

"Look at this." She spit the last word out with disgust. She picked up the centerpiece, a mason jar full of black and orange balls and stuffed with protruding ornaments on long plastic sticks ... pretty ordinary Halloween décor.

"Umm, help me out, Mrs. Bertelsen. What exactly should I be focused on?"

"Witches, goblins, gremlins, and something which looks like a devil." She pointed to each of the figures she found so objectionable. "Mrs. Olson bought these for the potluck. I should have done it myself when I was in Fargo. Now what are we going to do? She spent over sixty dollars from the kitchen fund and all we have are these evil sinful figures. Since when does the devil look like a sporty little cartoon character with a pointy tail?"

"I see your point." I truly did although I didn't share her conclusions on the evil nature of the decorations. "What would you suggest we do?"

"Do? Why, I'd like to burn the bunch of it. That's what I'd like to do."

"What would you replace it with?" I asked.

She had turned red by now ... her face, her neck, her flabby arms. I sensed she detected I didn't share her outrage which disappointed her. "Pumpkins, turkeys, and cornstalks. We have them left over from last year and they'd be just fine."

"Aren't those for Thanksgiving?"

"Okay, then, just pumpkins. I've a garden full of them. I'll carve them and we'll have a jack-o-lantern as the centerpiece on each table."

I didn't care to point out jack-o-lanterns had pagan origins as did the whole darn holiday. At the root of the problem was trying to fit yet another pagan celebration into a church tradition. "Fine by me, however, you'll have to deal with Mrs. Olson. Which Mrs. Olson by the way?"

"Oh, Mavis, of course. All right then, I'll take care of her and the pumpkins. What should I do with the devil's playthings?"

"You could burn them or perhaps the grade school would use them for the lunch room."

"Well, I guess it won't hurt those little heathens."

"Good luck with Mrs. Olson." I walked away and tiptoed up the steps. I was nearly to the restroom when Benny came running for his morning hug. With sneakers I'd learned to deal with his enthusiasm. Even in cowgirl boots, I could handle myself. On spikes stuffed with toilet paper I fell backwards onto the carpet. Benny landed on top of me.

"I'm sorry Pastor Kathy," he moaned.

"I'm all right, Benny, but get off me. You're heavy." I pushed on him, but without his participation in the effort wasn't able to free myself.

"Oh, my goodness, what are you two doing on the floor?" It was Mrs. Peterson, the Peterson who bakes the world's tastiest peanut butter cookies, with an armful of boxes. "Good gravy, now I've seen it all." Without an offer to help or waiting for an explanation, she marched away.

"Benny, get up."

He rolled and got on all fours looking at me like a naughty puppy.

I sat up, took the heels off, and bounced to my feet. I offered Benny a hand, got him to his feet, gave him a hug, and rushed into the restroom. I resolved this experiment had better work fast if I expected to keep my job. I was certain Mrs. Peterson would soon spread the word I had taken to dressing like a street walker.

Down at the café, Connie, with a new beehive hairdo, shouted a greeting from the grill as I marched in. Tammy waved from a table in the rear, the only one affording us some semblance of privacy.

Tammy's nails were indeed finely painted … a Halloween theme, black and orange. I'm not certain how she dared. I admired them and told her so. Connie ambled from her station behind the grill, served us coffee, and took our orders.

"I was expecting to see you all decked out," Connie said.

"News travels fast," I replied.

"I heard you were looking like a New York fashion model — or was it a New York hooker?" She grinned and waited for an explanation.

"Oh, I was just having some fun with Olive. She's always pestering me to dress in something other than jeans and sneakers. I do wear a dress on Sunday. Olive says I should maintain the same level of professionalism all week."

"Next time you are all fixed up stop in and show off a little. It would be good for business. Come around nine when all the old farts are sitting around telling whoppers. It'd give 'em something new to talk about. I'm darn tired of the same old stories and the same old jokes."

"There's one of my life's ambitions, entertaining old men like some exotic dancer I suppose."

"You might attract attention from some suitors, too, you know then." Connie winked.

"Connie, look around here and point out who you'd consider an eligible suitor," I said.

"Oh, you're just too fussy, you know, that's why you're still single. I've heard guys say they'd be interested, but they don't know how to approach a pastor. Gene Rasmussen, down at the pharmacy, heck he even told me he'd like to ask you out but wouldn't know what to talk about or if he could kiss you good night or just what the heck he could do, so he hasn't got the courage up to ask," Connie said.

"Connie, I'm content with what I have and I'm really starving …"

Connie waved her towel as if to say, "Oh the heck with you!" and left to fill our orders.

"Was your trip to Gabrielle's successful?" I asked Tammy with anticipation and relief my conversation with Connie was in the past.

Tammy flashed her nails. "You mean other than this wonderful nail job? I do have a few more personal facts you may find interesting and useful. Missy does the nails at Gabrielle's place. Gabrielle does the cuts and perms and color jobs. You could use one by the way."

"No."

"We'll work on that. Gabrielle's just colored her hair auburn."

"No."

"Ponder the possibilities. Anyway, Gabrielle's a talker. If she isn't talking with a customer, she's chatting with Missy. She blabs about every little detail in her life so I came away with some possibilities."

A large shadow appeared over our table. It was Mrs. Hildebrandt, a middle-aged woman about as wide as she was tall. She wore her trademark print dress that Tammy teased was made at Fargo Tent and Awning. Mrs. Hildebrandt made no apologies for being a busy body, a status enhanced because she was a weekly columnist for the local newspaper.

"Every time I see you two, you're together."

She was Tammy's congregant and it was Tammy who felt the need to respond. "Mrs. Hildebrandt, it would make sense that every time you see 'us two' we would be together."

She cocked her head like my dog does when I make little squeaky noises to tease him. She ignored the logic. "I wanted to tell you I won't be able to serve communion on Sunday. My daughter, the one in the Cities, needs my help down there. I'll be leaving tonight, then." Having dutifully reported, she turned and waddled away.

Tammy called after her, "Nothing serious I trust, with your daughter, I mean. We'll miss you."

"Isn't she the one you stole from Randy?"

"So Randy claims. I'm not sure Randy was as patient with her as I have been. She's a troubled soul. Evidently her daughter has a lifestyle which mom doesn't approve of. She's guarded in what she tells me, however, she once let it slip her daughter was arrested and in jail for charges unspecified."

The chicken-fried steaks were delicious but ruined my notion of dieting which I swore to start this morning. I'd done so well so far, just a ninety-five calorie Greek yogurt and an apple. I promised to eat spinach leaves, no dressing, for supper. That's how my diets go, feast or famine. Even better than my steak was the information Tammy gleaned from the hair salon. I felt a twinge of guilt as we conspired to use the new knowledge, although no more guilt than finishing my lunch with a piece of rhubarb pie, al a mode.

CHAPTER EIGHT

(Saturday)

The bride wore white. Linda was a plain woman who possessed the most beautiful complexion like one of the porcelain figurines in the display window at Macy's. Linda was nearing sixty, but her skin was as pure and unblemished as the day she was born. The countenance on her face reflected a peaceful soul. Someone you'd want and value as a best friend.

The groom had been down the aisle before, twice. Both wives had died from cancer. I'd officiated over the last funeral and now seeing the groom before me brought to mind how he had cried over her coffin at the service. Today, Harold beamed and with good reason, he was getting a prize. The bride and groom had been high school sweethearts, homecoming, proms, going steady, "the whole nine yards" as he described it. Then came a call to Vietnam and a war injury that left him limping up to the altar. He had not forgotten about Linda but didn't believe he was fit to be with her in his impaired condition. Soon he married the rehabilitation therapist who gave him back his manhood and self-confidence.

I had enjoyed the premarital counseling although given their age and experience there really wasn't much I could say. They each shared their story. Linda's was perhaps most remarkable. She'd never forgotten Harold. She had held out hope for this day for almost forty years. She confided to me that she was still a virgin. Linda had been waiting for Harold to return and somehow always knew he would.

I watched Linda march up to the chancel. The pianist and violinist played *Canon in D Minor*. My mind drifted back to my own wedding, more than a few years ago. I was only eighteen. John was a year older, at least by birthdays … maturity wise, maybe twelve. The trouble was he was so handsome – a full head of blonde hair, worn long and shaggy. A face and body like the romance novel covers only he was for real and mine. John worked on the railroad as a laborer. He came home, tanned and buffed after a day of pounding spikes and smelling of creosote from the wooden railroad ties. I still dream of him every time I smell the creosote. I was going to college, not sure why, other than my grandmother insisted and she was supported by my very determined grandfather who had a third grade education. "You'll never amount to anything other than a scrubwoman," my grandmother said repeatedly. She must have done some scrubbing herself in her younger days as she used that occupation as her example of how bad life could be without proper schooling.

One day, after finally coming up for air from between the sheets, I realized other than lust, and there was plenty of it, John and I had nothing in common. On weekends I'd study and John would watch football and polish off a case of beer. I wasn't suffering, but I did have the foresight to see how we'd look together at age thirty, forty, fifty. After only three years, we had already drifted apart. I still love John and we still "talk" on Facebook. I don't regret leaving and he understands why I left. He became a railroad engineer, bald, potbellied, and married for the third time.

I gave the standard wedding ceremony which Linda had wanted and waited for all these years. The ceremony was unremarkable; no one tripped, fainted, or cried out an objection. I came close to flubbing my lines when I caught a glimpse of Clayton Johansson pacing outside the vestibule. I gulped at the thought that Clayton might have Ron's casket waiting in the hall and the bride and groom's exit would be interrupted by the funeral procession. Nah, even Clayton wouldn't pull such a stunt, I reassured myself.

"I now pronounce you husband and wife!" I spoke loudly and with authority. I love that part, "I now pronounce you husband and wife." It shouts to the world the new status of two people in love and excited to become one. The piano player struck up *Wachet Auf* accompanied by a young lady picking an acoustic guitar. The guests stood out of respect for the couple who arm-in-arm strode down the aisle back to the narthex. I paused to let them complete the march then stepped down and greeted the relatives in the first row. I was shaking hands with Linda's sister when I heard a scream from the vestibule.

Pulling up my white robe, I rushed to the rear and out the double doors. He'd done it! Clayton had actually done it! There before me was a bronze casket, trimmed with flowers, the casket open. There lay Ron to greet the bride.

Linda's hands were to her face, tears streaming down her flawless, fair cheeks. Harold held her tightly. I moved quickly to their side and then ushered them towards the outside entrance where the rice throwers would soon be stationed. I motioned for the ushers to stop the exit of the guests. I scanned the vestibule and hallways. Clayton was absent as were the funeral home attendants who normally would stay with the casket.

I had no choice. Ron was a big man and the weight of a bronze casket made the task more strenuous. I pushed mightily to get the church truck rolling. Once it moved, like a sailboat in motion, it took its own course. All I could do was guide it and I didn't do that very well, bouncing off the wall and tipping over a display asking for Haitian mission donations which lay on a table. The first open door to the library was my target. Ron's final ship sailed through the doorway and came to dock against the plaid couch. I apologized to Ron for such rough treatment and retreated out the door, slamming it behind me.

I signaled the ushers to bring the guests forth. The couple stood outside in the bright sunshine ready to greet their friends, relatives, and neighbors. I made a beeline to Linda. "I'm so sorry. I can't believe it happened."

Linda's lower lip trembled. "I was mortified!" she said.

"No, just a misunderstanding. A schedule foul-up." I didn't want to make the matter worse by telling her the entire story.

"I thought it was a joke at first. You know, Harold and I being older and all. I saw the casket and thought someone was making fun of our age, like one foot in the grave. Then I saw someone was in the casket and I thought they'd gone too far."

"There's a funeral this afternoon and somehow the men from the funeral home arrived too early. I'm so very sorry."

"Did any of the guests see it?" Linda asked.

"I was the first out after you and I moved the casket. The ushers held everyone back. Please don't let it ruin your day. This is such a special day for you." Looking past Linda, I saw Clayton and the funeral attendants walking out the door towards the hearse which was parked directly behind Harold's Toyota.

"Excuse me." I grabbed Clayton's shoulder and spun him around. "What in hell are you doing? You've just ruined this wedding! The bride walked right into Ron's casket when she came out of the sanctuary." I pushed my finger into the funeral director's chest hard enough to move him back. "And you, what in hell are you doing leaving a body unattended in my church in the middle of a wedding?"

Clayton puffed out his chest. "Your church! Since when is this YOUR church. Do you ..."

"Clayton you've gone too far this time. You are dead wrong and you both need to apologize to the bride and groom."

"I will not. It was an accident, plain and simple."

"Ron's casket being left in the vestibule was no accident." I was beginning to shout and I could feel my face flush.

"You need to calm down and be more professional. We were just pushing Ron into the private chapel so a few relatives could spend some time with him. I had to show these men where to go. I wasn't certain they could make it down the steps. They're from Fargo and haven't been here before. So we just parked the casket for a minute so I could point out the two routes and they could choose the easiest. It was just an accident. Poor timing."

"Clayton, you are such an ass. You both get over there now and apologize. Don't you dare move Ron's casket from the library until all the wedding guests are outside."

"You're making a mountain out of a molehill. I'll tell the groom what happened and he'll understand," Clayton said.

"No, you will apologize and make no excuses. This is inexcusable."

"Your demeanor here is what's inexcusable. It was a simple accident and you're making a spectacle and embarrassing me in the process. I'll be taking this up at the next council meeting. You've not heard the last about your unprofessional conduct." Clayton stomped off toward the hearse.

I grabbed the attendant's arm before he could follow. "And you, move your damn hearse to the back of the church and do it now!"

CHAPTER NINE

(Saturday)

*T*he wedding reception was held at the American Legion, not every bride's dream venue although it was inexpensive, always available, and humbly functional. Linda's sister and friends had done a respectable job of decorating the hall with white ribbons and pink accents hanging from the suspended ceiling. The tables were covered with white cloths and sprinkled with those sparkly little things which are every janitor's nightmare as they are impossible to clean up. I have clothes in my closet which have tiny and sparkly wedding cake figures still attached from a wedding three years ago. On a tiny wooden stage an ancient accordion player, accompanied by a long-haired boy in a Bob Marley T-shirt strumming an electric guitar, entertained with danceable music. They, like the Legion hall, were always available and inexpensive. I spent time with the newlyweds and was fairly certain the incident with Ron's casket had for the moment been forgotten. I felt relieved but still anger burned deep inside. To make matters worse in an hour I had to muster up enough strength to give Ron a decent funeral.

I thought of joining in the many champagne toasts. Too much or even a little champagne might loosen my tongue for the funeral. Instead, I sallied up to the chocolate fountain. As only chocolate can, it brought great comfort.

Everyone expects the pastor to make the rounds meeting and greeting. Normally I enjoy this function. Today I could hardly force a smile. Clayton was indeed robbing my soul of peace and tranquility. Clayton had to be dealt with.

Tammy found me up to my elbows in chocolate. "You better slow down. You've got a long afternoon ahead. Pace yourself, girl," Tammy said what I already knew.

I told her how Clayton had come so close to robbing Linda of her dream wedding. She pulled me away from the chocolate and back into a corner next to where several men were passing a bottle of Everclear hard liquor to get up enough courage to dance. The men sheepishly moseyed away from Tammy and me.

"I believe I know who is sending me those hateful messages," Tammy said. She pulled folded notes from her purse. "Here, look at these." She handed them to me. "Read them."

"Dear Pastor Tammy,

I will not be able to join you as an escort to the Youth Convention in Dallas this year. Emile is taking me on a cruise to Jamaica for our fortieth wedding anniversary at the same time as the Dallas event. We fly out of Minneapolis the day you leave for Dallas.

My regrets,

Holly"

I read the second note.

"I'm tired of waiting for you to leave. You have until Halloween to fly your broom away from Pelican Falls to join the rest of the evil witches. UNTIL HALLOWEEN!!!!!"

It was the same card Tammy had shown me earlier.

"So?"

"So? Look at the handwriting. It's the same. Holly Hollenbachen wrote them both. A blind woman could see the similarities!" She grabbed the notes back and held them together so I could study them side by side. "See here, 'join' and 'join,' they're identical. And 'fly' and 'fly,' they're a match. She wrote both of them."

"I see similarities, but I'm no expert," I said.

"Look at the 'the's,' they are a perfect …"

I could hardly hear Tammy over the sound of spoons being tapped against the glassware.

"You may be right. I'm just saying I am no expert. Do you have some other evidence?" I asked.

"You bet I do. Look at this list." Tammy removed a piece of crumpled paper from her pocket. "Read this!"

I checked my watch, only forty minutes before the funeral. "Tammy, I've got to get going to the funeral."

"Just look at the list. It'll only take a minute."

I straightened the paper and read:

NRA

Dobson

Rush

Cross Your Legs

Homecoming Queen

"Tammy, I'm sorry. This makes no sense whatsoever."

"I know, those are just my notes to remind me of the evidence. I have to explain it all to you."

"Later, stop by the house after supper and we'll go over the clues then. I've got to get to the funeral." I rushed away.

"Wipe the chocolate from your face!" Tammy sang out loudly.

CHAPTER TEN

(Saturday)

"*Primoris Calix, Latin for the First Stone.* Who here among us would cast the first stone?" I had already provided all the prerequisite and somber words for the funeral service and moved on to the sermon. During the short drive from the Legion to the church, I had vacillated as to giving the sermon Clayton had demanded and speaking from the heart. My heart won.

"Jesus had gone to the Mount of Olives to teach. A group of religious leaders, scribes and Pharisees, shoved their way through the crowd of followers who had surrounded Jesus. They carried in their midst, a woman, and threw her at his feet. The Pharisees accused her of adultery, an offense calling for death by stoning." I paused and peered at Clayton, perhaps for too long. He'd been glaring at me until now when he cast his eyes to the highly polished oxfords he'd been restlessly shuffling and shaking throughout the service.

"Jesus heard the allegations and demands for her death. The Pharisees waited for Jesus to agree with the law and bless their actions. Jesus kicked at the dust with his sandals and then reached down and picked up a large stone, the first stone. I'm sure the crowd expected Jesus to throw it at her signaling the others to join in. She'd be dead in less than a minute.

"I bet just to heighten the suspense Jesus tossed the stone into the air a few times like a baseball pitcher will do before he throws a fastball. Then he turned to the scribes and Pharisees and said, 'You … you without sin, you cast the first stone.' Jesus dropped his stone on the ground and waited. None stepped forth and the accusers retreated, leaving the woman to Jesus.

"Like everyone in this church today, myself included, we are all sinners and not a single one of us is fit to cast the first stone. Ron was no saint and he had some demons running roughshod over his soul.

But when he meets Jesus at the gate, Jesus won't have a stone in his hand. He'll give Ron a big hug and welcome him. 'Come-on-in Ron you've already been through Hell on Earth. It's time to join the forgiven here in heaven.'"

I finished the sermon and the rituals as required, happy to have the funeral service end. The bronze casket, painted in Harley Davidson colors, was wheeled back down the aisle. I followed it, and Clayton along with his family, followed me. I stopped at the last pew in the sanctuary, stepped aside, and allowed the others to pass. A tall woman with lovely hair, the color a hardware paint chart might call Cajun Spice or Merlot Red, was weeping. I stopped to comfort her and let the procession pass.

I put my hand on her shoulder. She grasped it and squeezed tightly. Her arm was adorned with silver and turquoise jewelry. She wore a matching necklace dangling into her blouse cut lower than one might expect at a funeral. She had a pretty face and looked remarkably like my cousin, Sara. "I'm sorry for your loss. Are you related to Ron?" I asked.

"No, we dated for years. We were even engaged to be married but then he started ice fishing." Her proclamation brought on a new flood of tears. Her mascara ran down over the rouge on her cheeks making an embarrassing mess.

"Ice fishing caused you to breakup?" I asked with curiosity at such an unlikely declaration.

"No, not the fishing, it was then Ron began to drink. Before the drinking we had so much fun. Ron worked construction and had winters off. He collected unemployment and we would take trips to the Caribbean, Hawaii, and Mexico." The mention of the trips brought a hint of a smile to her face.

"Then he started drinking?" I asked.

"No, he started ice fishing. Have you ever been ice fishing or spearing?"

"No, I haven't ever felt the need."

"Don't. You spear inside a dark ice house, no light, and a big hole cut into the ice. You sit in the dark with a spear in one hand and a beer in the other and wait for a fish to come into your hole."

"Sounds deathly boring."

"Fishermen drink because it is so boring. Ron got so hooked on spearing fish in the winter we stopped taking vacations and he'd sit in his little house from November to March. It made him an alcoholic." The tears came again.

I drew her close until she calmed. When she stopped crying, the sanctuary was empty. "Come with me to the reception. There's a light meal in the basement."

"Oh, no, I couldn't. I mean it's been several years since I was with Ron and I'm not sure how the family would handle my being there."

"Let me worry about it. They're not going to say anything if you're with me." I led her out of the sanctuary and to the basement. The din of dozens of conversations filled the room. I chatted with my new friend as we waited in line for the bologna sandwiches, deviled eggs, and more bars and cookies than the Toot Suite Bakery on Main Street.

"You look so much like my cousin, Sara. She was a nurse in Biwabik…"

"Really, I'm from Biwabik. I left right after high school though."

"I don't mean to keep staring at you. It's just my cousin, Sara, died in a sky diving accident and I miss her so much."

"Ron and I used to sky dive. I still go up to Fargo and dive when the weather permits, which isn't very often."

"I have Sara's dog, a little pug who is so cuddly."

"I have a pug. This is really weird. I mean I look like her and sky dive and have a pug; I mean is it karma or what?"

We worked our way through the service line. My friend was met with a few glares from the ladies serving the petite sandwiches and potato salad, Ron's favorite I was told. It was near impossible for a stranger to win the approval of the kitchen ladies. They reviewed each guest and then traded assessments and criticisms while doing the dishes. "Her dress was too short. Too much makeup. She is just showing off a big diamond ring. Anyone with grey hair ought to keep it cut short and curled, not in a ponytail like some teenager." I imagine Ron's tavern friends provided fodder for some lengthy critiques. Judging from the overwhelming smell of hard liquor on their breaths, I'm guessing they'd just left the bar to attend the funeral and would be back at the saloon for a suitable wake after filling up on the sandwiches and potato salad. With my guest in tow, I led the way to the head table and took a seat next to Clayton. He said nothing. He glared at my companion.

"Clayton, this is Gabrielle Durand, but I suppose you two have already met. I mean she being engaged to Ron and all. Anyway, we've been chatting and find we have so much in common."

Clayton stopped chewing his bologna sandwich. His eyes met mine. They were full of hate and anger. "Yeah, hi Gabrielle, haven't seen you for a few years."

"I was just telling Pastor Kathy how much Ron and I enjoyed our vacations to Mexico. We'd hang-glide, scuba dive and go to bull fights …" her voice trailed off.

"Ya, Ron was a fun guy …" Clayton said and finished chewing.

"… until he started ice fishing," Gabrielle said.

We settled into our chairs and nibbled at the eggs and sandwiches. An uncomfortable silence hung over our table.

"I just love the way you do your hair, Gabrielle," I said.

"Where do you get your hair done?" Gabrielle asked as she inspected my short swished-back style.

"Oh, I do it myself, mostly. When I need it cut, I have a friend in Detroit Lakes who flunked out of cosmetology school but still does okay. I brought her a picture of Princess Di from People magazine and she tried her best to duplicate the same look."

"You just stop over to my shop sometime and I'll fix you up with a current style and maybe a color job," Gabrielle offered.

"I like your suggestion. What do you think, Clayton, would the board approve of a change of my hair color? Maybe the same color as Gabrielle?" I asked.

"Whatever." Clayton rose from his chair and walked away.

"I irritate him sometimes," I said.

"Oh, he's just a man. They can be grumpy sometimes."

"Gabrielle, you and I are going to become good friends," I said and held her hand in mine. "Real good friends."

CHAPTER ELEVEN

(Saturday)

*T*he *bonfire was magnificent.* The flames rose high enough to lick the twinkling stars. Weeks earlier, I'd written a long list of offenses Clayton Johansson had committed against me. With Tammy at my side, I threw the list into the crackling fire and watched it go up in smoke. "Soul sister, you may have just neutered old Clayton," I said with a deep sense of satisfaction. I felt free of burdens for the first time in months. As free as the day I signed the divorce papers.

"Are you convinced he's beaten?" Tammy asked.

"If you could have seen his face when he walked away from Gabrielle and me, yes, I think he's beaten."

"How about Gabrielle?" Tammy asked.

Max shifted his weight on the straw bales we were all sitting on and I fell off. Tammy giggled and Max came to lick my face. Max is so consistent – always there to provide comfort without asking for anything in return. Well, occasionally, I sense he may be hinting at an ice cream cone when we drive past the Golden Arches.

"I like Gabrielle — a little rough around the edges but grounded and honest. Oh my, here I'm touting her honesty and I was telling some major fibs."

"How bad were the 'fibs?'" Tammy asked.

"Bad. I told her she looked like my cousin Sara who had died in a sky diving accident…"

"You told her that?"

"I know, it sounds so bad, but it just flowed so well. I had all the information you'd given me about Gabrielle, like she was from Biwabik and traveled to Mexico and liked to sky dive. So I just used it as a means to get close to her."

"You sure stuck your neck out," Tammy said and whistled softly.

"I know. Maybe the most difficult tale is that I own a pug. You told me Gabrielle was in love with her pug so now I own a pug and Gabrielle wants for our pugs to have a date."

"Oh my goodness, you've spun quite a web of tales. Where are you going to get a pug?"

"I don't know. I'll ask around on Facebook or tweet my friends."

"Like maybe they'll have an old pug just laying around?"

"Oh what tangle webs we weave …"

"… when first we practice to deceive," Tammy finished the quote. She wagged her finger at me.

"Enough of that. We're here to celebrate. More wine? More chocolate?" I reached for both. I filled our glasses with a sparkling pinot noir.

Tammy raised her crystal goblet, "To the end of Clayton Johansson's reign of terror!"

"To his end, indeed!"

"I'm so happy this has worked out for you," Tammy said as she rubbed my shoulder gently.

"Now fellow warrior, we take on your dragon."

"I'm still convinced Holly Hollenbachen wrote the notes," Tammy said.

From my jean pocket, I pulled the paper Tammy had given me at the wedding reception. I smoothed it out and read by the light of the fire. "Okay first on your list is 'NRA.' What the heck does that refer to?"

"NRA. Holly drives a big black pickup with a National Rifle Association sticker on the bumper."

"Oh, there's some damning evidence. Her husband is probably a hunter."

"No, she's packing herself. I saw her gun, a small silver gun with a pink handle." Tammy formed the outline of a pistol with her hand.

"On her hip in a sequined holster?"

"Last year some of us from the church took a trip to St. Louis. We hauled a bus full of youth to a rally. As a side-trip we went to that monument, what's it called?"

"The Arch."

"Yeah, right and Holly didn't make it through the security check because she had the gun in her purse."

"Okay, so she's a pistol-packing mama, what about this 'Dobson' on your list?" I asked.

"Dr. James Dobson, you know the radio show host who is always railing against the gays? He is her favorite theologian."

"Jimmie Lee Dobson? He's not even a minister. He's a psychologist. I've listened to his show when folks claim homosexuality is learned and they can be cured with counseling."

"I know. Holly has all of his radio shows recorded. She listened to them the entire trip. In the evenings, she'd share the lessons with me."

"That must have been painful," I said. I poked at the fire with a long stick. Ambers flew into the crisp night air like sparkling Roman Candles.

"You see 'Rush' on the list?" Tammy asked.

"Let me guess, Rush Limbaugh."

"Exactly, she has a yipping little cocker spaniel that barks and whines incessantly. She named him 'Rush.'"

"I'm beginning to see your point."

"When she wasn't listening to Dobson she was glued to Limbaugh."

"What about 'Cross your Legs?'" I asked.

" It's the program she wanted to start at the church youth league. She called it, 'Just Cross Your Legs.'"

"And 'Homecoming?'" I asked reading from the list.

"A couple of years ago, her oldest daughter was named homecoming queen."

"Did she win by keeping her legs crossed?" I asked and then regretted the catty remark.

"I guess not because she graduated with a belly out to here," Tammy said and held her hand out a foot from her stomach.

"So much for the program."

"That's not the point. Holly was enraged because the homecoming king was one of the immigrants from Somalia. She raised holy hell. She made her daughter drop out of the coronation."

"You're thinking Holly is trying to run you out of town because you're Asian or what?"

"I wouldn't put it past her."

The wind switched directions and blew across the fire and into my face. I shifted my straw bale back a bit. I love the smell of burning maple logs and crisp leaves in the fall. I breathed deeply with my eyes closed.

"Now don't you agree she's a good suspect?" Tammy asked.

"I can think of several labels I could put on her."

"Don't forget the handwriting. Remember the 'the's,'" Tammy said.

"All right, I agree. With your circumstantial evidence, Holly is a suspect. What would you have us do about it?" I asked.

"Your friend, the one who was married to your cousin Sara, ask him to analyze the handwriting. That would prove it."

"Doc? Sara's ex? He's not a handwriting expert. He's a Special Agent with the State Police."

"Okay, but they have the lab and every lab has a handwriting expert. Give him the two notes and ask them to render an opinion. I'll bet the experts will say it's the same."

"I don't know. Is it even a crime?" I asked.

"Yes, it's a hate crime."

"All right, I'll call him tomorrow afternoon, after the potluck. Say, you're still coming to our Harvest Potluck, aren't you?"

Tammy didn't answer. I turned from the fire to face her. She was pointing a finger past the flames, towards the driveway.

"Don't look now, Kathy, someone's over there in the shadows," Tammy whispered.

Believing she was teasing, I said, "I hope it isn't your pistol packing mama."

"Seriously, I saw a shadow from the fire. It's moving along the driveway."

I looked at Max. His ears were cocked and he was looking in the direction Tammy had pointed. A slow growl rumbled from deep inside Max's chest.

CHAPTER TWELVE

(Saturday)

"*There's a .22 rifle in the barn.* I'm going to slowly walk over and get it. Keep talking and hold onto Max," I said under my breath. I stood and sidestepped towards the barn away from the firelight and into the shadows. Max continued to growl softly with a couple of concerned yips as emphasis. Tammy bantered, talking about how good the wine was and how the other women should be here any minute. As I neared the barn away from the crackling fire, I could hear steps, a rhythmic crunching of shoes on gravel. I slipped along the barn wall to the double door. The rifle I kept for coyotes and skunks was loaded and hanging up high near the light switch. In the dark barn, I felt along the rough plank walls until I touched the familiar stock. I took it down trying to be quiet and stealthy.

The steps grew nearer and I could make out a form, tall and lanky. Oh my god, I wondered if I pushed Clayton too far. Was he coming to kill us? To chop us up in the wood chipper? I wished I had returned the chipper to my neighbor.

Tammy continued to chatter away. She assumed two separate voices, one her own and the other very manly. In her male voice she said it was time to get back to work at the Sheriff's Department. I smiled at the absurdity and ingenuity and brought the rifle to my shoulder. I put the front sight squarely on the chest of the moving figure.

I watched the intruder progress towards the fire. I slid my finger on the trigger, careful not to fire, but ready to do so if he attacked Tammy. I'd remain still until I could assess the person's intentions. Why wasn't he announcing his presence?

Those intentions were difficult to make out when the figure suddenly stopped. Was he able to see Tammy and questioning where I was? Was he altering his plan? Then the figure let out a screechy wolf yelp and then another and another like some werewolf gone mad. I heard Tammy shout for me. Max barked like a rabid banshee. Smokey flew out of the barn door.

Tammy jumped up and threw a large log on the fire. The flames spread and shot skyward. I could clearly see the man for the first time. I dropped the rifle from my shoulder and put the safety on.

"Makwa, you scoundrel, I'm over here by the barn. Darn you anyway, you shouldn't come up on us like that in your Indian ways. I nearly shot you," I shouted more than a little perturbed. I walked out of the barn doorway, still cradling the rifle, and towards my old colleague.

"Kathy, you know it's against the law to shoot a bear out of season. Besides, I would see the bullet coming and dodge it. I have that power."

Makwa and I met at the fire. He'd lost some weight — maybe too much although he still struck a handsome profile in the dancing flames. I set the rifle down on the bale and we hugged. I suppose it was more of an embrace as it lasted longer than respectable. He lifted me a little off the ground and swung me in a circle, his waist-long ponytail swinging like a horse at a cantor. When he set me down, I introduced Makwa to Tammy.

"Tammy, this is my old friend and confidant, Dr. Joseph Auginaush. This is Pastor Chang, Tammy Chang."

"Call me Tammy, please, and nice to meet you. I've heard so much about you from Kathy." She held out her hand.

Dr. Auginaush kissed her hand and bowed. "*Anishinaabe*, my honor and you may call me Joe or Makwa if you like."

"Makwa? What does Makwa mean?"

"In Ojibwe it means bear. My mother gave me the name. On the day I was born, she saw a bear visiting our garbage cans behind the house and believed it to be a sign I would be strong and wise like a bear. There is a certain irony to being named after a freeloading bear who raids garbage cans, isn't there?"

Makwa was carrying a backpack in one hand. He set it down by a bale. "I see you ladies are enjoying some of the grape. Perhaps a thirsty traveler might have a taste?" He has the most enchanting smile, wide thin lips and pearly teeth – his brown eyes large and gentle. As always, he wore faded jeans and a pigskin blazer over a tattered cowboy style shirt. I poured some wine in my glass and handed it to him. He sniffed the bouquet and took a sip. "Ah, lovely." He handed me back the glass as I knew he would. He learned years ago alcohol was a demon not to be tempted. He'd take a taste just to prove to the demons he was in control. A strange little habit but one I respected.

"Sit, we're just having a fire and enjoying the …" I said.

"I apologize for frightening you. I was so intent on listening to Tammy's conversation as I approached, I neglected to sing out. Where is the man you were talking to?"

"Right here," Tammy said with a deep voice sounding comical and a bit like John Wayne.

"Ah, I see. I'm ever so grateful you didn't shoot me."

"Can I get you something to drink, eat?" I asked.

"I have water with me. Holy water from the sweat lodge. I was in South Dakota, at Pine Ridge, visiting a cousin."

"Rudy?" I asked.

"He's Running Bear now. He's 'running' three sweat lodges and can hardly find time to smoke the peyote. The poor guy's down to hundred and twenty pounds."

"Can I get you something to eat? I baked some pumpkin bars for the potluck tomorrow. They're not bad," I said.

"Maybe later. I just stopped at McDonald's in Fergus and had two Big Macs and a chocolate shake."

"How'd you get here anyway? I didn't hear a car drive up," I said.

"My cousin, Stretch, gave me a ride from the Pine Ridge Reservation. He's going up to the rez in White Earth. I told him to just drop me off at the driveway. He was smoking weed the last hundred miles and insisted on driving. I'd had enough and thought I'd stop and visit."

"Stretch, is he the one you use to call Skinny Weasel?" I asked.

"Not to his face. He's quick with the knife and short-fused when he's not smoking the weed."

"Tell us about the sweat lodge. How was it? You didn't do a sun dance again did you?" I asked hoping his answer was "no."

"No. No dance this time. I still haven't healed from the last time." He undid the top three metal buttons of his plaid cowboy shirt and showed his bare chest. Wounds, swollen and tender, were evident on his hairless chest. "They've been healing slowly."

"Excuse my ignorance, but what is a sun dance and why the scars?" Tammy asked.

"The Sun Dance is a spiritual ritual. The entire event can last for days. There is fasting, dancing, singing, and certain men perform a special rite requiring them to be pierced with sharp pegs and those pegs imbedded in the chest are attached by rawhide to a sacred pole. The men look into the sun and lean away from the pole until the pegs tear from their flesh. It is much more complex than I am describing, but you get the idea."

"Were there many participants?" Tammy asked.

"Not for the Sun Dance, although Rudy is running several sweat lodges every week. It'll slow down now with winter so near. In the summer, tourists and celebrities come from all over the world to smoke the peyote and attend the sweat lodge. Rudy won't do it, but some others will even let the celebrities participate in the Sun Dance."

"I suppose money changes hands?" Tammy asked.

"Of course, it's a shame rich folks can buy someone's spiritual ways. Many of us would like to see the Sun Dance remain sacred or at least not be purchased."

"Churches used to sell passes out of purgatory and bones from the saints. People have a long and rich tradition selling spiritual matters," I said.

"Oh, I almost forgot to tell you. The rez broke a record this summer."

"What sort of record?" I asked.

"Most church groups in a single season. I don't recall the exact number, well over a hundred counting just the organized ones. Bunch of folks come on their own each year. They built a new community center in town."

"The community center you guys keep burning down every winter so the church groups have something to do when they return?" I asked.

"Well, my dear, it serves such a noble purpose. Besides it gets cold in the winter and all the reclaimed lumber keeps the stoves burning until the summer. We can't find much buffalo poop anymore. Seems you guys killed them all."

Makwa could always make me laugh. He had such a light-hearted outlook on life. I was happy to have him join us although his entrance could have been less stressful. I left Tammy to chat with him while I went into the house and put together some lunch. I hesitantly cut into the frosted pumpkin bars destined for the church potluck. My grandmother always said one should never bring bars, a cake, or a pie with a piece missing. I buttered some bread and found some brie cheese which had aged, probably two more months in my fridge. I cooked some hot chocolate and added those tiny marshmallows making me feel like a little girl again.

Tammy and Makwa were laughing when I returned. He had told her some outrageous story of his youth on the reservation. He considered it his obligation to embellish the stories until they resembled a polished comedy routine. Just watching them so comfortable with each other made me miss Makwa. He had stayed gone too long.

"Here's lunch, be careful of the hot chocolate, I boiled it until it bubbled, just the way Grandma taught me." I set the tray of food on a straw bale between Max and Tammy. Max was drooling and whining. "Tammy, use discretion when it comes to some of the details of his stories."

"All fine stories get better with age just like this fine cheese. It gives the storyteller the opportunity to improve on the story," Makwa said with a wink.

"Without much regard for the truth, I might add," I said with a mouth full of pumpkin bar.

"Speaking of a fine storyteller, how is Father Gallo?" Makwa asked.

"Fit and still full of some of the finest stories this side of the Mississippi," I said.

"How do you know Father Gallo?" Tammy asked.

"We go way back. He was a young priest when I was in high school. Actually, I'd dropped out and was pursuing a life of crime, quite successfully, I might add. The good Father was assigned to the rez — the first of two times he had a parish at White Earth. My pals and I toyed with him for months. I began to want to be around him because he was so good natured about all the ribbing. He home-schooled me for my junior year. I learned more with Father than any other year of my life. He got me to graduate and then sent me with a scholarship to Notre Dame. Imagine me in Notre Dame with all those kids from Ward and June Cleaver families."

"So, you've stayed in touch?" Tammy asked.

"Of course, he got me interested in psychology and helped to get me admitted to graduate programs at the University of Minnesota. We even worked together for a while. He'd been sent to Minneapolis to work in the Little Rez down on Franklin Street. We ran a program for wayward native boys and girls." Makwa paused to sip his chocolate.

"It was there we met," I said. "I was working with felons on parole and some of them were natives. Our programs overlapped in some areas. We became fast friends, the three of us. It was Father Gallo who told me Grace Lutheran Church was looking for a pastor."

Makwa smiled. "Truth be told, I never thought your decision to enter the seminary would pan out."

"I've changed from those early years. I've changed a lot."

"Still, you've got an independent stubborn streak running through your core. I just couldn't imagine you bending to the will of a congregation or church council."

"How long were you standing out there listening to Tammy and me talk?" I asked.

"I was dropped off and walked right in. The only conversation I heard was between Tammy and her man friend. Why?"

"I didn't mean to imply you were eavesdropping, it's just that Tammy and I have been talking all evening about some problems we're both having with church members."

"I didn't mean to intrude," Makwa said with all sincerity.

"No, not at all. Perhaps you could provide some expert counseling ..." I said.

It was almost midnight when we finished with the entire story and I was correct, Makwa had some extraordinary insights and solutions – few of them legal, most ending with some felony. I called it quits. I had two church services tomorrow and more bonfire chats weren't going to help my performance. I told my companions I needed to retire.

Tammy excused herself and drove away in her Mini Cooper. Makwa and Max lingered by the fire. "Would I be too bold to assume my usual sleeping arrangement is still acceptable?"

I looked into his large brown eyes. They could make a girl melt.

"Of course, perfect," I said.

CHAPTER THIRTEEN

(Sunday)

I *was up before dawn, feeling young and chipper.* I made coffee, warmed up two bagels in the toaster, slathered both with butter and walked lightly with a tray full of coffee, bagels, and a jar of Olive's homemade orange marmalade out to the stables. A small fire still burned in the pot bellied stove and the aroma of burning maple lingered and mixed with the smell of horses, hay, and tack. If I could bottle that scent for horse lovers, I would retire. The air was cool but calm, a wonderful morning for a horse ride. I set the tray on the high table and pulled up a stool. I spread the marmalade on thick licking my lips with the knowledge I was about to bite into the world's best tasting jam.

"Makwa, get up and join me for some breakfast," I shouted wanting him to share my guilty pleasure.

Max returned a small bark, not worthy of his size, more like some Pekinese. I heard his tail banging on the upstairs wall like a drum at a native dance. Makwa had prevailed upon me last night to permit Max to sleep with him in the stable loft. "It's lonely in the barn and Max will keep the mice and rats from chewing on me."

I informed him the stables had neither mice nor rats thanks to Smokey's superior hunting skills. Nonetheless, I had to agree the stables could be lonely and Max was outstanding company although in a closed environment his excess gas may be unpleasant. So I slept with Smokey and Makwa with Max, an altogether acceptable situation.

I ate fast.

"Makwa, I'm going for a ride. I'll leave your breakfast on the table." Max barked. There was no response from Makwa who by his own admission was an impossibly sound sleeper. My buckskin mare, Whisper, munched on a handful of oats I'd thrown in her rubber feeder. Like her owner, she'd put a few pounds on and a full ration of oats wouldn't help her shed the weight any more than the half jar of marmalade I'd spread on my bagel. I pulled a saddle and tack from the rack outside the stall and had her ready to go about the time I finished my fourth cup of coffee. Still no Makwa although Max had crawled down from the loft and was sniffing around the table for handouts. He, Whisper, and I all needed some trimming of the waistline so I resisted tossing the big golden dog a bagel even though he was smiling at me. The dog had learned to smile as a puppy. Strangers often remarked Max was dangerous because his teeth showed as if he were snarling. Quite the contrary, the cuddly old guy just loved to smile at the world.

The sun was breaking the horizon as Whisper carried me at a trot over the first hill past the stables. Max ran at her heels. His tongue already nearly dragging on the ground. The lovely smell of fallen leaves filled the air. I forced my mind to concentrate on my sermon. Some may find me neglectful to leave such a matter to a few short hours before pulpit time. I find it to be the time when my mind is clear and I feel most close to my Maker.

Today was Reformation Sunday, the day Lutherans celebrated their founder's most famous deed. On October 31, 1517, All Saints Day, Martin Luther posted a protest against the sale of indulgences, loosely speaking some wayward priests were selling the forgiveness of sins. Such greedy and dishonest behavior was hardly condoned by the Good Book. As a studious monk, Luther knew it and his conscience forced him to nail this complaint and a bunch of others on the door at the Wittenberg University Cathedral for all to see. Luther's document came to be known as *The 95 Theses* and earned Luther an excommunication and a death sentence from the Catholic Church where he had been an extremely loyal and diligent priest. If he would have been caught, he'd likely been burned at the stake as had many of his peers. So on the Sunday closest to the 31st, the Lutheran Church celebrates its founder's act of rebellion by decorating the church in red cloth and speaking fondly of Dr. Luther.

I'd received and read the suggested sermon issued by the synod's headquarters. Every week, the synod president's guys type up a sermon they'd like to be preached. Sort of keeps us outlanders in line with the main office thinking. Maybe once a year, out of sheer laziness, I use the outline. So I read the Reformation sermon, crumpled it into a ball and made a three pointer in the office trash can. It was a bland bunch of rhetoric praising Dr. Luther, which I support, and then more or less dismissing his radical ideas and heretical comments as dated. The new Lutheran Church took no bold positions and strove to get along with everyone and every church. After all, bold positions may drive the members to become Unitarians which in turn causes the revenue flow to show a marked decline.

I was determined to tell the congregation how their founder was a rebellious monk who gave Rome the middle finger. Here was a man who defied the norms and married a nun. When the Luthers had their first child, the pope sent observers to witness the birth of what was sure to be a demonic baby. The union of a nun and a monk had to result in a Devil's child. Of course the baby didn't have horns or a tail — a disappointment to Luther's enemies.

Luther wasn't like the pious priests who pranced about their sanctuaries as if they weren't to be counted among the sinners. He was a theology professor who held court in the beer halls. Rumors abound, including that his church songs were adapted from traditional beer hall tunes and upon his death, his estate was left with a rather large bar tab to pay. Luther has been quoted as saying, "He who loves not wine, women and song, remains a fool his whole life long." He even went so far to say, "If you are not allowed to laugh in heaven, I don't want to go there."

I chuckled at the though — so loud Whisper cocked her ears back as if judging my fitness to ride her. At two miles out, I slowed her to a walk. I checked my watch. I still had an hour before I headed to town. I turned her around and held her at a slower pace.

I let Whisper have her head and lead the way back while I put myself into a trance and formulated my sermon. This year, I'd tell the congregation the truth about Martin Luther. I'd lay him bare with all of his flaws and blemishes. I'd tell them how Luther was steadfast in his belief a person was saved from their sins by grace alone – *"Sola gratia"* the Latin term for "by grace alone." This year, I'd shout from the pulpit: "no matter how many quilts you stitch and send to Madagascar, you will not be saved without grace." You cannot buy a ticket into heaven with deeds. That's what pissed Luther off. The church was selling tickets into heaven. Luther had a temper and wasn't bashful about using some rough language. I wondered what Martin Luther would say to Clayton Johansson? I needed to muster the gumption to be as brave as Luther.

Whisper brought me home just as I was putting the finishing touches on the sermon. Makwa and Smokey stood at the door of the stables waiting for our arrival. Makwa had a coffee cup in hand. He looked more handsome in the daylight. Makwa was one of those men who grow better looking with age, like they grow into their proportions. He kept his youthful figure even after adding some bulk to his upper body.

"Good morning, lovely woman, did you have a pleasant ride?"

"Good morning, handsome man, yes, Whisper and I had a wonderful ride and I was able to complete my sermon. Did you and Max sleep well?" I asked.

"Most excellent, although your furry friend has some extraordinary gastric activity."

"Yes, I know all about his weakness. It's especially foul when he visits my neighbor's bone yard. You found the coffee and bagel, I see."

"Just finished it when you rode up. Smokey came and woke me. He did a short jig on my head like Puss in Boots himself. I rose when you left and meditated with the rising of the sun."

"I hate to rush off, but I have two church services to attend. Care to join the congregation?"

"I think not. I'd be happy to do some chores while you're gone, clean the stalls, perhaps, make dinner?"

"You'll be missing a great potluck," I said.

"Will you be serving Lutefisk? For such a delicacy, I'd walk to town."

"Unfortunately the cod fish is for the first three weeks in December, Christmas food, you know, Lutefisk, mashed potatoes, and lefsa all for five ninety-nine."

"I'll be back in December. No, you go and I'll tend to Max and the horses."

"Would you feed Max and Smokey ..."

"And the horses and chickens, of course, I'd be delighted. Let me take Whisper now and you can get ready." Makwa moved closer and took the reins while I jumped off.

"Thank you so much." I gave him a peck on the cheek. He smelled so ... manly.

He led the horse away humming one of those native tunes which never end.

I finished the sermon in the shower. I even thought of a couple of feisty retorts to Clayton Johansson should he approach me with reproof after the sermon. I slipped into a black high necked dress and pumps. I added some turquoise jewelry of which I'm ashamed to say I was growing quite fond. I lavished on what I'd taken to calling "Gabrielle's" perfume. A final inspection in the full length mirror and I was off in the pickup which served me so well for the last decade. I practiced my sermon during the ten minute ride to town. It was an exact ten minute sermon. The brevity alone should win over half the congregation.

We opened the service with Martin Luther's *A Mighty Fortress is Our God* just to get into the reformation mood. During my firebrand-style sermon, I saw a few smiles, some nodding of the heads, several eyes closed and heard a single "Amen." Unlike a Southern Baptist Church, an "Amen" is a rare event mostly shouted out by some visitor who isn't familiar with the Lutheran ways. Should the poor soul attend a second service and repeat the heartfelt, "Amen," one of the kitchen women will set him straight.

We finished the last service with a rousing chorus of *Shrek's* song, which as I heard it had only religious significance because of the repetitive "Hallelujahs." I assumed my post at the rear of the sanctuary and shook hands and exchanged greetings. I was prepared for some harsh comments but received none and in fact heard a couple of whispered, "Atta girl." Clayton Johansson lingered at his place in the first pew. His wife, Liv, departed when the service concluded, but

Clayton remained bent over in what could have been a repentant pose. When only four were left in the greeting line, Clayton bounced down the aisle and brought up the rear.

"The synod didn't send the sermon you preached. As the president of the church council, I get a copy, too, you know."

"No, it wasn't and I'm not bound by those missives, you know."

"I don't think your sermon has a solid theological foundation, this 'solo gratis' business doesn't sound familiar to me. I was always …"

"It's 'Sola gratia' and …"

Clayton held his hand up to hush me. "I'm not impressed with the fancy French. I was always taught you got to heaven with an abundance of good works and deeds. I was always …"

"Clayton, you have something, maybe lettuce, between your front teeth," I said and pointed to my own incisors to show him where the offending food was wedged. "It's right about here."

Clayton stopped in mid-sentence. "What?"

"Between your teeth, there's something wedged in and it's distracting to talk …"

"Where?"

"Right here." I pointed a fingernail painted with lovely tiny flowers.

Clayton used his fingertip to clean his teeth. "Did I get it?"

"No, it's still there."

He turned from me and walked towards the restroom. It had been years since I'd used such a trick. It still worked, although I probably would not be able to use it on Clayton again. I joined the end of the line for the potluck. The basement was alive with conversation and laughter. The children ran unchecked with small decorated bags teeming with candy. I grabbed Benny at the bottom of the steps and asked him to join me for the meal. He clutched my hand until we reached the serving counter. With a clean plate in hand, I held it out for the ladies to serve ten different varieties of hot dish.

A large spoon full of tuna casserole was plopped next to a taco-hamburger hot dish which lay on top of a dollop of something with noodles and meat called Venison Surprise. The ladies managed to find room for a tater-tot dish and some more noodles and sausage swimming in cream of mushroom soup. I didn't protest or refuse any food as it would have been a breach of Lutheran potluck etiquette, something I'd learned the hard way at my first potluck as a new pastor. Such a display of poor manners had taken three years to recover from. I would have to run an extra hundred miles to burn off the calories presented by all the cream of whatever soups comprising the foundation of most of the hot dishes.

Benny, on the other hand, asked for seconds and delighted in making a single mountain on his plate of what had to produce heartburn within an hour after the great indulgence. We continued to the small sandwiches tables. As best I could tell and explain to Benny, each sandwich contained some sort of deviled meat, deviled chicken, deviled ham and the last plate deviled eggs. At the mention of the devil, Benny declined to partake – this was wise on his part. It was only two years ago the deviled eggs caused a rush to the toilet and for some an entire day of diarrhea. I'd ordered they never be served again although my orders were often overruled by the church kitchen ladies. They were their own governing body and even Clayton knew better than to venture onto their turf.

Benny and I paused just long enough to top our plates with olives — three varieties — and home canned pickles – at least six varieties. Those ladies could pickle anything … beans, beets, onions, cucumbers, gizzards, eggs. I sometimes joked with Tammy about sassy husbands being careful around canning season or an angry wife might take to pickling the family jewels.

I led Benny to the table reserved for the guests of honor including Clayton and his wife, Liv, Georgina Olson, the choir director, and her husband who everyone called Ole, Olive and a special guest I invited who had yet to arrive. Mrs. Johansson sat next to Brigit Bjornson, the Secretary-Treasurer of the Council, a slim woman with thinning silver hair. Her husband, Buddy Bjornson, was a cheerful man, always smiling unlike his wife who never even cracked a grin. Olive sat next to a seat she'd held for me. She reserved another for my guest. I noted with trepidation Olive had heaped a plate full of deviled eggs and hoped she would not be calling in sick tomorrow. I gave Benny the seat between Clayton and me. Benny went after the food with such gusto I was concerned he'd die of a cream of mushroom overdose.

Clayton joined our table and I was pleased to note he loaded up on the deviled ham sandwiches. Benny, ever alert to what others were eating, made the same observation and told Clayton "you are eating the Devil's own sandwiches.'" Benny's remark brought a scowl to Clayton's face which Benny laughed at and pointed out Clayton looked like a devil.

"You should be eating with the children," Clayton fired back.

"He's my guest, Clayton, and he's right, when you get a certain angry look on your face, you do look like Beelzebub," I said and speared a pickled beet which was as red as Clayton's face. Table talk came to an uncomfortable halt.

"Here we are!" Father Gallo's pleasant voice broke the silence.

"Ah, Father, thank you for joining us on this day of celebration. I'm touched you have reached out to our church and honored us with your presence. I've saved you a seat of honor." I pointed with my fork to the vacant chair next to mine.

"And I brought a guest. I trust that is all right?" Father Gallo said.

"Yes, yes, of course. We'll squeeze in another chair. Benny, could you get a chair from the kitchen for our guest?" I asked.

Benny sprung from his own seat and rushed to the kitchen.

"Clayton, as president of the church council, could I ask you to make the introduction to our guests?" I asked.

Clayton's eyes bulged and his lower lip quivered. He was on the brink of stroking out. He looked to his wife as if he'd forgotten her name and needed assistance.

"Ahhh, well, I'm Clayton Johansson, president of the church council and this is my wife, Liv," he said and finished by pointing to each and identifying by name and title.

"Thank you Clayton, and Father your guest …"

"I asked Gabrielle, Gabrielle Durand, to be my date. We were talking after mass today and having such a good time, I asked her if she'd join me. I need moral support coming into the enemy's camp on Reformation Sunday." He laughed heartily at his own joke.

Benny returned with a chair and, with gentlemanly manners, pushed the seat behind Gabrielle. I'd made room between Clayton and Benny. The young man cupped his hands and whispered in my ear, "Pastor Kathy, you look just like her." He pointed a stubby finger towards Gabrielle who caught the gesture and smiled.

Father Gallo could brighten up any table conversation. Most of the stories I'd heard before. He had an inventory of stories for all events and today was no exception. He had Benny laughing so hard, he blew a pea out of his nose. The pea bounced onto Clayton's lap and he stood brushing away like some burning ember. Mrs. Bjornson thought Benny's antics so amusing she was in tears.

I found Gabrielle to be charming. She was so down to earth. Being at the same table with Clayton and his wife didn't appear to daunt her a bit. I began to wonder if Father Gallo had somehow gotten his adultery characters confused. On the other hand, Clayton didn't speak a word. Such a welcome relief as he typically would turn any conversation into a monologue. I toyed with the idea of "stealing"Gabrielle from Father Gallo.

"… and so after being shot at and put on the Mexican drug lord's hit list, I moved to Pelican Falls where the only shots I take are from the sore losers at bingo," Father Gallo finished a lengthy story of how he came to his parish.

"I'm going to Mexico tomorrow. I'm taking a vacation in Cancun," Gabrielle chirped in at the mention of Mexico.

"Oh, my, and how lucky you are to get out of here before the next storm hits," the choir director said. She always had the most current weather information available. She feared ice and snow on the roads so much she watched worldwide weather patterns and jet stream movements starting in July. Local pilots would call her to get the most up-to-date conditions.

"Where are you flying out of, then?" Mrs. Olson asked.

"Minneapolis, I'm driving down tomorrow morning and flying out on a charter directly to Cancun," Gabrielle said cheerfully and then added, "I've been hitting the tanning booth in my shop for a month. Look how brown I am already." She pointed to her bare arm with a fingernail painted with lovely little flowers.

She was indeed brown when compared to our pasty Minnesota complexions. Even if we lay in the sun all summer, we'd always be pale by Halloween – we did save money on make-up by going to Halloween parties as ghosts or zombies.

"Well, even though I'm jealous, I hope you have a lovely vacation. Clayton, you're also leaving town tomorrow to go to Minneapolis, aren't you?" I asked recalling his lecture to me about how Ron couldn't be buried Monday because Clayton was traveling south.

"On business, I've got business in the Twin Cities all week. I should be so lucky as to go on a vacation," Clayton said rather unconvincingly.

"Well, I wish you both safe travels and if our choir director is correct and she always is, you'll both be missing a major Halloween snowstorm," I said. "Come on Benny, let's hit the table with the bars and cookies."

There were enough calories on the dessert table to fire up the Madagascar population for a week. American Crystal Sugar investors must have seen a sharp rise in sales last week. Cookies took a poor second to bars this year. The ratio of cookies to bars changes without explanation. Some soul might do a doctoral dissertation or get a Federal grant and find correlations between sun spot activities and the appearance of bars versus cookies at the Lutheran potlucks. Rhubarb bars, strawberry-rhubarb bars, strawberry pecan bars, and pecan chocolate bars – the procession went on in a clockwise presentation on a table bigger than Brainerd.

Benny and I had different strategies. Benny took one of everything. I vowed to limit myself to one dessert so I had to be certain I picked the perfect one. During my search I came upon a cake the size of our high school basketball court. It was a white decorated pan cake. The creamy frosting was adorned with witches, goblins, ghouls, and a couple of small red devils carrying pitchforks. I stood admiring the cake and trying to decide if this was the dessert I wanted to spend my calories on. I felt a tug on my dress sleeve.

It was Mrs. Olson, Mavis Olson. "Mrs. Bertelsen pulled my table decorations with the witches and ghosts so I thought I'd bake a cake with Halloween spirit. Do you like it, then?" Mavis asked. She looked up at me with large blue eyes waiting for an official declaration.

"Mavis, it is wonderful. I would have a piece, but I don't want to spoil the masterpiece," I answered.

Mavis produced a cake knife and a plate faster than a Japanese Sushi Chef with a new Kasumi Knife. She cut a corner and a zombie in half. I walked away from the table muttering a thank you. I noticed Mavis, with hands on her hip and still holding the big knife, staring defiantly at Mrs. Bertelsen. Under my breath, I made a prediction I had just witnessed the first shot fired in the next kitchen war.

CHAPTER FOURTEEN

(Sunday)

*C*layton and Liv Johansson were gone when I returned to my seat. So was my cake. I'd talked to a dozen people as I strolled from the dessert table back to my chair. As I chatted, I took small bites trying to make it last. Benny, on the other hand, still had half-dozen desserts on his plate. He was guarding them with his elbow because as he explained, "Father Gallo keeps taking pieces of my cookies."

Gabrielle was engaged in an animated conversation with Ole Olson about snowmobiling. Gabrielle had recently bought a Polaris snowmobile and evidently Ole was an Arctic Cat guy. Arguing over the superiority of a snowmobile model could be dangerous, perhaps topped only by a disagreement over which brand of farm tractor was better. Town gossips say these arguments cross generational lines and have resulted in fist fights and even gunfire in back of Antler's Bar and Grill.

Father Gallo gave me a wink and a nod signaling me to follow him. We were savvy enough to withdraw before we'd be asked to take a position in the snowmobile debate. Benny looked relieved Father Gallo was leaving and his cookies would be safe. He relaxed and became intent on eating and listening to the pointless discussion. I led Father Gallo upstairs, down the linoleum covered hallway, to my office. He shut the door and took a seat in the upholstered chair I'd rescued from an estate sale. I waited until the chair was marked down to a 90% discount before jumping at the purchase – risky business, waiting for the lowest price. In Pelican Falls, women had been known to engage in wrestling matches to get the bottom-line price. I've seen them perched like hawks on a telephone pole waiting for an item to be marked down for the last time before it gets tossed in the dumpster. It was a good chair, broken-in and comforting to the dozens of parishioners who wept, cried, and bawled over life and the loss of life.

"Makwa's in town. He's out at my place. Come out for supper?" I said before my cheeks even hit my leather swivel chair.

"Great. Did he just drop in like usual?" Father Gallo asked.

"Of course, I darn near shot him. I saw someone lurking in the shadows and until he let out his Makwa wolf cry, I thought it might be Clayton sneaking up to strangle me."

"Oh Poop, I forgot, I've got bingo tonight. I call the last few games every Sunday evening. Let's get together for breakfast tomorrow morning. How long is he staying anyway?" Father Gallo asked.

"He didn't say. I don't even think to ask. He comes and then he goes seemingly without a plan or a schedule. He goes when he's gone, I guess."

"Tell him not to be 'gone' until I see him. He can be so mysterious."

I took a sip of my tepid coffee and waited for Father Gallo to finish waxing about Makwa's puzzling nature. He was correct, Makwa did have some unusual powers of observations or insights or perhaps you'd call them magical qualities I couldn't explain. Makwa was not a religious man. However, he was one of the most spiritual men I've ever met. I think Jesus would have liked to have Makwa as a friend.

When Father Gallo finished his long description, I asked, "How did you like Clayton's reaction?"

"He was stunned. In Mexico I observed the same expression on the face of a poor fellow who had just been hit in the stomach with four rounds from a .45 Colt."

"Do you think it's working, our plan I mean?" I asked hoping he'd arrived at the same conclusion I had.

"Brilliantly, my dear, brilliantly. I do believe you are on the road to neutering that big stud, Mr. Johansson. Are you certain his wife knows?"

"Tammy says she does and so far Tammy has been spot on. Tammy is like a sponge. She soaks up every little word which is how I knew Gabrielle was going to Mexico."

"And she brought the trip up herself," Father Gallo said.

"Because of your rather lengthy story. I did have another way to bring it up anyway even if Gabrielle hadn't. I should have had Benny take a photo of Clayton's face when the trip was disclosed."

"Benny is going to have an upset tummy tonight, what with all he ate."

"I'm not so sure. I've seen him pack away a dozen hotdogs and still go back for more. He's a healthy eater," I said.

"On a different note, I've got news about the Vatican position…" Father Gallo began.

"Oh, oh, can I tell you about Tammy first? I'm sorry. I'm so excited. She thinks she knows who is sending the nasty notes," I interrupted my colleague.

"Who?" He leaned way forward in his seat as if to receive a prime piece of gossip. If he hadn't become a priest, I believe he would have moved to Hollywood and become a gossip columnist. He was always anxious to lap up the latest tidbit.

"Holly Hollenbachen, Mrs. Hollenbachen from south of town — you know her husband raises turkeys. You know those big barns which stink so rotten when you drive to Fergus Falls, that's the Hollenbachen farm."

"I know Holly and her husband – they call him Stubby. He's a big-shot down at the VFW, commander or something. I've dealt with him a number of times when we bury a veteran and the VFW is going to furnish an honor guard or a flag."

"You know, I remember the man — sort of an officious man who always looks like he's standing at attention," I said.

"What makes her think its Holly?"

"She has pieced together a string of circumstantial evidence which would make Perry Mason jealous. Have you got a few minutes?"

"Try to keep it under ten, I should get back to Gabrielle and I still want to tell you my news."

According to the left-handed clock on the wall over my friend's shoulder, I laid the details out in eight minutes and thirty-eight seconds.

"Well, your allegations are not altogether damning."

"What do you mean, back in the good old days you would burn a witch at the stake with less evidence," I quipped.

"I believe you have your historical facts confused. It was the Puritans on your side of the aisle who burned witches."

"You folks were too busy burning the reformers," I said.

"Exactly, and in the spirit of Reformation Day, I'll not be slighted with inaccurate history. I do have a bit of news which might add some weight to the scales of justice."

I was looking over Father Gallo's left shoulder to the full length mirror hanging on the back of my door. I've been told I have this annoying little habit of looking at myself in the mirror while carrying on a conversation. In my defense, I believe all women do this. Regardless, I saw the lipstick I'd applied so liberally had smeared. I took a tissue and tried to fix it. I wondered if I should add some gloss.

"Are you listening to me?" Father Gallo asked.

"Yes, of course, what do you have to tip the scales anyway?" I was becoming frustrated with the lipstick mess I was creating.

"My sisters used to annoy me by looking in the mirror when I was speaking to them."

I put the tissue down. "Sorry."

"When Tammy's church was looking for a pastor, Holly Hollenbachen was on the call committee. She had a friend whose son was a pastor over in Deer Creek and splitting his time between three country churches. Holly insisted he be selected."

"Where did you hear such news?" I asked.

"Well, if you must know, I heard it at the bridge club. Holly's gal pal from high school, they were cheerleaders together, said it out loud at the bridge table."

"I'm always amazed how much you learn playing bridge and even more amazed that Holly was a cheerleader given her size."

Father Gallo held his fist to his mouth and unleashed a dreadfully loud belch. "Excuse me! I think it was the Italian meatball hot dish."

"I understand. I feel some rumbling in my own overloaded stomach. Anyway, about the bridge match?"

"There's more. Holly actively campaigned against Tammy and when Tammy was selected, Holly swore she'd never last."

"May I share this with Tammy?" I asked.

"Certainly, although it may hurt whatever sort of relationship she has with Holly."

"I don't believe there much to salvage. Now tell me your news," I said.

"This morning, before sunrise, I received a telephone call from a Father Luiggi, a colleague in the Vatican. Luiggi is the ranking official who will be selecting the candidate for the position I've dreamed of for years. The good news is they have decided to leave the post open without filling it for some unspecified time."

"I thought you told me November 1st was the deadline."

"It was. However, the only candidate other than me is a quarrelsome priest from Romania. Father Luiggi is firmly against taking another troublesome soul into the Vatican. He says there is already more drama in the Vatican than in a girls' locker room in middle school," Father Gallo said.

I didn't bother to ask how a Vatican official would have knowledge of the social life of a girls' locker room. Instead I asked, "So, we've some time to work on Mrs. LeBlanc?"

"Yes, although I was warned the Holy See may intervene and force the appointment. He has some fondness for Romanians or so I am told."

"Now that we have Clayton on the ropes and Tammy's got a viable suspect, I say we turn our sights on Mrs. LeBlanc," I said.

"I agree, however we really need to get back to the potluck."

CHAPTER SIXTEEN

(Sunday)

"*I have to stop at the Cenex gas station to get some Tums or Rolaids,*" I muttered as I drove the pickup off the state highway and into the station parking lot. For a Sunday night, the place was hopping, a pickup at every pump and most of the parking spots taken – likely anglers buying minnows or those disgusting wax worms to go fishing. The hot topic at the potluck I learned as I was leaving was the crappies were biting on Beaver Lake. The tasty little fish were jumping in the boats.

"You need anything?" I asked Makwa.

"Ya, some No Doze. I'm not certain I can stay awake for an evening of bingo."

"You're not there to play bingo, you have a greater mission. Sit tight, I will be right back. I'll leave the pickup running to keep the heater going." I slid out of the driver's seat and onto an icy pavement. A few clouds had moved in right after the potluck and left a film of slick ice. I walked gingerly to the front door. As I was reaching for the handle the door flew open and knocked my hand. Something in my left thumb cracked and it hurt like heck.

"Careful there dear," Pastor Morgan Wentworth said as he emerged from the Cenex. "I nearly broke my nose when you stopped the door." He was wearing a University of Minnesota Golden Gopher sweatshirt and matching basketball shorts – unusual attire for the chilly fall evening.

"Geez, Morgan, I think you broke my thumb." I inspected the now throbbing digit. I couldn't tell if it was broken although it sure felt like it.

"Let me see." He grabbed my thumb and inspected it briefly. "No, it's all right, it's not broken."

"Thank you, Dr. Wentworth, for using your x-ray vision. How much do I owe you for the exam?"

"Funny, Kathy. I'd like to stand here and trade quips, but I have to get to a basketball game. My church is playing Pastor Randy's church and we're going to kick their butts."

"By all means, get to the game. Say, before you go, Father Gallo and I were just talking about the community autumn celebration."

"Oh, I forgot to call you. Pastor Randy and I are going with the games I talked about. Your people are welcome to put together some teams and join us. It'll be a great way to get together. I have to run." He brushed past me.

Sports, the new religion, seems to have consumed Pelican Falls.

My thumb really hurt. So did my feelings after the encounter with Morgan. I entered the store, waved to the clerk who I'd confirmed last year and went to the small medications display. I was conflicted whether to buy Tums, Ex-Lax, or Aleve. I bought all three plus some candy bars and returned to the pickup.

"Here's a couple of candy bars. They have enough caffeine and sugar to keep you awake through the bingo games," I said. I tossed two Snickers, giant-sized, the ones weighing about a pound a piece, onto Makwa's lap. He had one wrapper peeled back and the bar eaten by the time I was back on the state highway headed north to the Catholic Church.

"Who was the gentleman wearing the gopher shorts you were talking to at the gas station?" Makwa asked between bars.

"Pastor Morgan Wentworth. He's quite the athlete or so he tells me – high school quarterback, track star, college baseball scholarship. His church is the most physically fit congregation I've ever witnessed. If they had a potluck like we had today they'd serve arugula and spinach greens and kiwi fruit smoothies. You wouldn't find a single cream-of-mushroom dish on the serving table."

"He's a good looking man, fit for his age."

"Oh ya, his professional goal is to move on to a mega-church in the Twin Cities and then use the big church to launch a televangelism career and become an international star. He even had a studio built onto the church. He produces videos of all of his sermons and has brought in experts to help him with his delivery. It's some production, that's for sure."

I took a right on First Street and slowed for a jogger with a black dog. It was a dangerous night to be jogging on such slippery streets. We passed the Reformed United Church of the Redeemer, Morgan Wentworth's church. It was a newer building with three sprawling additions, the latest a gymnasium rivaling the local high school's decades old gym. I had to give Morgan credit, he knew how to raise money and support for whatever project he threw his weight behind.

I turned left on Sixth Street past the St. Mary's Church which was illuminated with million candlepower lamps. The parking lot was nearly full when we arrived. I found a space marked "Reserved for Father Gallo." I knew he parked in the garage and I reasoned he would welcome my use of his spot. As I recalled, bingo was in the basement. I'd been there once years ago. I hadn't planned on ever making a second visit. However, this afternoon as we walked from my office back to the potluck, Aldo served up an opportunity too delicious to refuse.

Makwa and I literally skated along the icy sidewalk and into the rear entrance. I led the way down the steps towards the sounds of 'B-6' and 'I-5'. The basement was alive with conversation and a flurry of players marking their cards. I searched the expansive room for Aldo. He was nowhere to be seen. It was already seven-thirty and he had insisted he would be waiting for us when we arrived. Makwa and I moved to the coffee and cookies table and helped ourselves. I know it sounds petty but I believe the Lutheran women can out bake the Catholic gals any day of the week. I took a cup of coffee and passed on the sweets. Makwa filled his big paws full of what passed for sugar cookies. I bet they didn't use lard. The Lutheran women are true believers in lard. Some even render their own lard using a baking sheet in an oven. I've watched them take big chunks of fat fresh from a butchered hog and reduce it to pure lard in no time at all. Sometimes I worry I'm getting to think and act just like the kitchen bosses. We took up obscure positions in the back of the hall.

I was worried about Aldo, what with the icy roads, and I knew he had to pick up Mrs. LeBlanc. Her estate has a long, steep driveway. Aldo, by his own admission, was a dreadful driver, except in Rome, where he claimed the other drivers matched his reckless style. We waited.

It was almost eight when I spied Aldo walking down the back steps. On his arm was a woman of striking beauty. Her thick silver hair was perfectly styled. She was draped in a short mink coat and covered with expensive looking jewelry from her manicured fingers to the diamonds hanging elegantly from her ears. She walked with a slight limp and hung tightly to Aldo. He wore a wide grin as if he was parading the Queen herself. I nudged Makwa and we strolled across the room to intercept the royal couple.

When we reached them, Aldo spoke first. "I'm so sorry we are late. We had an accident I'm afraid."

"I knew it. Was it serious? Did you wreck your car?" I asked as I examined him for wounds, blood, and broken bones.

"No, Mrs. LeBlanc fell as she was walking down the back steps to my car. Oh, it was my fault. I should have clutched her closer to me. The damn ice anyway. Oh, it's dangerously slippery out there tonight," Aldo said.

"Are you hurt badly?" I asked.

"No, my leg is bruised. Fortunately, I fell on Father Aldo. He's always there for me. Since my husband passed away, I rely on him for many things so it should be no surprise he'd be there for me to fall upon. I just couldn't bear to live without this dear man," Mrs. LeBlanc spoke slowly in a sophisticated voice with a hint of an accent. Not the Norwegian accent I was accustomed to hearing but more Canadian or perhaps French Canadian.

"Ahhh, my manners, please forgive me, Mrs. Sofia LeBlanc, let me introduce Pastor Kathy Johnson and Dr. Joseph Auginaush, both dear old pals of mine."

Makwa took Sofia's pale hand and kissed it adding a bow for an extra dose of charm. Sofia's face lit up like the Christmas tree star. She turned from me and clung to Makwa's hand with both of hers. I don't deny feeling a twinge of jealousy. She led him to a table at the front of the hall, right beneath the caller who was perched on top of a stool on an elevated stage of sorts. Sofia engaged Makwa in animated conversation. I couldn't quite hear the banter but it had to do with how much she missed a man in her life since the untimely departure of her husband. Aldo and I followed and joined them at a table on which rested a "Reserved" sign in bold black Gothic letters.

It was a welcomed relief when the bingo caller paused for a break between games. His voice was high pitched and squeaky. I could overhear Mrs. LeBlanc purring to Makwa.

"Now you simply must call me Sofia, Sofia with an 'f' not a 'ph'. And you, do you prefer to be addressed as doctor?" Sofia asked in a sweet voice reminiscent of my high school coquettish days.

"Mostly they call me Makwa."

"Bear in Ojibwe as I recall," Sofia said with a raised eyebrow, obviously been tattooed, although very tastefully.

"Very good, I'm impressed. How did you come by such a tasty morsel of knowledge?" Makwa asked.

"I was born into it. My family hails from Thunder Bay, Ontario. They go all the way back to the fur trading days. French men married into the Ojibwe tribe. You know, great-grandmother was from the Makwa Clan, the Bear Clan."

I missed the rest of the conversation amid the resumption of buzz of the bingo caller over a static prone microphone and Aldo pointing out a dozen or more parishioners we'd talked about but I'd never met.

"See that fellow over there in the green sweater? He's the gentleman who has me come out to his farm and bless his Holsteins every spring after calving season. I figure I've already blessed a thousand head of dairy cows. Who is to say how much extra milk in this village might be attributed to my blessings. Once a week, his kind wife brings me whole unprocessed milk, the kind the government warns against drinking. It keeps me fit as a fiddle."

"That must be a Catholic thing, Father, I mean the blessing thing. I've blessed plenty of babies and two motorcycles but never livestock," I said.

"Motorcycles?" Aldo asked.

"I married a couple staying at the B&B that went out of business last summer. You know the old grist mill that was remodeled into a swank bed and breakfast? Anyway this couple wanted to get married and they drove over from Little Falls on their matching Harley David-sons. After the ceremony, they asked if I'd bless the bikes. They were traveling to Banff and wanted some heavenly insurance, I guess. So I said a quick blessing and off they went. They sent me the nicest post-card and some Huckleberry Jam from the Canadian Rockies."

Aldo and I chatted without playing bingo until my cell phone about vibrated off my belt. I wrestled it from the holster and looked at the call I missed. The Caller ID read Ottertail County Sheriff. "Excuse me, I've got to return this call," I said and walked through the clamorous hall and into the women's bathroom where I had silence but only two bars of reception. I sat on a vacant stool and called into the dispatch center. I always make this call with great apprehension. I know the dispatchers are going to be the bearers of tragedy. This call was no exception. I finished and hurried back to Aldo.

"I'm so sorry, I have to leave. The Sheriff's Office is out at an acci-dent. A young man went off the road and into the Pelican River. A deputy is going to make a death notification and she'd like me to accompany her to the family home."

"Oh, I just hate this business. Why always the youngsters?" Aldo said and shook his bowed head.

"I'm meeting the deputy in ten minutes at my church. If I'm not back by the time bingo is over, would you be able to give Makwa a ride or perhaps he could stay …"

"Kathy, you go. I'll tell Makwa and don't worry, I'll take care of him." Aldo patted my arm and waved me on. He knew only too well what I'd soon be facing. We had talked many times about the mental toll of making these notifications. The grief is overwhelming. I can deal with that. Grieving is natural and a function of living and dying. The most difficult for me is when the family inevitably asks, "Why did God do this? Why did God let this happen?" Aldo and I burned a bottle of brandy one evening in our miserable attempt to understand

and form a reasonable answer to the family's question. Already I was rehearsing the inadequate lines I would deliver. I hardly remember getting into my truck and driving. A pretty deputy with a long ponytail was waiting in her squad car when I arrived at the church. She looked so young. I felt so old.

CHAPTER SEVENTEEN

(Sunday)

*I*t *was almost midnight when I turned off the county road* onto my long sandy driveway. A pair of tire tracks were faintly visible in the snow. Aldo must have dropped Makwa off at my house. In my mind, I replayed, for the fourth or fifth time, the sad scene at the young victim's house. His mother collapsed at the front door. The father just looked at his wife and stood frozen with disbelief. I did my best to comfort them and their two daughters but frankly felt totally inadequate. Someday, I promised myself, I'll have the answers. Someday.

I looked towards my house and could have sworn the barn was on fire. Big snowflakes driven by a north wind reflected whirling flames. I pushed hard on the accelerator and envisioned frightened horses trying to free themselves from the stables. As I neared the yard, it became clear the flames were only a bonfire and figures of Tammy and Makwa were huddled in front of the pyre. I slowed the truck and took deep breaths. Too much adrenaline for one day.

"Gosh, I thought the place was ablaze when I drove up. What are you two doing?" I spoke in a tone way too harsh.

"I should have called and told you. Aldo asked if I'd drive Makwa to your house. Aldo didn't feel well and wasn't up to motoring on the icy roads. I'm sorry," Tammy said.

"Oh, don't be. I apologize. I'm still a bit upset."

"And rightly so, come join us. I've been sinfully nipping at your bottle of Bailey's Irish Cream and have a glass for you." Tammy moved from the lean-to where they were seated on worn director chairs and gave me a much needed hug. She grasped my sweaty hand and pulled me out of the snowfall to a vacant chair. The fire warmed my outsides and the Irish Cream warmed my insides. Only one I told myself. That vow lasted as long as it took Max to plant his muzzle on my lap. I could always count on Max and Tammy.

"Was it bad?" Makwa asked.

"It always is, especially when it's a young person."

"What happened, if you even want to talk about it?" Tammy asked.

"The young man lived about five miles east of Pelican Falls and was a new driver. Of course his parents blamed themselves for letting him drive, but he was on his way to the church basketball game. It was as if they believed he'd be safe because he was on his way to a church function. He lost control of the vehicle outside of town, you know, the curve past the resort near the state park. He drove into the river and drowned."

"So sad," Tammy said.

"The family belongs to Randy's congregation. Randy was at the ball game until about ten. When he learned of the accident, he immediately came out to the house. I was relieved to see him and let him take over. I left and then spent another hour talking to the deputy. It was her first death notification and she was most shook-up."

We talked about the situation until I felt I couldn't anymore. I'd run out of wisdom and mental energy. Tammy sensed my exhaustion and changed the subject to the mundane. "When we got back to your place, Makwa and I got the horses inside and fed them along with Max and Smokey."

"Thanks so much. Tammy you have to stay the night. I couldn't bear the thought of you driving back in this weather."

"I've already planned to sleep over. I put an overnight bag in the house."

"Makwa, how was bingo?" I asked as I stroked Max behind his ears, his favorite spot.

"Aldo runs a rigged game."

"Oh, he doesn't," I said.

"Truly he does. Sofia and I were playing bingo while she talked my ear off. We never won a game. Then Aldo brought us some new bingo cards. He said it might change our luck. He left us alone and went to the microphone and called the last three games of the night. Sofia won two and I won the last game." Makwa reached into his leather vest pocket and brought out a thick wad of cash. "The game is rigged."

"Aldo does have a winning way with his loyal parishioners. To hear him talk, Sofia tithes about seventy-five percent of the church budget. Maybe it's just his way to give a little back," Tammy offered.

"So you and Sofia hit it off?" I asked.

"We did, famously. She is seriously interested in the native culture. She claims to have some blood from the tribe," Makwa said.

"You say 'claims' as if you don't believe her," I said.

"Kathy, every other person I meet has 'Indian blood.' By my count, there must have been two hundred million natives when the pilgrims arrived and for the first two centuries all they did was breed with the Europeans."

"Did I ever tell you about my…" Tammy said.

Makwa held his hands over his ears. "No, not you, too. And Kathy, do you have an Apache or Tohono O'odham somewhere in the closet?"

"Our family closet is packed but mostly with skeletons that rattle about. What was your impression of Mrs. LeBlanc?" I asked.

"Hmmm, that's complicated. Superficially, a bright and refined lady who is used to being pampered. She expects to have things her way. She knows how to use her money to get what she wants."

"And beneath the 'rich bitch' syndrome, is there something more?" I asked.

"I believe there is much more. She is deeply spiritual. She knows death is at her doorstep and is uncomfortable with what waits beyond."

"That's about ninety percent of the people I meet," Tammy said.

"Did you learn anything helpful?" I asked.

"Helpful?"

"Specifically, using your advanced degrees in psychology and your wisdom as a spiritual leader, did you discern any weaknesses or personality traits which might be exploited to make Mrs. LeBlanc free

Aldo so he can go to the Vatican?" I asked feeling less like a pastor and more like an attorney during cross-examination.

"Oh, sure, a bunch of them."

"Such a brilliant studious answer, 'a bunch of them,'" I said. Makwa could be a challenge to get an answer without some sword play.

"Since she lost her husband who was a domineering force in her life, she has been searching for a new leader — a new 'father figure' if you will — pun intended. Aldo is the new 'father figure.'"

"So she's not likely to let him out of her life?" I asked, already knowing the answer.

"Exactly!"

Tammy leaned across my lap and filled the empty glass I'd been cradling in my hands. "So, all we have to do is find a new 'father figure,' one even more potent than Aldo," Tammy concluded.

"Does anyone come to mind?" I asked liking the direction our conversation was going.

Makwa smiled. "Mrs. LeBlanc asked me to come to brunch tomorrow. She wants to discuss the spiritual aspect of the native culture. She was very interested in the sweat lodge and fascinated with the Sun Dance."

"Brunch? Did you bring your brunching attire?" I teased.

"I have to admit, I'm traveling light — just the clothes on my back and a couple of sets of underwear. I had planned on going to the rez where I keep some clothes at my auntie's place near White Earth. It was sunny and seventy when we left Pine Ridge and this snow has caught me unprepared."

"As I recall, you and I are about the same size. Come morning we'll toss those crusty jeans in the wash. I have some clean Carhartt shirts, a warmer jacket and hat you can wear. You're on your own for underwear though," I said.

Makwa winked. "Thanks, boots, you have any boots?"

"Cowgirl boots if you don't mind the fancy designs," I replied. "I've got a pair two sizes too large that I use to ride in."

"Kathy has some new turquoise jewelry which would go well with the boots and brunch," Tammy added.

"Tammy, I almost forgot to tell you what Aldo told me about Holly Hollenbachen and her husband, Stubby," I said.

"What?"

"I tell you this only as an additional piece of evidence to add to your list. Aldo said that when your church was searching for a new minister, Holly strongly opposed your selection because she had some pastor over in Deer Creek who was in the running. She wanted to see him called instead of you."

"I know who you mean. I met him during one of my early visits to Pelican Falls. He is a peach of a guy. I'd hire him. Now that you mention it, Holly has brought his name up several times. Just last week she said he was still looking to leave Deer Creek. See, my list of evidence is growing."

"Tomorrow, weather permitting, I'm going to meet my cousin's ex, you know the special agent with the Crime Bureau. He's in Detroit Lakes working on an old death investigation. He said he'd take a look at what you have," I said.

"Maybe he could follow her around or tap her phones," Tammy said wishfully.

"I don't think so, but at least he said he'll show the notes to a document examiner who can analyze the handwriting."

"You ladies make my head spin. I'd hoped to stop here for some peace and meditation and I find myself in the middle of some grand conspiracy," Makwa said as he stood. "I'm off to my humble bed in the manger."

"I don't have a manger and the cozy bed in the loft is better than the darn tepee you were sleeping in at Pine Ridge. Besides, I'm giving you Max again. What did you have to sleep with in Pine Ridge?"

"Oh, the coyotes were quite hospitable as were the Hollywood celebrities."

"Good night, Makwa!" Tammy and I said in unison.

CHAPTER EIGHTEEN

(Monday)

*T*ammy was gone from my house when I woke to the obnoxious alarm I had set for seven. I'd slept so soundly I didn't even hear her leave. I shuffled into the kitchen following the aroma of a brewing pot of pumpkin-spiced coffee. Tammy was like that, she'd made coffee and left me a cream filled croissant along with a note wishing me a good morning and warning me to be careful on my drive to Detroit Lakes. "...accidents always happen in threes," she wrote and signed the handprinted note "with love."

I drank and ate slowly, trying to make the pastry last. I checked my emails on the iPad. There was nothing urgent. The weather forecast promised a warm sunny day. I sent an email asking Doc, Sara's ex-husband, if we could delay the meeting until lunch time to let the ice melt from the highways. The response was immediate and we agreed to meet at the coffee shop on Main Street in Detroit Lakes.

I heard Makwa or Max snoring in the loft of the stable as I saddled Whisper. She was eager to leave her stall where she'd spent the night sheltered from the storm. I gave her a carrot and nuzzled her nose. I love the smell of a horse's nose. We exchanged breaths and it was as if our very souls were mixing. I warmed her snaffle-bit with my bare hand before asking her to accept the hard metal in her mouth.

The maples and oak trees had lost their last leaves but gained a glimmering coat of frost and snow. I inhaled deeply taking in the sharp fresh air. With a slight cue, Whisper broke into a trot taking me over the rolling hills and through the woods. I let my mind relax and relished the symmetry the horse and I achieved. With a nudge from my heel, she moved to a lope that felt like we were floating through some enchanted forest – her hoofs hardly touching the earth. Time ceased to exist as did all earthly concerns. As God intended, I was one with His noble creature in His magnificent creation.

We reluctantly returned to the stable. Makwa and Max were no longer in the loft. I turned Whisper out in the pasture and walked stiffly to the house. The 'boys' were sharing breakfast at the kitchen table — peanut butter toast and some sausage Makwa had dug up from the freezer. Max will be sad when Makwa leaves. They are soul brothers.

"Don't eat too much, you've brunch with the Widow LeBlanc in a few hours," I counseled.

"What do you think she'll serve? Foie Gras or quiches?" Makwa said while waving a fork with a speared sausage.

"Wild rice gruel with pemmican would be my guess, you know, keeping with your mutual native heritage."

"I pray you are wrong. I hate wild rice. It tastes like soggy cardboard. I don't see how those Indians can eat that stuff."

I smiled at the thought of chewing cardboard and had to agree with Makwa's assessment. Although buried in a cauldron of cream of mushroom soup, it is edible. "I don't believe the natives eat the rice. They harvest it and sell it to the tourists, all the while laughing in their hats."

"Max and I love the sausage, what is it?" Makwa asked.

"Venison. I shot the buck last year about three hundred yards behind the stable. He'd been entertaining several does all morning. I let him finish with his little pleasure before I popped him. Whisper never liked the buck in her pasture so she was pleased to help me drag the big boy back to the house. You and Max are eating the last package."

"I'll shower when we're done. I threw my jeans in the wash about thirty minutes ago. They should be ready for the dryer."

"I'm afraid to ask. If your only jeans are in the dryer, what are you wearing under my kitchen table?"

"Max and I are similarly dressed." Makwa wore a broad smile – the one he used to melt the hearts of most women he encountered.

"You and Max are a lot alike and I'm fairly certain that is not a compliment. You stay seated. I'll throw your pants in the dryer and put some shirts and boots in the living room. I'll leave a robe also."

"Won't need one if my pants are dry."

I retreated to the laundry room to throw the jeans in the dryer and then on to my bedroom. I scrunched into a fresh pair of jeans, tucked in a plaid shirt, and pulled on some boots I hadn't worn in a year. I ran a brush through my hair and was ready. Mondays are my day off and I did my best to dress casually and comfortably. I found a couple of shirts, a pair of boots, a hat, and a robe and brought them into the living room. I heard Makwa in the kitchen talking to Max. I went into the three season porch to pray. I'd start with Makwa and Max.

The ride into Pelican Falls was precarious. I stopped twice to help travelers who'd slipped into the ditch. We were able to pull one back onto the road with a long nylon rope I kept in the back of the truck. I called a wrecker for the other deeply buried car. Max sat proudly between Makwa and me. He loved a good road trip and was excellent company. I dropped Makwa off at the bottom of Mrs. LeBlanc's steep driveway. It looked too slippery to chance the drive up. Makwa appeared quite dashing in my shirt, jacket, and turquoise colored boots. Max and I continued on to the church. I parked the truck in my usual spot and after Max did his business, we strolled in through the rear door. The hall lights were turned off. Benny often switched all the lights off after someone told him leaving them on would cost him his job. I could easily see light coming into the glass doors at the front of the church and aimed for the luminescence. Max is not a growler or a snarler so when he did, it caught my attention. He continued with this low rumbling the length of the hallway. I wouldn't have given it a second thought except Max does this some times when he enters the church. His canine behavior is spooky enough, but I have had this feeling of some invisible spirit being present at times. I feel it most often when I am at the pulpit, preaching, and I sense a presence behind me as if the spirit is listening to make certain I'm getting it right. Grandma always said I had a vivid imagination.

Olive didn't approve of Max being in church and the dour look on her face didn't soften when Max presented himself to be petted and scratched. She held her skinny arms high, squealed, and shooed him away. He looked hurt.

"Any calls?" I asked when I paused at her desk.

"Max, you go into her office, go on now, scoot. Just one, some Sheriff's deputy called. She wanted to thank you for being there for her last night. What was all of that about?" Olive asked.

"It's a long story, Olive. I'll tell you when I have more time."

"I have time now."

"I have to get on the road. I'm going to Detroit Lakes. Do you need anything?"

"Can I make a list?" Olive asked.

"Sure, I'm leaving in ten minutes."

I turned to go into my office when Olive inquired, "What was the deal with the woman Father Aldo brought to our potluck?"

"Gabrielle? Oh, she goes to his church and he just asked her to join him. It can be awkward when one comes to those functions alone. I imagine he just wanted some company."

"I understand. I meant to say there seemed to be some bad blood between her and Clayton and especially with Clayton's wife, Liv."

"I didn't notice. Do you really think so?"

"Yes, I do and so did Bridget Bjornson. She called me this morning already and talked for twenty minutes about the matter. She said Liv was staring daggers at Clayton and Gabrielle."

"I don't know … maybe Liv had a bad hair experience over at the Curl Up and Dye. Ask Clayton sometime."

"Oh, I almost forgot, Clayton called from the airport in Minneapolis. He said I was supposed to call a special council meeting when he gets back into town."

He's going to resign was the thought which popped into my mind. It was going to be a good day.

Chapter Nineteen

(Monday)

*M*y special agent friend, Doc Martini, was already seated on the couch facing the fireplace which warmed the only Internet coffee house in Detroit Lakes. He was watching the burning log and nursing a mug in both hands. Doc is a handsome man in a tough sort of way. He has a chiseled face favoring his Italian heritage. Thick dark hair cut high and peppered with grey, although not as much as one would expect for his age. He wore the scars of a combat veteran and a few decades of being a cop. In his younger days, Doc was an all-state hockey player. He had maintained his athletic build into middle age. I met Doc when he married my cousin, Sara. Like Doc's first two marriages, this one had not lasted long. By his own admission, his first love and lifelong mistress was "the job." Maybe he should have been a priest like his mama wanted and he would have avoided the conflicts of marriage and a job. Long after the marriage to Sara ended, we kept up a warm and cordial relationship.

Doc stood as I approached. I didn't even notice he had seen me coming – must be some sixth sense cops have. "Doc, it's so good to see you." We embraced with gusto. He even lifted me off my feet although I was as tall as he.

"Kathy, you get more beautiful every time we meet. If only I'd met you instead of your cousin, I would have taken you back to Italy and bought you an estate in Tuscany where we'd spend our days growing grapes and drinking fine wines."

"Doc, you are such a BSer. I mean the part about buying me an estate ... on a cop's salary yet?"

"Come sit next to me. I've ordered you a caramel latte. I asked the waitress to bring it when she saw the prettiest woman come prancing through the doorway." He sat and patted the cushion next to him – always such a charmer.

I shucked my Merrill boots and sat with my stocking feet curled under my seat. It was so good to see Doc again. I wished he had stayed with Sara. He was good for her ... settled her down. She would've stayed too, if she could have had children. She always wanted to raise a big family. She learned from her doctor that children were never to be and she left to return to exotic dancing

"Are you still riding horses?" Doc asked.

"Yes, I was out early this morning."

"Sara loved horses, too."

"We grew up on horseback. During the summer, when the tourists came to town, Sara, her sister, Barb, and I worked at the horse stables leading the trail rides for little buckaroos. The Johnson girls everyone called us. We were inseparable."

"I remember Sara saying you three were back to back homecoming queens in Detroit Lakes," Doc said.

"Here's the latte to the prettiest woman in the shop," a petite blonde gal served the steaming cup over my shoulder and left as abruptly as she'd appeared.

"You remembered my favorite latte. Thank you for the cup and for remembering." I patted his shoulder with my free hand. His muscles were rock-solid.

"I can imagine the Johnson girls being pursued by every boy in town," Doc said.

"And a fair number from out of town. In the summer, Detroit Lakes filled with teenagers on the beach and cruising the streets. Every weekend there was a dance at the lakeside pavilion. Those were the days, my friend," I said recalling the old song with those lyrics.

"Have you heard from Sara?" Doc asked.

"We are Facebook friends. She's in Rio," I replied.

"Dancing?"

"I imagine, that's what she does."

"Send her my love next time you Facebook her," Doc said.

"You don't Facebook?"

"Yeah, one of the interns set me up an account. Turns out I don't have any friends. She offered to give me some of her eight hundred friends. I don't know, seems tacky to me. I'm content with no Face-book friends."

"Oh Doc, I'm sure you could have friends."

"Anyway, enough about my solitary life … you have some evidence for me. Let's see what you have."

I pulled the three pieces of paper from my purse and handed them to Doc. "Now, we're not alleging a crime here. My friend, Tammy, is just worried about these notes. I mean, just read them."

Doc, with his lips moving, read them quickly. "It may not be a crime although I can understand why she'd be concerned. These matters should never be shrugged off. They can become very serious, even dangerous."

"What do you think? Did the same person write all three notes?" I asked.

"Frankly, Kathy, your opinion is as good as mine. I never have been sold on my ability to analyze handwriting. We have experts who do our guessing."

"Tammy is convinced the woman who wrote and signed the innocent note also authored the other two."

"Maybe, what would you like me to do?"

"Could you ask your expert to look at the three notes?"

"Yeah, sure. The expert, she's a friend of mine. She owes me a favor. A while ago, some guy was stalking her in the apartment complex where she lived. I had a visit with the man. He moved to Kentucky, somewhere back in the hills, and she owes me a professional courtesy. I'm not going to log this in officially as evidence. If I do, I have to open an investigation, take out a case number and do a report naming Tammy and yourself. Probably not something any of us wants, eh?"

"No, can we just keep it informal?"

"We can and we will. If the handwriting expert says it is the same writer and this becomes a crime like a terroristic threat, we'll go the formal route," Doc said.

"Thank you so much. Tammy is very worried."

"I don't know Tammy, all right …" He paused as if searching for the right words. "… however you need to know sometimes notes like these are authored by the 'victim' as a means to get attention or sympathy. I'm not saying your friend is writing the notes. I'm just sharing my experience and professional knowledge. No offense meant, okay?" Doc asked.

"I don't take offense. I know Tammy and she wouldn't …"

"Seriously, it wasn't meant as an allegation and you don't need to defend her to me."

We suffered an uncomfortable moment of silence while I contemplated what Doc was telling me in a professional sort of way.

"What brings you to my old hometown anyway?" I asked to change the subject.

"I'm assisting another agent on a cold case. A while ago, a gal named Brenda Fairbanks went missing from the White Earth reservation. A pretty and bright woman working in the reservation village of Ogema just vanished." Doc pulled a photograph from his pocket and handed it to me. Even though the photograph was grainy, Brenda was indeed attractive – dark skinned, high cheekbones and long black hair with a killer smile. I handed the photo back to Doc.

"You said she disappeared some time ago. Why are you looking for her now?"

"One of our agents had an informant call. He may know where she is."

"Alive or buried?" I asked.

"Yes, one of those two." Doc smiled the sly grin I found so endearing. Sara probably shared my feelings. In our younger days, we often chased after the same boy.

"Are you going to dig her up?"

"The agents are interviewing this informant as we speak. I don't know if he is going to say Brenda was put through a wood chipper or she's alive and well in Vegas. If the informant has some credibility, I'm going to interview some of the folks who last had contact with her."

"Sounds gruesome …"

"It is a gruesome game I play, my dear." Doc stood and stretched his arms. "Can I buy you lunch? I see they just opened a Maid-Rite. I haven't eaten one of those crumbly little hamburgers in years."

"Yesterday, my church had potluck. The kitchen ladies packed leftovers and gave me enough to last until Thanksgiving, when we have another potluck and then I'm good until Christmas when we have another …"

"… and you're good until Easter," Doc finished my thought.

"Not quite. I run out around Valentine's Day. I'm thinking of a potluck for Valentine's Day which would get me to Easter. After Lent, it is only a few weeks until the 'lake people' return to our church and I have an invitation every week to a BBQ at someone's lake home." I rose and took his arm. "Come join Max and me for a picnic down at the lake. I've enough for all of us and a dozen begging geese."

"Let me make a phone call, run an errand, and then I can meet you at the lake."

"I'll wait by the pavilion. Do you need directions?"

"No. Sara showed me when we came home to visit Grandma. I'll be there in a half-hour."

When I crawled into the pickup, I found Max had moved into the rear seat and had nearly succeeded in prying the top from the wicker basket which held our lunch. I scolded him and he returned the most pitiful look. I drove off in the direction of Big Detroit Lake. I slowed as I passed the modest cottage where I grew up on Summit Street. I have only fond memories of living with Grandma and Grandpa. They were the kindest people on earth. On Grandpa's small salary from the railroad, they provided for Sara, Barb, and me long after their children, our parents, had struck out on their own without us. I wanted to stop and run into the house and give them a big hug, but they both passed away last year. It was the saddest time of my life. At least the new owners were keeping the place up. Grandpa would smile at the sight.

Steam rose from Big Detroit Lake as the sun warmed the surface after the hard freeze last night. Hundreds of coots, the stepchildren of the duck world, swam in endless circles as two bald eagles took turns diving at the flocks. The attacks seemed more for entertainment than food. Like the two-legged earth-bound hunters, the eagles evidently also didn't appreciate the not so delicate taste of coot. Assisted by Max, I unpacked the picnic basket full of sandwiches, vinegar and sea salt chips, Doc's favorite, and a variety plate of bars. Max took a seat on the picnic table and waited politely for Doc to arrive. My companion wore a smile on his face warming my soul. If people had the hearts of Goldens, I'd be out of business.

Doc pulled his black SUV into the parking lot. He exited with a cigarette, probably a Camel, dangling from his lips. He walked towards us with a slight limp, old hockey injury turned to arthritis, he explained last time I asked. He'd been destined to play in the NHL until the draft notice for the army arrived. As Doc described the situation, he hated snakes and the jungle so he enlisted in the Navy where they made him a medical corpsman and sent him to the snake-filled jungles of Viet Nam with a company of U. S. Marines. Such is life, humans plan and God laughs.

"Here's some hot chocolate and please help yourself to sandwiches. I picked up your favorite salt and vinegar chips. I hope you still like them," I said as I pushed the unopened bag across the pine table. Max snuggled next to Doc, leaning his long snout on Doc's shoulder.

We ate without talking much. Max did bark at a squirrel but refused to budge from his catbird seat where bits of sandwich came his way. When we finished, we sipped thick hot chocolate from heavy ceramic mugs – a gift from a local potter. Finally, Doc said, "I spoke with the case agent on the way over. She said the informant appears to be honest and has a fair amount of information about Brenda Fairbanks."

"Does he know where she's buried?" I asked.

"Probably not seeing as how she's alive."

"Where is she?"

"Good question."

"Why did she leave under such mysterious circumstances?" I asked.

"The informant claims the county has been giving logging rights for timber not standing on state forest land but on Indian lands. The tribe has never collected a nickel for the millions of dollars worth of trees taken from their land. Brenda found out about this and was about to expose the matter."

"Did she tell anyone? I mean did she go to the media or the prosecutor?" I asked.

"It's too early to know. We are going to begin conducting interviews. My first interview is in Pelican Falls. I could have saved you a trip and met you at home."

"Pelican Falls? Who is connected with this mess from Pelican Falls?"

"Father Aldo Gallo, I presume you know him?"

CHAPTER TWENTY

(Monday)

Supper was a leftover hot dish of rice in a creamy marsh of chicken soup and some sort of sausage. More bars, lemon sprinkled with powdered sugar, were served for dessert. Tammy, Makwa and I retired to the overstuffed chairs in front of the stone fireplace. Tammy and I swore off wine and chocolate for the rest of the week even though a friend had recently given me a bottle of chocolate wine and I was excited to taste it. Max and Smokey snuggled next to Makwa. Smokey purred and Max snored, at least Makwa blamed the poor dog for that impolite behavior. Outside, the north wind howled and occasionally the house lights dimmed foreshadowing a possible power outage.

"You've been keeping us in suspense long enough. Let's have the low-down on the Widow LeBlanc," Tammy insisted with her best pouty face.

"She's a lovely lady. I feel uneasy with our plotting against her."

"We are not against her, dear, we are simply helping to free Aldo from her bondage which prevents his departure to Rome," I said.

"You must admit, it is selfish of her to deny Aldo his lifelong dream of toiling in the bowels of the Vatican Library," Tammy added.

"Yes, it is selfish I will admit. Still, she is such a nice lady."

"You've fallen under her charms. See, you're about to become a victim of her wily ways," I said hoping to sway his allegiance.

"Let's put my guilt aside. Sofia wants to have a sweat lodge. She is fascinated by the spiritual nature of the ceremony. She tried to persuade her deceased husband to let her attend an annual ceremony up at Grand Portage. He refused alleging the entire ritual belongs to the devil."

"What did you tell her? Did you offer to take her to Pine Ridge?" Tammy asked.

"No, she can't travel for medical reasons and besides Pine Ridge would be a challenge for an old gal like Sofia."

"White Earth, does anyone have a lodge on the White Earth reservation?" I asked.

"In Naytahwaush, a dangerous place to venture into when you're a stranger. I'm not even fully accepted there – too educated — too much a white man. Some call me an apple, red on the outside and white inside."

"So no sweat lodge for Sofia?" Tammy concluded.

"I promised I would bring a lodge to her," Makwa announced and waited for our reactions.

The fire crackled and spit sparks into the black iron screen. The wind rattled the century old windows and the three of us simply looked at one another. A sweat lodge in Pelican Falls? The spiritual connotations could stir up quite a controversy. Mrs. Bertelsen was still burning over the inclusion of witches and goblins on the potluck cake. I could imagine that a sweat lodge might incite folks to grab their torches and pitchforks and storm the castle walls at the Chateau de Fleur Roses.

"How are you going to accomplish that?" I finally asked.

"The country club has a sauna. Could you use the club?" Tammy asked.

"No. That would be like you holding church in an outhouse. We, the three of us, are going to the rez tomorrow to find Skinny Weasel. He has, in the back of his truck, the buffalo hide lodge I brought back from Pine Ridge. We will get the lodge and bring it to the estate. In the rear of the rose garden, there's a secluded place sur-rounded by red pines where we can have a fire and erect the lodge."

"Why tomorrow? I have to work." I objected thinking about the piles of messages Olive would have stacked on my desk.

"Why do you have church on Sunday?" Makwa asked.

"Seriously, the timing of this all, what's the big rush?"

"Seriously, Sofia is like a fragile rose. She insists we have the sweat lodge on the 31st of October."

"Why on Halloween?" Tammy asked.

"On the 1st of November, All Saints Day, Sofia believes there is the strongest possibility of contacting a newly departed soul who may be parked in purgatory."

"Her husband?" I asked.

"Yes, she insists I help her contact her deceased husband, Serge."

"Why you and why the sweat lodge?" I asked now growing impatient with Makwa.

"Why do *you* perform baptisms and communion, why not Clayton or Olive for example?"

"Those are holy rites, sacraments, to be performed by ordained …"

"And the sweat lodge is some pagan custom performed by heathen medicine men?"

"I apologize, Makwa. I have this theory, 90% of what we say is misspoken or misunderstood. I try to be a mindful speaker and now I've added myself to the 90%. I'm sorry," I said almost in tears.

"The Buddhists have the Concept of Mindful Speech." Makwa spoke softly, "The followers of Buddha ask before you speak to answer these questions: Is it true? Is it kind? Will it hurt anyone? Is it the proper time? Will it improve on the silence?"

"I violated all of those rules," I said.

"Apology accepted, my dear. Said and forgotten."

"Okay, back to what we need to do," Tammy interrupted the awkward conversation.

"Let me just finish what I had started to explain. Sofia knows I am of the *midewiwin*. Tammy, I don't expect you to know the term. It is a small society more secret than the Masons or Opus Dei. The members have healing powers and great spiritual insights."

"Just like the twelve disciples," Tammy interjected.

"I'm certain we could make all sorts of comparisons to Christianity. I am a *midewinini*, a medicine man if you have to translate into English. I must say the English term isn't doing justice to what a *midewinini* is capable of doing for the physically and spiritually sick."

"The lodge is part of this society?" Tammy asked.

"The lodge is an independent function. The purpose of the sweat lodge is for purification. It is an opportunity to return to the warmth of the womb with the innocence of a baby and be close again to God. You see Sofia has a very troubled soul. She is carrying an immense guilt and believes strongly as a *midewinini*, I can bring her in contact with her deceased husband, Serge, on All Saints Day. Only Serge can relieve her of the burden she is carrying. The sweat lodge ceremony will be used to purify Mrs. LeBlanc in her journey to reconcile with God."

"I know this seems cold, but will the lodge ceremony relieve Aldo from Mrs. LeBlanc's clutches?" I asked.

"Burrrrr. Yes, I believe she will be free from dependence on Aldo. You see, Sofia and Aldo share a secret burden binding them together. I don't know the secret, but I'm convinced Sofia believes she will be relieved of the burden at the lodge ceremony."

"What can Kathy and I do to help?"

"I'm in need of a ride to the rez tomorrow. I need to find Skinny Weasel and get the lodge back from him. It will fill the back end of a pickup. Then we need to find Lonesome Dave to get some smoking tobacco, sweet grass, and sage for the ceremony. I will ask Lonesome and Crow Boy to drive back with us and be the two other spiritual leaders needed for the cleansing ceremony."

I stood and moved towards the kitchen. "I'm a little hungry. Can I offer you two a snack? Plenty of bars and sandwiches leftover from the potluck."

"I'll have three sandwiches. I don't care what kind and four lemon bars. You two should eat also. This will be our last supper together," Makwa rose and started for the kitchen.

"Why?" Tammy asked and followed Makwa.

"Because as of midnight tonight we fast."

"Why do Tammy and I have to fast?"

"Because you will be touching the lodge, the sage, all of the instruments of the ceremony. When we get the lodge back to Mrs. LeBlanc's estate, I'll need help with the ceremony to set it up."

"What sort of help?" Tammy asked.

"The lodge is sacred. It must be set up just a certain way. The aspen branches which make the frame have to be woven together in a prescribed manner. The buffalo robes must be purified. A floor of conifer branches must be cut and spread. The rocks must be gathered and cleaned. The fire wood should be blessed and the fire started to have coals to heat the rocks. Clean water from the river must be collected. There is much to do and it requires clean hearts and clean flesh to make the ceremony successful."

"I'm on board. Tammy can you take the day off?" I asked as I laid the basket full of assorted sandwiches on the kitchen table.

"Ya sure, you bettcha," Tammy replied in a miserable Norwegian accent. "Although I must admit this is not what I envisioned when I agreed to help Aldo with his problem parishioner. I hope this works."

CHAPTER TWENTY-ONE

(Tuesday)

I rose early, skipped my run and horseback ride. I left a note for Makwa asking him to do chores and promising to be back by ten. When I entered the church office, Olive was parked at her station, humming a tune I didn't recognize. It might have been *Bringing in the Sheaves.* Her cat, Mel, lay sprawled on Olive's lap and ignored my arrival – so catlike. Olive handed me a few telephone messages. I read them as I continued to my desk. There was an invitation to give the invocation at the Muskrat Lake Lions Club meeting in December. The answer would be a "yes." They have the best lunches at their quarterly meetings and December meant they would be featuring the game harvested during the fall hunting season, roast pheasant, elk chops, and grouse on a bed of wild rice.

The Darlings called to cancel their November marriage counseling session. A relief as I could bear no more details of their dysfunctional sexual encounters. Mister had no interest and Missus, by her own endlessly wagging tongue, was evidently insatiable. I believe she had just worn the old guy out. I am no prude but certainly would not share the intimate details provided by Mrs. Darling during these counseling sessions.

Mrs. Olson, Margie, called to express her disappointment in my Sunday sermon. I surmised she believed Martin Luther was ancient history and had no contemporary relevance. Margie didn't expect a callback, she was just venting. I know, because when I first came to Grace Lutheran, I spent days trying to please her over how babies should be baptized. She insisted their tiny heads be dunked in the blessed water. I believed a few drops from my fingers would suffice. After all, it's all symbolic. Finally, I was rescued when her husband took me aside and told me to just listen but not act on any of her complaints. His advice was golden and virtually every week, Margie leaves a message which I ignore. I made two points in my waste basket with her latest outrage.

I sat on the edge of my desk and played back the recorded messages. A single request for a private baptism of the Michelson's newly born infant who had Down's Syndrome. I would call them back tonight and urge a public baptism next Sunday before the congregation.

Mrs. Tollefson called and asked me to contact her immediately. I dialed the number she provided. I was about to hang-up when she answered. She got right to the point.

"Pastor Kathy, there are just too many of them coming to church and besides they should not be given communion, that's for us!" She was on the verge of tears judging by her quivering voice.

"I'm sorry, who are the 'them' you are talking about?" I asked although I suspected it was the usual "thems."

"Oh, you know, those turkey workers."

"You mean like Doris and Kevin McKay?"

"Oh, of course not, you know, the foreigners!"

"Ahhh, the three families who always sit in the back, the dark-skinned ones?" I asked.

"Yeah, they have so many kids and they all parade up for communion like they own the place. They are not even members!"

"We have an open table policy, everyone who believes is welcome."

"Oh, that policy means like if your cousin from Nebraska is visiting and he is Missouri Synod, he's still welcomed. It was not meant to ..."

I interrupted her before my blood pressure blew my ear drums out. "Mrs. Tollefson, you've been the leader of foreign missions for as long as I can remember. You've sent hundreds of quilts to Africa and coats to Peru and missionaries to Bora Bora. I fail to understand why you would want them to hear the Word and then deny them the sacraments when they are in your own church."

"Oh, it's just not the same thing. I can't explain it over the telephone. I will talk to you in person when you're not so emotional." The phone went dead.

I walked a few steps into Olive's domain. It was definitely *Bringing in the Sheaves* she was humming. She directed her own musical with a pencil waving about like Leonard Bernstein himself. Mel's eyes followed the baton as if he might leap upon the flying "bird" at any moment.

"Olive, in a few hours, please call Mrs. Tollefson and schedule a half-hour appointment with her. And send her some flowers from me. Take it from petty cash."

Olive nodded but didn't miss a note. I was only mildly confident she had paid sufficient attention so I wrote her a note and left it in my outbox which she checked every hour regardless of whether I was even in the office. I have never figured out why or how she thinks papers get added to my outbox when I am absent. I tended to a few more matters and left. Olive wasn't at her desk although Mel the cat was and he appeared to have everything under control.

"Morning hug, Pastor Kathy?" Benny came at me with unbridled love and enthusiasm. I braced and bladed myself like a golden gloves boxer. He stopped inches short. "I fool you." A broad smile spread over his face.

"Yes, Benny, you fooled me again. Come here you big lug and get your hug." I pulled him tight and ruffled his hair for good measure. Benny has always been a bright spot in my day, so innocent and pure in his motives. When Benny tells me something, I never have to wonder what he meant or if he had some ulterior motive. I pulled away before he became permanently affixed to my torso which he was given to do.

"Benny, watch after Olive and Mel for me. I will be gone for the day."

"I will. I take good care of them." He patted me on the back and trundled off towards Olive's office.

Makwa was waiting on the porch when Tammy and I arrived home in my pickup. He had donned his backpack and was obviously ready to head north. I left the truck running and rushed into the back entrance to grab the pack I'd prepared for the trip. Max looked forlorn when I told him he couldn't come with and even worse, Smokey the cat would be in charge for the day. I was back at the truck and headed out the driveway before I remembered to ask Makwa if he'd done the chores. When I did ask, he described in great detail, every task he'd completed. I suggested he stay on as a ranch hand. Tammy rolled her eyes and reminded me of what a scandal such an arrangement would be.

"Do you know how to get to Naytahwaush?" Makwa asked when I reached the intersection of Highways 59 and 10.

"Don't you?" I asked.

"Yes, I just wasn't going to boss you around if you knew."

"Highway 59 to Waubun and 113 to Naytahwaush, right?" I responded.

"Good, you ladies visit, I'm going back to sleep. Wake me when we get to the lodge at Twin Lakes, Crow Boy is going to meet us at the lodge." Makwa kicked "my" cowboy boots up near the back window and by Callaway was snoring so loudly I turned up the volume of the radio to drown him out a bit. Tammy and I were content to listen to the tunes blasted out by the Detroit Lakes radio station, a moldy combination of country and pop, all from decades earlier. I couldn't have told you the names of the tunes as my mind replayed the conversation with Mrs. Tollefson. I could have handled it differently. I could have placated her with meaningless words of comfort and understanding. However, I was so offended by the hypocrisy of her words and the blackness of her heart. It was only three weeks since she was standing tall at the altar and beating the drum to collect for the missionaries to roam the world converting the very same people she didn't want in "our" church. A tap on my shoulder brought me back to reality.

"There's Highway 113, take a right by the convenience store," Tammy said from the front passenger seat.

"No, stop there. I've got to use the restroom, real bad, and I want to talk to Crow Boy's cousin. He works at the store, most days any way," Makwa said from his makeshift backseat bed.

I pulled the truck into the lot and we rolled up to the gas pumps. Geez, almost fifty cents higher than the Walmart in Detroit Lakes. I pumped while the other two went into the little store which, according to the posted signs, sold everything from lottery tickets to native made trinkets. I needed neither nor anything in between so I waited in the cab of the warm pickup for my friends to return. As is normal, the wind was howling and blowing loose snow and dirt, snirt we called it, across the highway. A few sad-looking crows tried to feed on a skunk carcass although between the wind and passing cars, they were making little progress. You'd think one of those darn black birds would drag the flatten road kill into the ditch where they wouldn't have to fly away at every approaching vehicle. And they're supposed to be so smart.

I didn't have to wait long. Makwa returned first and took the front seat. "I'll sit up here so I can give you better directions. Crow Boy's cousin says the entire clan is at an encampment east of Naytahwaush, in a stand of pine west of Hogback Hill. I know the trail to their camp," Makwa said.

"Camp? Do you mean they are all in a camp with a bunch of tents? Is this safe for us to go to?" I asked in all seriousness.

"I've read that General Custer asked his Indian scouts the same question just north of the Little Big Horn River where all of my brothers were encamped."

"Really, can't they meet us somewhere, like the Lodge at Twin Lakes?"

"There is no good way to reach them. I spoke with Crow Boy's mother last night. She works in the cage at the casino up in Mahnomen. She told me to stop here in Waubun and the cousin would know where Crow Boy was hanging. Anyway, they mean us no harm. You're letting your notions of my people play tricks on your mind — too many bad movies."

I wasn't so sure. Tammy returned with a small bag and crawled into the rear seat. I heard the rustling of paper behind me.

"What are you doing?" Makwa asked. He turned and was glaring at Tammy.

"Skittles, I'm eating Skittles."

"We are fasting. No food!" He lunged for Tammy's rainbow-colored treasures.

I couldn't see the tussle but Tammy must have won because the argument continued. "Tammy, you can't eat food. We all agreed."

"Skittles aren't food, they're Skittles," she said with much determination and a mouthful of the sugary morsels.

"If they aren't food, what are they?" Makwa asked sounding more than a little irritated.

"Who knows! Chemicals, they are just a mixture of chemicals like crack cocaine which keeps us Skittleheads addicted."

Makwa looked at me. "If Crow Boy and his band turn on us, Tammy's the first to go!"

"What's this turn on us stuff? What'd I miss?" Tammy asked.

"Just enjoy your chemicals, junkie," Makwa said and then began to softly sing one of those Indian chants that seemed to never have an end.

It was exactly an hour later we pulled into the camp. Our arrival was met with the hostile stares of a dozen or so men – at least two had rifles slung over their shoulders. I saw no women or children and chills ran down my spine. Had Makwa misjudged his "friends?" I proceeded slowly. One short skinny fellow with hair down to his waist removed the rifle from his shoulder and held it pointed in our direction.

"STOP!" Makwa yelled.

I braked hard causing Tammy to fall off her seat. Makwa slowly opened his door and slid out of the truck with his hands in plain view. He shouted what I took to be greetings and immediately calm came over the gathering. The rifle was put down and the men came forth to welcome Makwa and I hoped Tammy and me. He waved us out and, amidst barking dogs, we were introduced to each. I almost slipped up and called Stretch by his nickname of Skinny Weasel. Makwa caught my blunder and gave me a dirty look. I sensed Tammy and I should be on our best behavior. I looked at my surroundings – pine trees as tall as skyscrapers, virgin forest – a thick mat of toasty pine needles blanketed the floor. The air smelled of evergreens and smoke from the healthy fires burning in rock circles. Eight tents, three shaped like tepees, were in a crude circle around the campfires. Off to the side was an array of conveyances, trucks, ATVs, a buggy, and a tired looking pinto pony tied to the metal bumper of a pickup truck on blocks. The carcass of a small deer hung behind the horse. Still, I saw no sign of women or youngsters. Evidently this was the native version of deer hunting camp.

Makwa pulled Tammy and me aside. "Would you two mind waiting in the pickup. Seems a couple of the men believe women will bring misfortune onto the camp. I'm sorry, it's like bringing a woman aboard a sailing ship or something, I guess. I forget being here is like stepping back five centuries. I'll get the sweat lodge from Skinny Weasel and we'll be on our way."

"Perhaps I could win them over with some Skittles." Tammy said.

"You will be the first to be sacrificed you know," Makwa said and opened the rear door for Tammy. "And don't you come out again," he shouted for all to hear. I retreated to the warmth of the cab and locked the doors. I closed my eyes and offered a prayer asking for the Holy Spirit to be present in the hearts of all.

The men retreated to the larger tepee style tent and the camp fell silent, even the yelping and howling dogs and curs. An owl flew low and landed on a pine bough next to the tent as if to listen to the hooting of the men inside. I wished I too could hear their conversations but then thought better of it. No, I didn't want or need to know what foolish talk they were undoubtedly about.

Tammy and I had chatted for maybe forty-five minutes when the men, single-file, left the tent and Makwa returned to my truck. I powered my window down to hear him speak. "Please pull up next to the trailer parked on the far side, behind the horse corral. It is where Stretch has the sweat lodge stored. We'll load it up and be on our way. Sorry about the chilly welcome. I should have known better. They thought we were the game warden when you pulled in. The game warden drives the same truck and they have some illegal deer and a bear hanging out back."

"I'm just glad they waited to find out and didn't start shooting..."

"They wouldn't have shot. They just didn't want the game warden to give them problems. It's all fine. I apologized for the intrusion and they've welcomed all three of us to stay for dinner. They have a bear rump and venison stew in the pot. We can stay if you'd like." Makwa wore a large smile assuring me all was well.

"Tell them we're fasting but next time we'll stay and I will even bring Skittles for dessert," Tammy suggested. I agreed.

I drove the pickup behind Makwa as he walked to the trailer. Two men, Crow Boy and the tallest man, Lonesome Dave, met us at the trailer. I jumped out to offer my apologies for the intrusion. Lonesome resembled the Disney cartoon character, Goofy. He was gangly with big ears and, I'm ashamed to say it, sort of a dumb look on his face. He was, however, most gracious.

"Pastor Kathy, we'd be the ones asking forgiveness."

Crow Boy, who was no young man, he had snow white hair tied behind his back, added, "It's Skinny Weasel what's the problem. He's got himself a arrest warrant and was 'fraid the warden would arrest him. We'd like you to stay and eat with us."

"Thank you, however we are fasting. Perhaps we can return, with some notice of course. You and Dave will be following us back to Pelican Falls. We'll share a meal after the fast."

"Didn't Makwa tell you? Lonesome Dave and me can't come with. We got a sweat lodge over at Red Lake with our cousins. Lonesome split our sage, sweet grass and smoking tobacco with Makwa. Our spirits, they be with you all, but our old bodies will be elsewhere."

Tammy and I helped the three men load the lodge in the back of my truck. We tied a canvas tarp down and prepared to leave, feeling much better about the men we met in the forest. I extended my hand to Crow Boy when I felt intense pain in my lower leg. I looked down and saw a rangy grey dog snarling and shaking my leg. He had a grip on my leg just below the knee. Blood oozed down his yellow teeth. He shook and a frothy drool flew into the air. A second brown dog was about to join the attack when Lonesome Dave let loose with a kick sending the dog across the field. Crow Boy beat on the grey dog with a broken pine branch. The dog gripped harder and dodged the club. The pain was intense. I collapsed into Makwa's arms.

CHAPTER TWENTY-TWO

(Tuesday)

"*Father, over here, we're over here behind the gazebo,*" I shouted and waved my hands high for my friend to spot our location.

The priest wore his long brown robe, something he seldom did outside of the church walls. He strode down the cobblestone walkway, through a maze of arbors and hedges, towards the sound of my voice. Tammy, Makwa, and I had been building the sweat lodge in the back acres of the Chateau de Fleur Roses. Makwa had located a fine hideaway, a grassy area surrounded by towering conifers and bordered with thick lilac bushes, sans leaves and lilacs. The sweet scent of pines hung in the air. The site afforded the lodge ceremony protection from the wind which this time of year could, as Tammy sometimes put it, "freeze the testicles off a brass monkey." Indeed, the wind was screaming through the heavy pine branches which when they swayed caused bizarre shadows cast by the distant sodium yard light. The location also provided protection from prying eyes. I was feeling no pain after taking a double dose of medication prescribed by the emergency physician at the hospital in Detroit Lakes.

"My dear lady, how are you? I was so concerned to learn of your encounter with the canine," Father Gallo said when he finally located our small haven of seclusion.

"Better, much better after the initial trauma of being attacked," I replied.

"Shouldn't you be at home in bed?"

"No, I'm going to be fine. It was more the shock and the memories than the actual pain." I explained to Father Gallo how I'd been attacked by a cocker spaniel as a child. I showed him the scars on my arm and the faint scar on my face. Fortunately, I've never had a fear of dogs, even after the earlier bite by the spaniel. "When the dog grabbed my leg today, the panic and terror I had as a child came back to me and was overwhelming. I told the emergency ward physician my heart was still racing hours later. He gave me a prescription, a tranquilizer, which mellowed me out."

"Shouldn't you get rabies shots?"

"The doctor gave me a tetanus shot, a strong antibiotic, and a shot of rabies immune globulin. The bite is wrapped and really doesn't hurt too much."

"Because the doc gave you a shot of Novocain or something in your leg," Tammy interjected.

"It is the salve I rubbed with loving hands on her leg. The salve is what has repressed the pain," Makwa said.

"Oh, my, you let Makwa use some of his mysterious remedies? The last time he treated me for psoriasis I turned two shades of scarlet for three weeks. You didn't use the same wonder cure on her, did you?" Father Gallo asked.

"Aldo, you **exaggerate**, you were already red from the psoriasis. And no, I used something special for Kathy, a sweet potion of perineal glands of the Castor Canadensis, poplar buds, calendula, and a handful of other useful ingredients which shall remain my secret. After all, one doesn't learn of Pfizer's secret chemical recipes either," Makwa said all the while swinging a bulging leather medicine bag before the priest's face in a teasing sort of way.

"Regardless my leg is still numb which is fine with me. If I went home, I'd just sit there and think about the bite. No, I prefer to keep busy with what we started here."

"She's being brave," Makwa said.

"Did you capture the dog to be tested for rabies?" Father Gallo asked.

"No, the dog ran off into the forest," I said.

Makwa put his strong arm around my shoulder. "He was a rez dog. None of them have rabies shots and they mostly all look alike. They are such a blend of breeds they've assumed the appearance of African bush dogs."

"It happened so fast I'm not sure we could even point to one dog and say, 'That's the one,'" Tammy said.

"Frankly, I'm resigned to having the rabies vaccine. I watched an uncle die from rabies. It was the most horrible death. He begged his brother to shoot him. I'd get the rabies shot even if they produced a dozen suspect dogs and they were all disease-free."

"How is your sweat lodge coming? It looks like a bad jigsaw puzzle," Father Gallo said.

"We are just about done," Makwa said.

"Done? It's just a pile of sticks," Father Gallo commented as he rubbed his chin.

Makwa frowned and shook his head. "I've dug the fire pit you will have to tend. It's over there." Makwa pointed to a hole in the earth surrounded with large stones taken from a farmer's rock pile abutting the backside of Mrs. LeBlanc's estate. "I've prepared the lodge pit where we will place the red hot rocks you pass into the lodge." Makwa pointed to the stone circle he had just completed.

"Kathy and I have the saplings laid out," Tammy said.

"So all we have to do is erect the sapling posts," I added.

"It's sort of like the modern tent poles where you just throw the darn posts in the air and the tent is formed by the time it hits the ground," Tammy said.

"Wrong! Each sapling has its proper place in the structure. I like it to be symmetrical and where each is placed has special significance to the ceremony. We will tie them together with buffalo rawhide. When the frame is constructed, we will cover it with buffalo robes, except for the rear, we'll use cow hides," Makwa explained.

"Because he ran out of buffalo robes," Tammy said.

"I didn't 'run out.' I had to split the entire operation with Crow Boy and Lonesome Dave. We'll make do with cow hides. Come on, let's finish," Makwa said.

Under Makwa's watchful eye and gentle instruction, Tammy, Father Gallo, and I bent long thick saplings and bound them together with rawhide. As we joined the poles in the order prescribed, Makwa explained the significance of each pole's location and how it symbolized life, death, reincarnation and a host of other serious matters. I paid reverent attention until my leg began to throb and the pain was all I could think about.

Makwa was correct in claiming we were nearly done with the construction. Within thirty minutes, the saplings had been formed into a sturdy geodesic dome.

"Now, we all lift the frame and get the entrance to face east. That being the direction the sun rises and symbolizes the rebirth as each participant emerges from the lodge, from the mother's womb. The entrance is low so one must crawl on his belly to remind us of the humility with which we need to enter and leave mother's womb."

The four of us easily lifted the wood frame and placed it over the stone pit so the entrance faced precisely to the East. Makwa had used a metal compass to determine the exact direction. Tammy and Makwa brought the hides from the stack we'd made earlier and Father Gallo and I laid each carefully onto the frame. Those hides were heavy and dusty. I sneezed several times before we finally finished. My hands were black with dirt and sore to boot.

"I will stay the night to keep the fire burning so the coals will heat the rocks. I'd suggest you three go home and get some rest. Remember, you can drink only water and no eating. Not even Skittles," Makwa said. He sat cross-legged on a Holstein cow hide facing the fire. He began to chant. To my ear it was a lonesome and eerie chant the powerful wind carried across Pelican Falls.

The three of us made some wrong turns in the garden maze as we ambled back to the house and then down the lane to our waiting vehicles. We chatted with anticipation about the sweat lodge. When conversation drew to an end, I was surprised Father Gallo didn't bring up his interview with Doc. Out of respect for Doc's wishes, I didn't ask either.

It was pitch black when we reached my pickup and parted ways. "Good night, ladies. I might be a tad late for tomorrow's activities. I must drive to Waubun for an urgent meeting. I'm afraid I can't put it off, so just bear with me, please," were Father Gallo's last words as he entered his car.

Tammy and I shivered in the damp night air until the truck's heater began to slowly warm the cab. Even the seat heater didn't seem to shake the chill from our bones. The pain in my leg was growing as if a red hot poker was being held to the wound. I would double the dose of painkiller before bed.

"Did Aldo seem distracted to you?" Tammy asked when her teeth stopped chattering.

"I didn't notice. He must have seemed so to you?"

"He did."

"Sometimes, when his mind is chasing some academic theory or solving some philosophical riddle, he will appear distant and distracted," I offered.

"No, it was not one of those moments. I sensed his soul was troubled. He was not at peace with himself as he normally is. Did you notice how he took some digs at Makwa's medicine? It's not like Aldo."

"Maybe he is conflicted about the sweat lodge, you know, with tricking old Mrs. LeBlanc. Maybe there's some internal ethical conflagration," I said.

"Maybe," Tammy said and dropped the subject.

I pulled my truck next to her Mini Cooper which was parked in the Cenex parking lot. The windows were already frosted over as the cold front worked its misery on every aspect of life. "Do you want to start it up and let it defrost? You can wait in here."

"No, you look like you're in pain. Get home and take the meds and a long hot bubble bath. I left some on the tub last time I was at your place," Tammy said and hopped out into the frigid night air.

"Watch my truck, I'm going to leave it running while I go in and buy some more Advil." I didn't wait for an answer.

When I returned to my truck, Tammy was sitting in the passenger seat. She held a crumpled piece of paper. "Holly Hollenbachen has struck again, damn, look at this," Tammy said. She passed the paper to me and I read, "Only one more day and you are on your way. Get on your broom stick and fly back to sin city!!!!"

"Not very poetic, I mean it reads like some third grader penned it out as a note to pass in the classroom."

"It's how Holly writes!"

"Tammy, Holly left town this morning! She won't be back for another day!"

CHAPTER TWENTY-THREE

(Wednesday)

A pain shot up my leg when I stepped out of the pickup truck onto the pavement of the Gentle Days Nursing Home parking lot. Honestly, I was becoming used to the pain and comforted myself with the knowledge it would diminish with each passing day. Not so lucky were some of the residents at Gentle Days. It was Wednesday, October 31, Halloween, All Hallows' Eve, and the day of the week I visited the only nursing home in Pelican Falls. Each visit was bittersweet. It's sad to see so many folks in poor health and waiting to die, sometimes even pleading to die. On the other hand, there are some residents who share joy and a wisdom which is only available to those with wrinkled faces and scars from a thousand battles fought and mostly won.

Genevieve Cecilia Langer was one of those cheerful souls I looked forward to visiting. I was always greeted with a smile, a squeeze of the hand, and a new joke. Today was no exception when I strolled into Gen's cozy room decorated with photos of adult children and grandchildren and a few dozen works of art the youngsters had delivered to Grandma. As always she directed me to the only chair and brought out a tin of cookies. I have to admit, I broke the fast with a couple of shortbread cookies. Filled with lard and sugar, they melted in my mouth. I reasoned it was more spiritually pure to break the fast than to break Gen's heart. Everyone called her "Gen," although one could be certain upon initially meeting her, she'd introduce herself as Genevieve Cecilia. One afternoon, she confided the name had a ring of aristocracy. I had to agree it made an impression more than Sue or Pat, for example. I liked the name so much I named my favorite barn cat, the Persian who acted like the queen herself, Genevieve Cecilia.

I munched, sipped tea and chatted away for half an hour when I received a text message from Makwa reminding me to be at the lodge by nine this evening. The text message tickled my memory of a long list of tasks to accomplish before the sweat lodge. I had best be moving on.

"I've brought the sacraments to give you communion if you'd like," I said and reached down into my canvas tote bag to remove the bottle of wine and bread which I had blessed earlier.

"Oh, Pastor Kathy, I don't think I'm ready today."

"Are you sure? You never miss communion."

"Frankly, Pastor, I've been a bad girl and my heart isn't so pure. I'd feel like I was being blasphemous."

"Oh, I can't imagine. How much sinning can you do here at the home? You don't break the Ten Commandments, you live a pure life, you get along with everyone ..."

"I'm afraid I got along a little too well with someone!" Gen said. She sat on her bed and looked down at her pink fuzzy slippers.

"You don't mean ..." I began to ask although not believing I was on the right track.

"Yes, I do. Mr. Olson, Arlie Olson ... well he and I ... right here on this very bed ..." She patted the hand-stitched patchwork quilt and looked at me as if to ask, "What now?"

I turned red and for a moment was speechless. This was a first. My mind raced through the long list of possible sins and related consequences which in the Lutheran doctrine are limited. This didn't seem to fit into any specific category. A man and a woman both single and in their eighties engaged in sexual intercourse in the privacy of her room. Hmmm. No Old Testament virginity issues, no children or birthright issues, no adultery issues, no harm to anyone. I reasoned, even if I was missing something, isn't communion meant to accept the grace of He who directed all to partake in the sacrament?

Finally I got my wits about me and a most stupid question rolled off my tongue. "Was this the first time?" Now I really blushed and at my own question.

"Not if you subscribe to the Jimmy Carter principle of having sinned if there's lust in your heart. Arlie and I grew up together, we taught high school together, we even sang together for over thirty years in the same church choir. And I have to confess, over many of those years, I had lust in my heart for Arlie, and so did he for me, least he said he did. Now, last night was the first time we acted upon our lust."

"Was he able to perform at his age?" I don't know why I was so intrigued with the idea. I just could not seem to drop the subject.

"I should say. Surprised me to no end. He gave me quite the ride. Evidently we got a bit carried away because one of the staff knocked on the door to inquire of my well being. I moan at such moments, sometimes a bit too loud and this old bed, well the springs squeak."

I took another shortbread cookie just to keep from asking any more nosey questions. I washed it down with the remaining tea and proclaimed, "You've confessed and your sins are forgiven." I didn't think there was a sin, but Gen obviously was feeling some twinge of guilt and the most generous act I could perform was to pronounce them, whatever sins there might be, forgiven. "Now Gen get your soul ready for communion."

I can't recall a more beautiful sacramental act than I had with Genevieve Cecilia. Tears filled both of our eyes as I provided the symbolic body and blood and she provided a willing soul. I packed my tote and stood ready to resume my visits, although none was likely to top this one.

"You're wondering how two old farts can have sex?" she said with a twinkle in her eye.

"Not so much how, I assume it's the same as the rest of us. I mean as younger folks, you know, I mean there's only so many ways you can do it, right?" I was stammering.

"Until last night, I would have agreed. Arlie had a few new tricks up his sleeve and wow, I have to confess, last night may not be the end of this affair."

"Maybe it was the culmination of sixty years of repressed lust," I said. "Let me give you a big hug, wish you and Arlie the best, and we'll leave it at that."

We hugged and I turned to leave when Gen said, "I'll let you know next time you visit if Arlie has any more surprises. I almost forgot to give you my sage advice for the week: Stand up for what you believe in, even if you're standing alone."

It was midday when I left the Gentle Days Nursing Home. None of the other residents were as entertaining or joyful as Gen although I truly appreciate each one of them. I had only a block remaining to get to Grace Lutheran when I heard a short burst of an emergency vehicle siren behind me. I glanced in my rearview mirror. A shiny black Durango was riding my bumper and had blue and red lights flashing behind the grill. The siren blared a second time and I pulled to the curb. I wasn't speeding. The roads were still too slippery. The Durango didn't belong to the local police or the sheriff's office. I know each of those officers and their squads. I parked and looked in my side mirror. The Durango door flung open. My heart beat was at the losing weight rate one sees on the exercise posters in the gym. "Now what?" Grandma had uttered the short phrase on almost a daily basis and it seemed a suitable expression for the occasion. The familiar face of Doc answered my question although it begged a second, "now what?" was Doc doing in Pelican Falls and pulling me over like some common criminal. Darn, Pastor Kathy being pulled over by the State Police could put me on the front page if it was a slow news day, or even if it wasn't.

Doc approached on the passenger side of my truck and jumped in.

"Geez Kathy, I've been waving at you to pull over for six blocks …"

"Doc, please, turn off those goldarn lights. I'll be the talk of the town!"

"Oops, sorry, I'm too used of my big city ways. I forget …"

"Please, don't explain or apologize, just turn them off."

I exhaled a deep sigh of relief when the Durango grill lights went dark and Doc returned to the pickup cab. "Truly, I'm sorry. I saw you pull out of the nursing home and tried to flag you down so we could talk."

"Why didn't you just call me?"

"Because I wanted to talk to you privately and there you were right in front of me. Mea Culpa."

"Wrong religion. Anyway, no harm done. Wassup to use worn street jargon you big city cops must be familiar with." A smile had returned to my face.

"Yeah, about a decade ago all the punks said wassup. It's been replaced about five times. I wanted to ask you about Father Aldo. Now, if you don't feel comfortable with this discussion, just say so. I don't know what your relationship is to the priest."

"He's like a father to me and not in the priestly sort of way. We are close."

"Then maybe I should leave it alone."

"Now you have tickled my curiosity. Ask me the question and I'll tell you if it is out of bounds, okay?"

Doc squirmed in his seat, clearly regretting he'd opened the door to this conversation. He paused as if reconsidering then said, "I interviewed him yesterday and frankly, he was not telling the truth or at least not the entire story. I'm asking you if he would have something to hide."

"Don't we all? I really can't respond to such a broad question. Did he cheat on his golf handicap? Maybe. Does he run a rigged game of bingo? I recently heard he did and perhaps for the greater good of the church. Honestly, Doc, I don't have a clue what you are talking about."

"You're right, bad judgment on my part. I'm frustrated and was hoping you'd tell me the guy is as crooked as a dog's hind leg. Let's just forget I asked. I do have something else I was going to tell you."

"What?"

"The document examiner is down in Fergus Falls putting on some crime scene training. Between interviews I drove down there and showed her the documents you gave to me."

"Was Tammy correct?"

"No. Now you have to understand, examining documents is, in my opinion, like reading Tarot Cards or tea leaves. The examiner said the two nasty notes were not written by the same person who wrote the known exemplar. She suggested both 't h e s' were the same style although the similarity may be explained in part by the two writers having the same teacher when they were young students."

"I'm not surprised by the results. I meant to give you a call today and tell you Tammy had another note put on her car last night. The person we suspected was out of town so she couldn't have been the guilty party."

"Tammy needs to go to police. She should take the matter to a local detective. I know there's the desire to keep this low key, however sometimes what may appear to be a prank can be deadly."

"I'll tell her although she may not heed the advice."

"When the note was left last night, where was her car parked?" Doc asked.

"At the Cenex station — the note was left under the windshield wiper blade."

"Did you actually see the note under the wiper?"

"No, I had to run inside to get something and when I returned, Tammy was back in my car and had the note in her hand."

"So how do you know it was under the wiper?"

"Tammy told me ..."

Doc grabbed the door handle and began to slide out of the seat. "I apologize for turning on the lights. I know what it's like to live under public scrutiny. For ten years I wore a uniform and drove around in a police squad. Believe me I know what it's like to be in the glass house."

"Thank you Doc, please forgive me for being so irritated. There's been a lot going on these last few days. I guess I'm a bit on edge."

"Let me know if I can be of help." Doc grabbed the door handle again.

"You have me so curious about Father Gallo. Can you at least tell me the circumstances? I promise it will go no further."

Doc stared hard into my eyes, so hard, I was frightened, no, more like intimidated. I could imagine he had used his menacing glare a thousand times on tough guys. I regretted resurrecting the subject.

Finally he spoke, "The informant said the priest was like a 'father' to Brenda Fairbanks, the missing woman. The agent asked the informant who Brenda would confide in, who could she trust? The informant named Father Gallo."

"The information is consistent with the Father Gallo I know and trust and confide in."

"Yeah right, and when I interviewed the priest, you would have thought I was asking about someone he'd met for ten minutes a decade ago. I showed him a photo of Brenda and he acted as though he'd never seen her."

CHAPTER TWENTY-FOUR

(Wednesday)

"*Who's winning?*" I asked when I entered the church office and saw Olive playing Uno with Benny.

"Mel and me is winning. Olive has made some big mistakes," Benny replied with Mel sitting upright on his lap. "Olive, show Pastor Kathy the score."

"She's not interested. She's got business to attend to. Now play."

"I have time to look at the score." I reached across the table and picked up the post-it with Olive's distinctive chicken scratching using the pink ink she favored. "Hmmm, Benny, you and Mel are surely beating Olive today. You better give her a chance to catch up."

"Okay Pastor Kathy, me and Mel will give her a chance."

"Olive, I'll be here for a few hours and then unavailable for the evening," I said and moved into my office ignoring Olive's inquiry whether I had "some hot date," and the same inquiry echoed by Benny. There were a few telephone messages left in the inbox. The top message was from Mrs. Peterson and said, as best I could decipher from Olive's note, "Mrs. Peterson called and invited you to join her family for Thanksgiving. Call her back today!" Beneath were Olive's editorial comments: "Mrs. Peterson's nephew, the bachelor from Brainerd, is going to be visiting on Thanksgiving and she is trying to hook you up with him. If he's thirty-five and still living at home with his mother, there's got to be something terribly wrong with the man. Be Careful!!!!"

I've eaten turkey dinner with a different family each year and I appreciate their hospitality. This year I thought I'd take a break. After the Thanksgiving church service I planned a drive to my favorite spa just outside the Twin Cities and pamper myself for two days - maybe even take one of those chocolate baths I saw advertised. I'd have to think of a polite way to decline.

The next message was from an anonymous caller. It read: "Can't something be done about the crippled boy in the wheelchair? His parents let him make all those disgusting noises during the church service. He sounds like an animal and it's very distracting. Please move him to the nursery." Olive added her thoughts on the bottom of the note: "I think the caller was Mrs. Tingstad. She tried to disguise her voice. She's talking about the Craven kid who has cerebral palsy. He does howl like a banshee but God doesn't care so we shouldn't either. For all I know he's singing praises to the Lord!"

That's why I love Olive and keep her on despite her shortcomings. She can articulate in her pithy manner the essence of what really matters. I crumpled the note and made a three-pointer off the miniature bank board and into the wastebasket. I set about reading the latest missive sent by the synod headquarters.

"Can we come in?"

I looked up from my work. Morgan Wentworth and Randy Peterson stood smiling in the doorway. They were dressed in matching jogging attire. This was the first visit either had made to my office. I braced myself for bad news or some startling revelation. I was as surprised as if Ed McMahon himself was delivering a million dollar check from Publishers Clearing House. Am I the only American who still returns those phony notices and even buys several magazines in hopes the subscriptions will increase my odds?

"Yes, of course, have a seat. Can I get you some coffee? Cookies, there's a bunch left over from the potluck."

"Never touch the stuff. I get enough of a boost from life itself," Morgan said emphatically.

"Me either. Morgan got me to kick the habit," Randy echoed.

"Randy and I were just out for a run and thought we'd drop in to talk about a really exciting opportunity for Pelican Falls," Morgan said wasting no time with banalities or chitchat.

"Yeah, Morg here found these really neat folks who can ..." Randy was so excited he was stammering.

"I can't take the credit for this one. It was Clayton Johansson who turned me on to these guys. Clayton has a pastor friend in the Cities who swears by this organization."

"You've got my attention, Morgan, don't hold me in suspense any longer," I said. I marveled at how Clayton's long arms could reach out and grab me all the way from Mexico.

Morgan produced his smart phone and put his fingers to work punching in commands, "Here, watch this, it's a video from Jocks for Jesus. These boys are athletes in the service of God. They have a dynamite program and they'll come to Pelican Falls."

The video was as slick as any televangelist I'd ever seen. Buffed men in skimpy muscle shirts and matching Zubaz sweatpants told a story of how God wants every believer to be wealthy, rich beyond their greatest dreams. They cited some cherry-picked Bible quotes as proof God wants a Mercedes in every man's driveway and a mink on every woman's shoulder. In between quotes, the "dudes" performed amazing feats of acrobatics and lifted weights which would break the back of an ox. The athletes, who took turns speaking on the video, concluded God was looking to bestow lavish gifts on the true believers and how could He identify the true believers, the blonde "dude'"with the spiked hair asked the audience who by now had been worked into a slobbering frenzy. The true believers were those who gave the most to God's church. The more you gave the more you would get in return. Tenfold, twentyfold. The video concluded with some "dupes" testifying they'd given the church a tithe of 20% and now a Ferrari was parked in their garage. Another, looking fit and tan, had written a $5,000.00 check and just got back from a month in Hawaii — a trip she'd won within a week of the gift. I could take no more and handed the phone back to Morgan.

"What would you have me do?" I asked the pastors who wore the excited looks of fresh converts.

"I called Allen. He's the one who was the first speaker in the video. They had a cancellation and are available the same weekend as our autumn festival. The hand of God intervenes. This program would fit perfect with the sports activities Randy and I have planned for the celebration," Morgan said with the slickness of a car salesman.

"Morg and I are in already. We're on the court and ready to play. We are here to recruit you to join the team," Randy said.

"We'd include Aldo and Tammy, too, the five us coming off the bench like a team of hoopsters. It would be great. The five of us could even take on all challengers in five minute games. I know you were a superstar for the Detroit Lakes girls' team. We'll be God's team."

"We have to think of a catchy name," Randy added.

"Other than being on the 'team,' what further commitment does this require?" I asked.

"Nothing … you join the team and make the announcement your church is on board. Randy and I will make all the arrangements. We'll put the Jocks for Jesus up at Clayton's Skull Lake Resort. He already said we could have the run of the place. It's too early for snowmobilers and ice fishermen so the resort is empty. We'll put the program on in my church gym as the climax to our other events."

"It will be like Pelican Falls' own Olympics and we'll make money to boot," Randy said.

"Make money?" I asked.

"I'm not saying how much. I spoke with a couple of pastors in the Twin Cities who sponsored the Jocks and they cleared over twenty grand. They were out in California at one of the mega churches and made five times as much."

"Morgan, Randy, I appreciate your offer however I'm going to have to decline."

"Why?" Morgan asked looking like I'd just kicked him the groin.

"Let's just say, theological and moral reasons. Jocks for Jesus is using false teachings. There is no basis in the belief that the more one gives to church the more God will 'bless' them in kind, no basis whatsoever. Besides the name is thoroughly offensive."

"Kathy, you miss the point."

"What am I missing?"

"Sports are the new religion, like it or not. Take a look at your own congregation; how many vacant seats do you have because the family left town to attend a kid's soccer tournament? These guys are the new disciples. They'll bring the kids in with the sports angle and where the kids go, the parents will follow."

"Okay, I do get it now. I do see the point. The parents will follow with their checkbooks and when those simple minded souls hear that God, like Santa Claus, is waiting to deliver gifts, the money will fill the offering baskets and we'll all make a bundle."

"How cynical," Morgan said. He stood and shook his head. "Clayton will be back Saturday. He may have a different opinion. Thank you for the time."

They were gone as quickly as they arrived. I felt soiled and ashamed to even be a party to such a conversation. I knew Clayton would side with them. Last summer he insisted I move Bible Camp two weeks later on the calendar so his cousin's boys could attend hockey camp in Fargo. I closed my eyes and asked for wisdom and strength to withstand the attack I knew would come upon Clayton's return. I prayed the sweat lodge ceremony would cleanse my soul of the anger I felt towards my peers.

CHAPTER TWENTY-FIVE

(Wednesday)

"*Now what?*" I said more to myself than Tammy who was seated next to me in the pickup. I'd just made the turn onto the narrow street leading to the driveway of the Chateau de Fleur Roses when we were met by a parade of fire trucks, police cars, and an ambulance. I pulled over to allow them to pass. The last vehicle in line was the bright red SUV driven by the volunteer fire chief, Wally Hildebrandt. He stopped the Suburban inches from my front bumper, the large emergency light still flashing on the top of the dash. When he didn't move and didn't make an effort to get out of his vehicle, Tammy suggested we get out and talk. I could smell smoke in the air as we walked the few short steps to Wally's truck.

"What's going on Wally?" I asked. I shielded my eyes from the rotating light. How could he even drive with the blinding light?

"Fire at the LeBlanc place." Wally is a big man who spoke in small sentences as if there were a limit on the number of words he could expel in one day.

"Is anyone hurt? Did the place burn down?" Tammy asked in rapid succession.

"Naw, nothing like that," Wally said. He reached down and pulled the plug on the red light. I could hear the county dispatcher clearing the responders from the scene. Wally turned his radio off. "No, everything's all okay."

"What happened? Where was the fire?" I asked.

"Every time, I see you two, you're together." It was Mrs. Hildebrandt's screeching voice. She was seated next to Wally, something I could not see earlier having been half-blinded by the red light. "The neighbor saw smoke coming up from the top of the hill and heard this strange voice like someone might have been injured."

"So they sent the department to the scene," Wally declared in an officious sounding tone.

"Well, was there a fire?" I asked growing impatient with the couple who were not being very forthcoming.

"Yeah, some Indian was up in the back garden area. Mrs. LeBlanc said it was okay. The Indian started the fire and was singing if that's what you call it. When the police talked to him, it turns out he is having a sweat lodge for Mrs. LeBlanc. She claims to be part Indian herself, not enough to get the welfare checks." Mrs. Hildebrandt was finally beginning to spill the beans.

"Like she'd need more money." Wally chuckled at the thought.

"Yeah, then, so Mrs. LeBlanc's going to have a sweat lodge. Now there's a story for next week," Mrs. Hildebrandt concluded as if she already had the opening paragraph of her column written.

"Is everything all right? The fire didn't spread out of control or burn down a building?" I asked.

"Oh, hell no, just an Indian sittin' by a smoky fire with a bunch of rocks and singing his songs," Wally concluded and used about half his daily allowance of words at the same time.

"Can you back up and let us pass?" I asked.

"What are you two doing up there anyway?" Mrs. Hildebrandt asked. She would be adding a second paragraph: "Two local pastors were seen taking the back alley to the sweat lodge ceremony." "Are you two going to join Mrs. LeBlanc and the Indian?" She waited for an answer while munching on her third Halloween-sized Baby Ruth candy bar. She tossed the wrapper out the partially open window.

"Mrs. LeBlanc is a member of St. Mary's Catholic Church and Father Aldo asked us to join him and Mrs. LeBlanc for a meeting. It is a private matter. I'm certain you can respect there is confidentiality among the clergy not to discuss such things," I said knowing it would only stimulate her imagination and curiosity.

"Wally, you back up and let these preachers pass," Mrs. Hildebrandt spoke with the authority of the Pelican Falls Volunteer Fire Chief's Wife.

Tammy and I were soon past the SUV and parked below the hill next to the stone steps leading to the estate. I took my gym bag from the truck box. Having no experience with a sweat lodge, like all women, I agonized over what to bring. After all, what does one wear to a sweat lodge ceremony? I made three telephone calls to Tammy and we finally agreed, one piece bathing suits, nylon gym pants, T-shirts, sandals, two beach towels, and a case of bottled water should see us through the event. I also packed an ample supply of sand-wiches, chips, and cookies to be consumed when we could break the fast at sunrise. I hoisted a backpack on my shoulders and carried the gym bag, alternating hands. We paused often to rest and frankly delay an uncomfortable situation — mostly because of fear of the unknown. I recalled the tragic sweat lodge in Sedona where partici-pants became deathly ill. I told myself Makwa wouldn't let that hap-pen, still ...

We were blessed with a balmy evening without a hint of a breeze, a rare event in these parts. At the half-way point there was a cobble-stone ledge. We stopped and dropped the bags. In the distance, a hundred moving lights lit the night. They were carried by youngsters making their rounds while dressed in costumes and gathering bags full of candy. The mobile home park where hundreds of turkey fac-tory workers lived was filled with trick or treaters. Many of the chil-dren belonged to parents who, legally or otherwise, had recently immigrated to America. I was gratified the children had embraced such a wonderful custom as Halloween.

As Tammy and I had driven through the streets, we were delighted to see green turtles, princess fairies, pirates, and ghosts prowling our town. We shared stories of our own wonderful experi-ences and wistfully wished we could have one last stab at going door to door begging treats and playing tricks.

Such was not our plight tonight so we hoisted our packs and trudged to the top. The mansion windows were full of orange candle lights. As many of the townsfolk claimed, it surely looked haunted. The house was built of stone and had large windows, a roof with many gables, and gargoyles perched beneath the soffit as if ready to pounce on any intruders. I could smell the wood fire as we neared the lodge. I braced myself and continued. I was having second and third thoughts about the wisdom of our actions. Was this really likely to result in Mrs. LeBlanc freeing Father Gallo? Would this backfire on all of us? Was this even morally justified?

Makwa sat cross-legged near the smoldering fire. He softly chanted as he held his hands above the rocks which were glowing red from the heat. It appeared as though he was blessing the stones. I imagined this scene had been repeated for hundreds, maybe thousands of years. Makwa had stripped to a loincloth. His lithe body, covered with sweat or perhaps oils, glimmered in the firelight. Suddenly, I felt totally at ease with the situation. It all seemed so natural, so innocent, and so pure of spirit. Tammy and I set our bags down and joined Makwa at the fire ring. He didn't acknowledge our presence. Frankly, he seemed to be in a trance as if he was not totally of this world, perhaps communicating with some spiritual being beyond my ability to perceive, beyond my reality. I was mesmerized by the sight and Makwa's barely perceptible chant.

"Are we ready?" Mrs. LeBlanc had slipped behind us and stood wrapped in a plaid trade blanket.

"We are waiting for Father Gallo," I said softly not wanting to interrupt Makwa.

"I'm right here," Father Gallo said. He stepped out of the shadows. He wore his ankle length brown robe and matching stocking cap. "I apologize for being late. I was delayed in Waubun. I'm ready to tend the fire, so let's get started."

Makwa stopped singing. "Please, all of you, this can't be rushed. We have much to do but no reason to hurry. Sit, please, join me around the fire. I've placed pine boughs for you to rest upon. Soon it will be All Saints Day and we will enter the lodge. Until then, I ask you to join me in quiet contemplation and reflection. Gaze into the fire and prepare your minds and souls for purification."

Tammy, Father Gallo, Mrs. LeBlanc, and I sat in that order on the prepared Scottish pine boughs. I drew deep breaths and relaxed my shoulders, tension drained from my body. I gazed into the flames and the glowing embers. Nearby two owls traded hoots and in the distance some hounds shared in a chorus of a song known only to them. Slowly, I shut the world out of my mind, out of my senses, and tried my best to connect my mind with my heart, not the heart that so faithfully pumps my blood through my veins, but the heart where my soul resides. I felt a sense of peace and joy envelope me and yet felt or thought of nothing.

I had no idea how long I'd been beside the fire when Makwa gently squeezed my shoulder and brought me back to another reality. "We're ready," Makwa said in a barely audible voice. He helped me to my feet. My legs felt a little unstable.

The others were already standing in a circle. We joined them, Makwa with a bound bundle of smoldering sage. He ritualistically waved the bundle over our entire bodies. "This is to purify you before you enter the lodge which I've already cleansed. Remember, not only your bodies but your minds must be pure when you enter."

When he finished, he laid the remaining sage near the fire. "Aldo, we will soon enter. I would like you to select seven stones from the fire pit and the first stone should be the largest. We will enter, take our places around the stone pit and Aldo will pass the heated rocks in through the entrance. He will be the keeper of the fire for the entire ceremony."

"How long will you all be in there?" Father Gallo asked. He seemed impatient and preoccupied.

"Maybe forty-five minutes at a time. We will leave for a short time to cool down and restore our strength with fresh water. We will repeat this until sunrise when we will leave the lodge for the last time," Makwa said.

"Can you explain my duties?" Father Gallo asked.

"Certainly, come with me." Makwa led the priest to the bed of hot coals and rocks heated until they almost glowed. He picked up a rustic pitchfork and handed it to Father Gallo. "Once the four of us enter, pick up the top seven rocks – one at a time with the pitchfork. Slide the fork with the rock under the doorway and I will place it in the fire pit. When the rocks cool, I will ask for more."

"Won't we run out of rocks? There can't be more than a couple of dozen in the pit now," Father Gallo said.

"There are fourteen rocks in the fire, there are seven more piled right there." Makwa pointed to a pile next to the neatly stacked split wood. "After the first stones are passed, each time you send a new hot stone inside the lodge, I will pass a cooler stone back to you. Add those and the seven by the wood pile to the fire."

"So, I'm just rotating them?"

"Exactly, so you will always have hot rocks to pass through."

"And the fire?"

"You have enough to last to sunrise. Keep adding wood throughout the night. Can you stay awake?" Makwa asked.

"Unlike St. Peter, I will stay awake or die trying," Father Gallo declared as if taking an oath.

"Good, this entire ceremony rests upon your ability to do so."

"Makwa, what about us? Are there some rules we need to abide by?" Tammy asked.

"First, and perhaps foremost, bring a pure heart and a clear mind to this ceremony. We will be seated close together, not touching but close, and any negativity brought into the lodge will be felt by each of us."

"Can we talk?" I asked.

"If you can do so with your mind clear of any thoughts, you may speak. Your speech best come from your heart."

"Do you mean my soul?" Mrs. LeBlanc asked.

"Call it what you want," Makwa replied.

"Will I be able to communicate with my departed husband, Serge?"

"Let me remind you all, we are entering the lodge to cleanse ourselves, to purge not only our physical impurities but our spiritual impurities. If during the ceremony your inner self encounters and communicates with another spiritual being, the experience would be most pleasing."

"I'm of the belief All Saints Day is an opportunity to communicate with the recently departed souls, especially one who is being refined in purgatory," Mrs. LeBlanc said. "Am I correct Father?"

"There are those who hold such beliefs. I am not one of them, although I am not a denier either," Father Gallo answered.

"Sofia, you are free to explore the possibility while in the lodge. The lodge is not a place of rules and restrictions. It is a place to be open to all possibilities and all opportunities," Makwa explained.

"Are there any restrictions, you know, anything taboo?" Tammy asked.

"Respect one another and respect the ceremony – if you do both, there is no need for rules."

"Mrs. LeBlanc, is there someplace Tammy and I can change into our bathing suits? Are bathing suits appropriate, Makwa?" I asked.

"Yes, dear ..." Mrs. LeBlanc began to answer.

"No!" Makwa sternly interrupted.

"No?" I asked.

"I mean no disrespect and perhaps I should have discussed this with you first. I didn't think about it because I expected Lonesome Dave and Crow Boy to be assisting me as spiritual leaders. We must enter the lodge without clothes just as we entered this world from our mother's womb."

"No! Makwa, I am not going in the lodge without a stitch of clothes! I am NOT!"

CHAPTER TWENTY-SIX

(Thursday)

*T*hankfully, *it was much darker in the sweat lodge than I antic-
ipated* – much hotter also. Could hell be much hotter I asked
myself? Over the course of an hour we negotiated a settlement, a
compromise, concerning the nudity matter. Mrs. LeBlanc took an
early lead in the discussion insisting we follow Makwa's traditions
and customs. Father Gallo abstained saying he had "no skin in the
game." Tammy's initial reaction was similar to mine and then she
migrated to Mrs. LeBlanc's side with an "Oh, what the heck, I'm in."
After Makwa assured me the lodge interior would be so dark we
would not even be able to see each other, I negotiated for blankets,
furnished by Mrs. LeBlanc, to be used to shield our disrobing and
entrance into the lodge. So it was that the four of us entered. We sat
cross-legged and I folded my arms in front of my bashful bare breasts.
Soon my thoughts drifted to Eve in the Garden of Eden. Eve had been
driven from the innocence of the Garden where she and Adam wore
no clothes into a world of strife that required attire. Inside the lodge,
which Makwa had likened to a mother's womb, I felt innocent again
and safe. My arms dropped to my lap. I closed my eyes and visited
my soul, a pure spiritual soul not tainted by the evil of the world. I
felt an overwhelming sense of peace.

"We may leave and take our break now," Makwa spoke from the
blackness interrupted only by the fading glow of the heated rocks. For
what might have been an hour, not a word had been uttered. The
only sound was of our breaths which had taken on a mutual rhythm.
"I will go out first and hold the blankets with Aldo for you ladies to
exit. As I slide through the entrance, some light may come in so I'd
suggest you divert your eyes or close them so as not to be shocked,
offended, or amused."

I closed my eyes then opened them a slit, just to see if Makwa was through the entrance I told myself. He wasn't and he was correct in saying some light may illuminate his body. Frankly, I got a shot of Makwa on all fours with his privates swaying in a most seductive manner. I glanced towards Mrs. LeBlanc. Her eyes were wide open and her lips curled in a smile. I closed my eyes and scolded myself for violating the very matter I insisted required blankets, closed eyes, and backs facing us women as we egressed.

As long as I'm being honest, this wasn't the first time I'd seen Makwa in such a natural state. Before I began my journey to the seminary, Makwa and I had a dalliance, not a long relationship, as Makwa never stayed put long enough. I knew it to be the case when I submitted to him. He was a great lover, thoughtful and gentle, and pleasing. Our relationship had been many years ago, before I took my vows, and before I swore my horse would be the only living thing which would ever come between my loins again. Darn, here I was in the sweat lodge to be purified and my mind eagerly pursued such lustful thoughts of Makwa. My heart is willing and strong but my flesh so weak.

Tammy, Mrs. LeBlanc, and I crawled out, modestly separated and were met by the two men holding blankets high in the air and with their backs to the lodge. We wrapped ourselves in blankets and quilts. The crisp air filled my lungs and was so refreshing – as wonderful as my first breath here on earth, I suspect. We moved to the fire ring and downed copious amounts of cool water from earthen pots.

"Is everyone okay?" Makwa asked. He looked into our faces for signs of discomfort. Seeing none, he declared, "It is a good lodge!"

I had nothing to compare it to and agreed the experience had been cleansing, except for my momentary indiscretion at the time of Makwa's departure, I felt refreshed, physically and spiritually.

Tammy and Mrs. LeBlanc agreed out loud expressing their satisfaction and desire to return to the sweat lodge. I wasn't as enthusiastic, so when Makwa announced it was time to return, I was the last of us three women to crawl back through the tiny low entrance. When Makwa entered, I closed my eyes and forced myself to think of nothing, except the visual image of Makwa's exit forced its way back into my mind's eye like a scene from a movie trailer.

We repeated this process five more times before finally exiting at Father Gallo's declaration the sun was rising. On the third cycle Makwa broke the silence with a chant lasting the entire length of the sweat. At first I found the chant to be irritating because it intervened in my personal soul-searching efforts. As time wore on, I grew to find the song pleasant and even aided my quest for finding inner peace. When Makwa stopped, I yearned for more and didn't want to leave the lodge. Makwa insisted for health reasons we all leave, cool our bodies, and rehydrate.

I was on an emotional roller coaster. Initially I felt trepidation and even some remorse for having entered into this alliance. The idea had taken on the stench of doing a bad deed for a good cause. I rolled up the tracks to anger then down to guilt and shame. I'd gone up to euphoria and a smooth decent to peace and tranquility. Now, I was just exhausted, mentally and physically. Despite having consumed gallons of water, I'd yet to retreat to a restroom during a break. I began to identify more with a wrung out washrag than a human. I mustered up the last of what Grandpa called gumption and crawled back into the entrance no longer caring if the men caught a glimpse of what I privately called my "fat ass."

It was during our last session, forty-five minutes before the 7:50 sunrise, when Makwa said we could speak during the sweat. "We've all spent hours together in a ceremony binding us forever with one another and the Creator. We've not spoken, instead letting our souls communicate in ways we don't even understand. Now is the time, if you so desire, to allow your flesh to speak."

I passed as did Tammy – a rare instance when neither of us had words to share. Not so with Mrs. LeBlanc and perhaps as is right, this was her event, her fulfillment of a wish to join in the sweat lodge ceremony. "I've wanted to do this since I was a young woman. Thank you Makwa and Kathy and Tammy for making this happen. It is a life dream."

"Was it what you expected and hoped for?" Makwa asked.

"Yes, but for my desire to communicate with Serge. I had hoped to speak to him. I tried so hard."

"Sometimes it is just not to be and as we discussed a few days ago, one must be careful what one wishes for," Makwa said.

"Yes, I understand. I'm certain Serge is lingering in purgatory and this day, All Saints Day, is the most likely time to speak with him. I never had an opportunity to say good-bye. When he fell down the stairs, it was unexpected, I mean his death from the fall was so sudden. I never was able to say good-bye. It has been like a wolf gnawing at my soul all these months. I just want to say good-bye."

"We have about forty minutes before we leave this ceremony. Perhaps you would like to try again. Perhaps we could all come together to make this happen."

"Yes, oh, it would mean so much, yes, please may we try!" She pleaded like a toddler asking for an all-day sucker at the checkout counter.

"I'm going to sprinkle some dried plants on the hot rocks. The smoke they produce may help us on our quest," Makwa said. I could smell the incense. He must have poured a bundle on the stones because my lungs were suddenly filled with the potent smoke.

"Join hands, all of us, join hands," Makwa said.

I was seated between Makwa and Tammy. I found Tammy's hand easily. I groped for Makwa and it wasn't until I felt his hand against my breast that I was able to clasp his large hand. He gripped mine tightly and without a tremble.

"Each of you, ask your Inner Selves to join Sofia in her quest. Send your spirit to join her. Focus on nothing else. Do not speak or let your minds think, the mind will lead you down a dark tunnel without end, allow your spirits to join Sofia and search for the Light," Makwa said and then began a most eerie chant. I squeezed my eyes shut and tried my best to force my mind to go blank. Years of mediation and prayer came to my aid and so I was without conscious thought. In hindsight, I've wondered if I'd reached such a state on my own or as a result of the smoke I couldn't help but inhale.

I can't pinpoint exactly when I became aware of Mrs. LeBlanc talking. Time was suspended in the smoke of the lodge. I recall catching her in the midst of a conversation and not the beginning. Her voiced was hushed but somehow urgent.

"Serge, you must forgive me!"

"I understand purgatory is a terrible place to be. I've made a plea to the church to intervene and hasten your departure."

"Yes, of course, the plea was backed with silver."

"Well, don't blame me, I didn't lead your life."

"I understand you wish I were there with you."

"Father Gallo told me purgatory is a murky muck you can't escape."

"No, he's still here. I've asked him to stay instead of leaving for the Vatican."

"Because I need him."

"No, I need him."

"That's not true."

"You made me so mad. I didn't mean to push you down the stairs. Honestly, I was so furious at what you had done. You put our entire fortune in jeopardy."

"I'm sorry. I truly am sorry!"

There was a long pause as if she'd lost contact.

"Yes, I understand you can't take it with you."

"I still have to live and to keep this place up."

"Yes, I could give it to St. Mary's although I'm not certain but what the police may confiscate the funds should they find out what you and Clayton have done."

"No, he never stops over."

There was again a pause.

"Tell him to have faith and walk towards the light." It was Tammy speaking in a voice sounding as if it came from some inner place in her soul.

"Serge, have faith and walk towards the light."

"Have faith, Serge, have faith."

"You see the light?"

There was a pause.

"It's magnificent, you say? Serge, Serge."

Then there was silence. I opened my eyes and the lodge had cleared of smoke. I realized my right hand was empty. I felt for his body. "Makwa?" There was no answer, he was gone.

I slowly returned to reality, crawled to the entrance and through the opening. Naked and unashamed of it, I was greeted by the most spectacular orange colored sunrise. I was overwhelmed with joy. I looked at Tammy who'd crawled out ahead of me. Peace was written on her face. We embraced.

CHAPTER TWENTY-SEVEN

(Thursday)

"*Then she says she killed her husband, Serge,* by pushing him down the stairs. I don't know what to do," I said. Max, my Golden Retriever turned his head and cocked his ears as if to agree, it was quite the predicament. I sipped my steaming coffee and nibbled at the second peanut butter sandwich.

I'd hope to sleep until late afternoon. However, Olive called at ten waking me with a reminder of a dinner engagement. "I wanted to remind you the Hansons are expecting you for dinner tonight," Olive said in a cheery voice. I drearily thanked her. "Mrs. Hanson just called to cancel because Mr. Hanson has the flu. It's coming out of both ends and she doesn't want to expose you." I mumbled how much I appreciated her thoughtfulness and hung up with the intent to sleep until Friday morning. I couldn't get back to sleep so, with about an hour of rest, I hauled myself from under the down comforter and trundled to the kitchen where Max was waiting.

I brought the second full pot of coffee out to the stable along with the lunch I'd hauled to the ceremony but didn't touch. I had been too tired to eat. Midway through the second pot, I began to tell my story to Max, Whisper, and Smokey the cat. Frankly, I didn't know who else I could talk to. After we'd left the sweat lodge and were again properly attired, there was a brief celebration. We all agreed the experience was exceptional and surpassed our expectations. There was no mention of the declaration of Mrs. LeBlanc. "Max, I'm beginning to question if she even said she pushed Serge down the steps. I don't discount the possibility I was hallucinating, particularly because as I drove Tammy back to her house and she didn't mention it."

Max shifted and curled his long bushy tail under his rear legs. "Yes, I suppose it is possible Mrs. LeBlanc was hallucinating. Makwa did add something to the hot rocks producing a powerful smoke. I imagine we all could have been in dreamland." Smokey purred on my lap with his eyes closed. I left him out for the night and suspect he was worn out from a night of mouseing. Whisper watched me with her gentle brown eyes and accepted all I said as gospel. I chewed on my sandwich and gnawed on my situation. My three friends waited patiently for me to speak.

"All right, guys, here's how I see it. Clayton has been defeated. Our little scheme worked and he has called a special church council meeting when he returns. I fully expect he will resign. He's been neutered, no offense meant to you boys who have that in common with Clayton.

"Tammy made it past Halloween without any of the threats being carried out. We still don't know who left the notes. I am concerned with what Doc told me about how many 'victims' of these sort of notes are also the perpetrators. I know Tammy has some issues, we all do. I just don't know if she would use such a dreadful prank to get attention. On the other hand, the years she spent on the theater stage have given her a lively imagination and a honed talent for acting.

"Now, Father Gallo's situation has been complicated. You see, Doc has planted the seeds of suspicion the Father is hiding something. Does that play into why he is so desperate to get out of town? I don't know. Getting back to the original plan, Makwa was to act as a substitute for Father Gallo. I believe the plot worked. When we were done with the lodge, I thought Makwa would return with me to sleep with you, Max. Mrs. LeBlanc took him aside and they spoke for maybe ten minutes. When Makwa returned without Mrs. LeBlanc, he told me she insisted he stay in the guest house as she had many matters to discuss with him. She received great revelations during the ceremony and needed his interpretation. She dismissed Father Gallo out of hand. I'm of the opinion, and Makwa alluded to his concurrence, Mrs. LeBlanc has no further need for her priest. Makwa will press the point today and tomorrow."

Max sat at my feet and listened intently. Some call me crazy at my insistence Max and I communicate without words. I don't agree and neither does Max. It isn't that Max can talk, he can't. However, through repeated effort, I've learned his language. Nonetheless, I've become cautious who I tell.

"Now, I recall Makwa told me Mrs. LeBlanc and Father Gallo shared a secret. Was the secret that she murdered her husband? What about the remark she made about Clayton being involved? Did Father Gallo have prior knowledge? Was that why he shared the secret of Gabrielle Durand being Clayton's lover? Why did he leave the lodge so abruptly like someone had just pooped in the punch bowl? Was he listening to Mrs. LeBlanc's conversation with Serge? I mean he just left as if he wanted nothing to do with us. I know Tammy felt the same, although we were too numb to speak a word of any of it. if Olive hadn't called and I hadn't drunk two pots of strong coffee, I wouldn't be rambling like some crack addict."

Max moved closer and pushed his muzzle under my hand. I could always count on the Golden to listen, not judge me or correct me, and keep his gums closed. Likewise with Smokey, although I wasn't sure he was even listening. I miss my Grandma. She had the same qualities as Max. I could always count on her to end our conversation with a hug and an affirmation. I wish Grandma were here with me today. It wasn't long before I dozed off, my head resting on the table using my arms as a pillow. I dreamed of talking to Grandma.

When I woke, I did the chores early and headed into town with a new idea, evidently conjured during my slumber. Maybe, I could put one of the questions to rest. I pulled into the Cenex station, parked at the end of the lot, and powered down my window so Max could hang his head out.

A young woman was on duty as the store manager. I recalled having confirmed her although I couldn't remember her name. Her name tag read Pat. Fortunately, she remembered me and greeted me cheerfully. "Pastor Kathy, how are you?"

"Pat, good to see you again," I replied.

"I know, I haven't been to Grace Lutheran, but I have been going to church. I joined the Community Church, you know, Pastor Morgan's church. I'm on their basketball and soccer teams. So I am still going to church."

"Great, Pat, I'm proud of you. But, I'm confused, weren't you Julie when I confirmed you?"

"Yes, Pat is my middle name, actually it's Patricia. Morg thought Julie sounded too girlie for an athlete so I'm using my middle name."

"Julie Patricia, I've a favor to ask of you."

"Of course, I owe you. I am so grateful for the guidance you gave me when I broke up with my first boyfriend. So ask away."

"Two days, ago, on Tuesday evening, a friend of mine had her car parked in your lot, about four spots south of the front door. Someone pulled a joke on her and it is very important for us to find out the identity of the prankster."

"Unfortunately, I wasn't working on Tuesday so I'd be of no help."

"You have cameras in the lot for security and drive-offs don't you?"

"Sure, twelve cameras all together, heck there are three cameras the counter clerks don't even know about," Julie Patricia replied.

"I'd like to look at the videos of Tuesday evening. Would it be possible?"

"It has been a few years since we had 'videos' although I can download Tuesday's activity and you're welcome to view it."

"Perfect. Is there somewhere, I can sit and watch?"

"If you can wait ten minutes, I'll load it to a flashdrive and you can go home and watch on your computer. The only thing is, please bring the drive back. I do this for the police and never see the drive again. Those things are expensive."

"Yes, I can bring it back tomorrow," I said.

"I don't work tomorrow. I've got a high school game and a church game, back to back. Saturday morning would better."

"Saturday it is," I said. "Say are you still pursuing your interests in photography? You did such an outstanding job photo shopping and making those great picture books for the young folks. I remember how you switched heads and bodies and put faces on camels and giraffes. Your work was so funny."

"I'm still doing some when I have time between basketball practice and games and camps."

"I hope you continue working on the photography and by the way good luck with your basketball season."

"Thanks, our church team is undefeated. Your church should start a team."

"Yeah, good idea."

It took thirty minutes and I spent the time at the magazine rack catching up on the gossip. I hadn't known Bill Clinton had fathered a love child with a space alien, although I must admit, I'm not surprised. I was secretly pleased to view the surreptitiously taken photos of the celebrities in their skimpy bathing suits. Some of those stars had plastered on serious weight. And of course the royals continued to be up to mischievous antics, some sans clothes. After last night's sweat lodge, I felt a new sense of sympathy for the celebrities who have unexpected photos taken. I couldn't imagine what I would do if a paparazzi snapped my naked body crawling into the lodge.

Julie Patricia rocked me from the foreign "realities" of the world of celebrities and notables when she tapped me on the shoulder and said, "Pastor Kathy, I've got your flashdrive ready."

I turned away from the magazines and accepted the drive with an expression of appreciation. I was about to leave, anxious to view the contents of the media, when Julie Patricia meekly blocked my exit. "I just wanted you to know I miss you and Grace Lutheran. Like we really had some great times and I learned so much, thank you, Pastor Kathy!" She put me in a bear hug and squeezed me tightly.

"Thank you for telling me and stop by anytime and see your old gang."

"Like I see them at school all the time. Like what I really meant is I miss you."

"If I remember correctly, you like to ride horses. Let's make a date for you to come over and we will ride together," I said.

"Like that would be awesome. I never wanted to leave Grace Lutheran, you know."

"So why did you, leave, I mean?"

"My high school basketball coach and parents wanted me to play more ball and Pastor Morgan has an awesome program. He is always bringing in special coaches and one time like he even brought a player from the Timberwolves. My parents want me to get more attention from the college scouts so like I can get a scholarship, you know."

"Julie, just always hold close to your heart what we studied. If you do, frankly, it doesn't matter what church you attend. Here's my cell phone number, call me next week and we'll go ride and renew our friendship," I said. I fished a calling card from my purse and handed it to her. She had a tear in her eye as she accepted it.

I left with the flashdrive buried deep into my North Face quilted jacket pocket. My fingers played with the little piece of plastic, spinning it, and wondering if it would contain the answer to our mystery. Who was sending these mean notes? I identified, to myself, a short list of suspects although with each, I refused to believe even they could be so cruel, except Clayton and he was in Mexico with Gabrielle. By the time I'd parked the truck behind Grace Lutheran, I'd eliminated all of the suspects and was resigned to the hope the surveillance cameras would provide the answer.

It became evident walking down the hallway to my office it was nearly as cold inside the building as outside where the wind chill temperature was about thirty degrees. Olive was parked at her desk next to an electric space heater and bundled in her long wool coat and a stocking cap festooned with sequins. I'd given her the cap last year after purchasing it at the church craft sale. This was the first time I'd seen her wear the decorative purple cap. I suspect it may have been stashed in the bottom of her desk drawer.

"I've already called Lakes Plumbing and Heating. They have two other emergencies and they'll be here," Olive said without me asking.

"What happened to the heat?"

"The furnace just stopped. I heard it rumble, snort, and then with a loud bang, she gave up the ghost. She is over twenty-five years old, you know."

"I do know. The furnace has been on the budget committee agenda for five years. Bud warned us back then the Beast wouldn't last too much longer," I said.

"I looked it up, a year ago, $13,233.78 was the estimate," Olive said holding up what I surmised was the written estimate.

"We can add another two grand now."

"I already called Bud over at First National and told him to get a loan ready. Lakes Plumbing is going to want a check, you know," Olive said.

"Because when they remodeled the kitchen plumbing the church took a year to pay the bill," I said.

"I added the furnace to the church council agenda Clayton sent by email this morning," Olive said. She handed me a single piece of paper. I read it as I passed by her and into my office which was heated by five candles Olive had lit. She must have gotten into her stash of candles she'd laid up from the craft sale. Surprisingly, it was perhaps two or three degrees warmer, or so it seemed.

I arrived at my leather swivel chair at the same time I read the last agenda item, 'RESIGNATION.'

I could hardly believe my luck. Clayton was going to resign as president of the church council. My nemesis, my tormentor, would be gone. I felt like an anvil had been lifted from my chest. I offered words of thanks.

Now, if I could just find Tammy's tormentor, I'd have as Clayton was fond of calling it, "a hat-trick." Still wearing a smile of victory on my face, I inserted the flashdrive into my laptop and opened the file. Immediately a familiar scene of the parking lot at Cenex jumped on the screen. I played with the cursor trying to learn how to fast forward and stop the action. By the time Olive had brought me a cup of hot chocolate and the Lakes Plumbing service technician had stopped by to ascertain if the church had proper funds for a new furnace, I'd figured out how to speed through the scenes. I slowed when I saw Tammy's Mini Cooper arrive and then stopped when someone came close enough to the windshield to place a note under the wipers. Doc's words of caution about how Tammy could be the perpetrator of her own scheme circled in my head. I concentrated on the screen to prove that not to be the case. I refused to believe my best friend and confidant was capable of such a lie. Hours ticked by. Olive went home with Mel the cat cradled in her arms. The furnace technician stopped by to tell me he'd turned off the entire water supply so the water pipes wouldn't freeze and break. He promised they'd bring a new furnace down tomorrow, one that would "save" the church thousands of dollars in efficiency benefits over the life of the heater.

The sun had set and the office temperature was just about unbearable when I found what I was looking for. It couldn't have been more than an hour before Tammy and I drove into the Cenex lot to retrieve her Mini Cooper that a figure appeared next to the little car, paused momentarily and departed. I played the scene over a dozen times looking for clues as to the identity. I slowly dissected the movements. The figure, larger than average by a substantial amount, comes from the side of the service station out of the camera's view. He or she has their back to the camera the entire time. I'm never able to see the facial features. In fact, the scene was very similar to the poor quality video the television news plays when someone robs a convenience store. The figure stops next to the Mini Cooper for no discernible reason. Again the person's back blocks the view which would show with some definite clarity the note was placed on the windshield. When the person waddles away from the car, with back to camera, there appears to be something under the wiper blades. The window was covered with frost and the notepaper was white so if there was the note, it blended in too well to say with certainty.

My teeth were beginning to chatter so I pulled the flashdrive and packed the laptop into a nylon carrying case. I blew out my only source of heat, the flickering candles, and wasted no time getting to my pickup. I'd punched the remote start on the truck about ten minutes earlier so it was toasty warm. I can hardly recall driving home as I mentally listed and then eliminated dozens of possible suspects. By the time I parked in front of my porch steps, I had whittled the list down to less than a handful.

CHAPTER TWENTY-EIGHT

(Friday)

"*I know it's her!*" Tammy said for the fourth time after having watched the computer screen playing the Cenex parking lot scene for the sixth time.

"I don't disagree with you, it may be her," I said for the third time. Tammy was so certain she'd identified the author of the notes. I still had some doubt. I was still straddling the fence.

"Tammy's right," Father Gallo said. "That is definitely ..."

Tammy interrupted, "There is no other person in Pelican Falls who is as wide as her. I mean look at her backside. It's wider than my Mini Cooper. Look when she stands next to the car, she's bigger than the front fender — it is her!"

I spent a restless night, tossing and turning in bed, worrying about the rabies treatment I'd get first thing in the morning and mulling over what I'd seen on the recording of the Cenex parking lot. My mind pondered the next move. I settled on showing the video to Father Gallo and Tammy. We had started down this trail a little over a week ago. Perhaps, I concluded, we should finish together. I had not called ahead to tell Aldo that Tammy and I were stopping by and I was a little surprised to see he answered the door still wearing his flannel pajama bottoms and a t-shirt commemorating the 1990 visit to Mexico by Pope John Paul II. His Holiness, seated in the Popemobile, smiled sweetly and waved broadly from the front of Father Gallo's t-shirt. I'd never seen him dressed so informally or, for that matter, without his clerical collar, at least not at eleven in the morning. I must have telegraphed my thoughts concerning his appearance because he immediately explained.

"Maria didn't wake me this morning. She had to return home for an emergency."

"To Mexico?" I asked.

"Mexico?" Aldo replied with raised eyebrows.

"Isn't she from Mexico? I never wanted to ask but I always assumed she came from Mexico," I said. Tammy and I stepped through the doorway and took our coats off, half expecting Maria, as she always did, to take them to wherever it was they were hung until our departure.

"She's not from Mexico. She's Ojibwe from the White Earth Reservation. Why did you ever think she was from Mexico?" Aldo asked.

I was embarrassed to tell him 1) she looked like she was from Mexico, 2) I'd never heard her speak so I assumed she spoke only her native tongue, Spanish, and 3) Aldo was hiding her in the rectory because she was in the country illegally. Consequently, I just said, "Tammy had mentioned Maria was from Mexico," which was true as Tammy had been the first to draw those conclusions and share them with me.

"You two, what can I say?" Aldo shook his head and crunched his lips like Grandpa used to do when Sara and I were late for curfew.

"Well, she never spoke," Tammy said as if now feeling the need to defend herself.

"I know, she is the quiet sort. She is very self-conscious because she speaks with a backwoods dialect unique to natives who come from Naytahwaush."

"So you weren't hiding her from the *Federales*?" Tammy asked while giving me an elbow to the ribs.

"Why would you two ever think such a thing?" Aldo turned away and led us into the library. "I'll go put some coffee on. I wasn't expecting early visitors." He left Tammy and me to hang our coats on the side of chairs and sit at the large mahogany table. I removed my laptop computer from the nylon bag and set it on the polished surface. My computer was on the verge of being given to the museum, it was so ancient. It needed a five minute warm-up before I could even consider giving it suggestions. Years ago I stopped striking its keys with the idea I was sending commands or instructions. Our relationship had grown to one wherein I would tap a key, "enter," for example, and my laptop would take the keystroke under consideration as a suggestion. When she, my computer is a "she," finally came awake and the screen lit up, I pushed the flashdrive into her and hoped she wouldn't be offended with the intrusion. She was not and I opened the file.

"Can one of you ladies help me make the coffee? I'm afraid I don't know how this one works, it has so many bells and whistles," Aldo said from the library doorway. He was holding a coffee pot filled with water in his hand.

"Oh, forget the coffee," Tammy said. "I want to see this, come join us." She waved him to the table.

"This is going to take me a few minutes to find if you want to help him," I said.

"Yes, please, I don't function without my caffeine first thing in the morning," Father Gallo said. "I was up most of the night getting ready..." He never finished his sentence as to what he was getting ready for.

"It's not the 'first thing in the morning.' That was five hours ago. Give me the pot, I'll make the coffee while Kathy finds the right place on the recording," Tammy said.

Father Gallo passed the pot and came to my side. He pulled up a leather padded chair and sat next to me. I forwarded the recording as fast as I dared without offending the laptop. She was sensitive to being asked to overexert herself, sort of like Olive could be at times.

"Oh, look, there goes Pastor Randy and he is with Morgan. My ... is that a twelve pack under Randy's arm?" Aldo said and pointed a stubby finger at the computer screen where it did indeed look like Randy had tucked a pack of beer under his arm like a running back.

"Probably Mountain Dew, Randy doesn't drink, you know," I said.

"Well he should, it might cause a smile to replace the scowl on his prune-face," Father Gallo said and then chuckled enough to make his tummy shake and the Pope wave.

"Okay, it's not long after those two left, it's coming up soon. I'm going to pause it here until Tammy gets back. She won't like it if she's the last to see."

"Fine, I can wait. Let me tell you what I did last night," Father Gallo said.

I hoped he would explain his strange behavior these last days and perhaps even explain why he had been alluding Doc's questions. I knew my father confessor, my consoler, and spiritual guide had some honorable explanation that when presented, would cause me to shout, 'Ah Ha, I knew he had nothing to hide.'

"I met with Mrs. LeBlanc and Makwa. She called me and insisted I join them for dinner last night. Makwa made the most delicious rump roast with some of those herbs he picks. Bear rump roast and parsley potatoes, Yummmm."

"Yeah, and?"

"And Makwa announced he is moving in with Mrs. LeBlanc…"

"Nooo," I said, jumping to the wrong conclusion about his use of the phrase "moving in with."

"Oh, no, Makwa is going to stay in the guest house and provide some spiritual guidance to the grieving widow. They have hit it off nicely. Makwa is writing a book …"

"I know, he's been working on it over three years," I said recalling how he had me edit his initial attempts until he decided my remarks were too cutting.

"Makwa has about two hundred pages completed and even has a literary agent interested in his work," Father Aldo said.

"It is a fascinating work. He tells of his spiritual journey from atheist to Catholic to Ojibwe *midewinini*," I said.

"The literary agent made Makwa promise he'd be finished by the first of the year. Makwa was hoping you would ask him to stay on at your place and if not, he was going to stay at his auntie's place in Waubun. Since you never made the offer, he's thinking this garden house would be just the ticket. Mrs. LeBlanc even offered to help with the editing and hire the local English teacher to proof the manuscript."

"*Cafe Lattes, mon amis*," Tammy announced when she entered the room carrying a silver tray filled with frothy white mugs and shortbread cookies. "You didn't start without me, did you?"

I accepted the hot mug and took a sip, "Very good, my compliments to the *barista.*"

"That is a complex coffee maker you have in the kitchen. I understand why you might have difficulties making a cup. I, on the other hand, spent two years working at Starbucks in San Francisco's Chinatown. In other words, I am a pro."

"Very good, my dear…" Father Gallo said.

"Now, let the show begin," Tammy said.

"I was telling a story. Let me finish my story."

"I want to see the culprit Kathy has found," Tammy said.

"Let him finish," I suggested.

"I'm just about done anyway. So, I have dinner with Mrs. LeBlanc and Makwa …"

"They had rump roast in case you were wondering," I teased.

"So, it came up during our dinner conversation, the position at the Vatican is still open."

"Who brought the topic up?" I asked.

"Makwa, like it was scripted, he asked, 'Is the opportunity for you to study in Rome still an option?'" Father Gallo said.

"What did Mrs. LeBlanc say?" I asked.

"You are getting ahead of my story. I, of course, replied matter-of-factly, the once-in-a-lifetime chance was still a possibility if I could only get the Bishop's concurrence. Mrs. LeBlanc spoke up as if she'd always been a supporter of my departure. 'Why,' she said, 'I'll call the Bishop right now and tell him to send you post-haste.'"

"Did she call?" I asked sensing certain victory.

"She did, I sat there in the overstuffed chair and watched her call. She didn't ask the Bishop, she told him he needed to send me to Rome and waste no time doing so. The woman's got some juice because there was no discussion and within two minutes, she was off the phone and told me to go home and pack."

"Hurrah, I'm so happy for you," Tammy said. We both hugged our good friend and generally created such a commotion causing the long lazy dog, Brandy, with ears dragging, to check on our welfare.

"I called my friend at the Vatican and woke him up to tell him the news. He told me to waste no time before some official changed his mind as they are oft given to do." Father Gallo looked as if a great burden had been lifted from his shoulders. His old dog gleaned the benefit of the emotional high in the form of an intense scratching behind the ears. It looked as though the priest might shake the long droopy ears right from the dog's head.

I wondered if Makwa had, during their dinner, mentioned the dramatic statements I attributed to Mrs. LeBlanc. Tammy hadn't talked about it since the ceremony and I was full of self-doubt as to whether I'd actually heard Mrs. LeBlanc declare she killed her husband, Serge. I wanted to ask, however, I couldn't quite conjure up a way to introduce the subject. "How 'bout that Sofia, killin' ol' Serge, then?" or "Did the topic of Mr. LeBlanc's untimely death surface during the serving of the rump roast?" I decided I would watch for an opening and play off that. Then again, I recalled Makwa had said Aldo and Sofia "shared" a secret. If that were the truth, then Aldo might not be so apt to talk about the death. Or, as I had concluded several times during this mental ping pong match, maybe I hadn't even heard the confession. It was strange neither Tammy nor Aldo brought the matter up for discussion. I mean, it's not every day one hears a murder confession.

I decided to serve up an easy ball to Aldo, "Did you talk about any other important matters during your eventful dinner?" I asked not feeling exceptionally clever.

"Like what?" was Aldo's only response. If he'd seen the bait I had cast under his nose, he chose to ignore it.

"Like murder" flashed through my mind although, "Like how did Mrs. LeBlanc feel about the sweat lodge ceremony?" was what came out as a lame stab to at least bring up the topic.

"She found it delightful. Sofia said the ceremony had cleansed her soul of guilt and remorse and she looked forward to another ceremony within the month. Makwa agreed and has already contacted his spiritual compatriots, oh, I forget their names ..."

"Lonesome Dave and Crow Boy," Tammy filled in the blanks, "looks like we've been replaced after our debut as holy women."

"Other than sitting cross-legged and naked, we didn't seem to have much of a role anyway," I said without regret I had been replaced so readily.

"Let's get on with the show," Tammy said. She pulled up a chair in front of the computer screen and I prompted her, the computer, to play the recording.

I immediately see Tammy's Mini Cooper on the screen. There does not appear to be any paper under the windshield wiper. Several people walk in front of the little car, none stop near it. On two occasions a pickup truck pulled next to the compact and the driver stepped out. The view of the windshield is obstructed by the hood of the truck. When the trucks leave, there doesn't seem to be a note on the windshield. Then a figure comes out of the shadows of the store as if having walked not near the store entrance but from behind the store, out of sight of any other cameras aimed at the entrance. The figure waddles over to the Mini Cooper, pauses so briefly as to be barely discernible on a time lapse camera, and retreats in the same fashion it had arrived. The figure was clad in a long black coat and wore a hood and ball cap over its head. What with the hood, ball cap and large sunglasses, there were no distinguishable facial features to be viewed. Most notable was the duck waddle of a heavy person coupled with the sheer bulk of the figure. Male or female? Impossible to say. Age? Over twelve and under one hundred. No one so large lives past one hundred.

"Play it again, Kathy, play it again." Tammy was noticeably excited like a dog closing in on a treed cat.

On the third playing of the recording, Tammy declared, "That is Mrs. Hildebrandt!"

Chapter Twenty-nine

(Friday)

*I*n the rear of the Grace Lutheran Church, I pulled the pickup into the parking spot marked with the sign which read RESERVED FOR Pastor Johnson. The sign was looking faded and no longer wore the luster it had years ago on the day I arrived for my first calling as a minister. I remember feeling proud and confident upon parking my Subaru and seeing the departing pastor waiting at the door fully prepared to literally hand over the keys to the church. He gave me an abbreviated tour, pointing out the furnace was on its last leg, and took me into his office and shut the door. "Kathy, this church is full of sinners," he said. I entertained the possibility he was teasing me until he laid out the facts of life in plain terms. "A church like Grace Lutheran hires as pastors, those who have just graduated, like yourself, and those who haven't 'worked out' at other churches, like myself, and then they pick up senior pastors who are retired and looking for part-time work. They can't afford to pay enough to support a pastor with a family."

"I'm not looking to get wealthy from this ..."

"Good because you won't. I'm the eighth pastor in as many years. This is not a bad town, but you will be in a glass house. The congregation will know more about you than your own family, more than you know about yourself. Sometimes what they don't know, the gossips will make up for a good story. And they will have expectations of you that Christ himself would struggle to meet. If you last six months, there will be a faction asking to form a call committee to find another 'more suitable' pastor — one who will 'fit in' the community. When you can't turn water into wine and can't double the contributions, the council will turn on you. I wish I could paint a rosier picture."

Well, he was correct in most of his assessment which continued past an hour. I had experienced all of his prognostications and a few more he hadn't enumerated. Still, I prevailed and have grown to love my "sinners" knowing deep down I was not better than the worst of them, except Clayton, who would soon be gone. So though my "Reserved" sign had faded, I still looked forward to each day's challenge.

I let Max out of the truck. I had ditched my little Subaru after the first winter when we had a record snow fall and icy roads until May. Max ran to his bush, sniffed, and tinkled. The bush was like a doggy Facebook, with every canine in Pelican Falls and each adjacent township checking in on a daily basis. The bush had long ago died. I considered replacing it until Olive pointed out no bush could survive so many visits by so many dogs.

With Max by my side, I strolled into the church and past the empty Sunday school rooms. Benny was busy pushing his Oreck vacuum across the grey Berber carpet. He did it with such gusto I was concerned he'd wear paths into the tough floor covering. I walked past the colorful flannel board with little biblical figures of Jonah, a whale with mean eyes, and a God who sat on a gold throne looking perturbed. I'm conflicted with the idea when we teach the wee ones stories which can easily be misunderstood. When a six or seven year old hears a story how God made a whale swallow Jonah, what do they think? When they are told the armies of Israel marched around a city blowing trumpets and killed the residents, what do they think? I'm beginning to believe we are teaching the little guys about things they can't possibly understand and worse, perhaps planting scary and wrongful ideas taking a lifetime to undo. I feel the same about Santa Claus. What bright youngster is going to question why her parents and teachers would lie about Santa but tell her the truth about Jesus?

Max and I continued past the library and into my office. I noted the church was once again warm and concluded the furnace had already been replaced. Olive was napping with her cat on her lap. When she napped, she tossed her head back with her mouth open and looked dead. It took me a year to get used to this scene. I hustled Max past Olive so he wouldn't wake her with a cold nose to her arms triggering a heart attack. The candles were flickering – time for another craft sale to replenish the candle inventory. I saw a few Olive notes in my inbox. On top was a note stating Mrs. Aaronson called to ask if I would perform the marriage ceremony of her daughter at Grace Lutheran if she was marrying a Jewish boy. She also asked if a rabbi could be included in the ceremony and whether they could blow the Shofar horn. I called her back and assured her I would perform the ceremony and the rabbi was welcome to join me at the altar. I went through her long list of concerns and ended with the blowing of the horn. Heck, I told her, they could bring the entire flock of rams to the wedding if it pleased them. I'm not much for standing on rituals and ceremonies — except baptism and communion – on those sacraments I won't compromise.

For the last five minutes of my telephone conversation, Mrs. Bertelsen stood in the office doorway listening and occasionally participating with facial expressions of disagreement or approval. This is what I get for having an "open door" policy. Olive must have taken Mel for his bathroom break out to the sandy area under the dogs' bush in back of the church. I motioned for her to enter although she already had when the phone touched the receiver cradle.

"I don't think we should be so tolerant. If you invite the rabbi then you have to allow the Grand Mufti himself. A lot of those turkey workers down at the mobile home park are Muslims, you know."

"And there are some Mormons living out on Muskrat Lake ... should I exclude them too?"

"Mormons, I'm not so sure. They're Christians too, aren't they?"

"Depends on who you ask. Did you come to talk about church policy or did you have something less serious on your mind?" I asked fearing I would regret the question no matter what her answer.

"No, more serious. I'm here to resign from the church kitchen board. I've had enough!" Her face flushed and lips trembled as though a flood of tears was sure to follow.

"I didn't know we had a church kitchen board."

"We do ... it's all of us ladies who toil and slave in the kitchen week after week, year after year, to make this a happy place where people want to come."

"All of you ladies do so well."

"I'm done. I've had enough. You'll just have to find someone else. And by golly, I'm not the only one who is fed up." Now the tears flowed and her nose ran. I moved beside her with a box of pink Kleenex I replaced every week. I went through a case every six months. Clayton once questioned why I was spending so much on tissues. "Why don't they bring their own?" he asked scornfully.

"What happened? Did someone say something mean to you?" I asked.

"It's that damn Lutefisk, excuse the French, Pastor. The annual Lutefisk dinner is in a few weeks and I was about to put our order in at Olsen's Fish Company down in the Cities when Mrs. Olson ..."

"Which Olson?"

"Mavis, of course, she says that Finlander, Mr. Aho, has a better source for Lutefisk from Canada. Mavis says it's cheaper and better because they make it with birch ash instead of lye, who ever heard of such a thing? What'll you call it BjrøkFisk?"

"Is that true?"

"Oh, I don't know, and she said Obama's EPA has listed lye cured Lutefisk as a hazardous product. She says lye is so caustic the EPA has prohibited it from consumption. I called the EPA in Minneapolis and asked them if it was true."

"What did they say?" I asked.

"They just laughed and hung up."

"Did you tell her?"

"No, but I did some checking, on the internet, you know, and it turns out the Finlanders up in Canada have been selling Pollock instead of Cod and preserving the fish in tree ash instead of lye. I called over to the Sons of Norway in Fargo and they said they tried it a few years back and it was a failure. Nobody came back to the Lutefisk dinner until they got the real stuff again."

"Did you tell Mavis?"

"No, you know she's so stubborn she won't listen and besides she has already ordered it and it's been shipped. I quit!"

I sat back in my chair. Solomon had the dilemma of choosing which woman got the baby and it was a difficult decision he resolved by offering to slice the baby in two and giving half to each. The woman who wanted the baby the most gave up her demand for the son and Solomon awarded her the babe. This Lutefisk controversy could grow into a battle which will be recorded in the Lutheran Church history book alongside Martin Luther's rebellion and the Hundred Year War. I needed the wisdom of Solomon.

"Place your order with Olsen's for the Lutefisk. We will have a side by side taste test of the old and new *fisk*. If you are correct and this other fish stinks, the controversy will be settled. I need you to stay in the kitchen. You are the cornerstone of the board. Please?"

Mrs. Bertelsen, after all the fuss, was not going to give in so easy. "What about Mavis? Will you talk to her?" She blew her nose with finality and I knew I'd won her over if I agreed to negotiate the deal with Mavis.

"Yes, you place the order, cut back a few pounds, and tell Olsen's Fish Company we are experimenting with this new fish. If they would lower their price a bit, it would sweeten the pot. And order extra meatballs. I'm going to call some pastors from nearby churches to see if they would lend a hand to drive our numbers up. I know the Cormorant Church had to cancel their Lutefisk dinner this year so there must be a bunch of Norsk junkies looking for a Lutefisk fix."

"Thank you so very much Pastor Kathy, you're the best."

I turned to Max after she left, "Ah, if all our problems could be so easily solved. Yes, Smokey and you will undoubtedly be eating leftover Lutefisk for a week, making Smokey a very happy cat. We best get moving, I told Tammy I'd meet her for dinner at Connie's."

*   *   *

"Connie, I'll just have a toasted cheese sandwich," I said with little enthusiasm.

"What, it's the all-you-can-eat Friday fish fry?" Connie said.

"I've lost my appetite for fish. Did you know the Finns from Canada are peddling counterfeit Lutefisk?" I asked.

Connie slapped the side of her head. "What next? First we had 9/11 and now this! Where did you hear that?"

"Mrs. Bertelsen, and on second thought, let's not spread the rumor. I'm on the brink of a Lutefisk war at the church. Say, can we put a flyer in your window advertising the Lutefisk Dinner?"

"Yeah sure, be my guest, that event has never cost me a single customer. In fact, if you'd like, I'll sponsor a lottery for free tickets to the dinner."

"A lottery?" I asked.

"Yeah, I'll put the old goldfish bowl on the cashier counter and sell tickets for a buck a piece. The customers will give me a dollar for a chance to pull a winning ticket from the fish bowl. The old farts will love it. I'll donate the proceeds to Grace Lutheran," Connie said.

"Thank you, I'll put it towards paying the loan for the new furnace."

"Tammy, what'll you have?" Connie asked.

"I'll take your fish and I'll bet you the chance to pull the first ticket that Kathy is eating off my plate when she finishes her cheese sandwich."

"I'll bring you both coffee in a second," Connie said as she walked away still scribbling our order.

"Have you heard from Makwa?" Tammy asked.

"Not a peep. Perhaps no news is good news. I am happy for Aldo. He will be leaving within a week."

"They have a replacement for him so quickly?"

"They're bringing a semi-retired guy off the bench to fill in until they can bring in a long-term replacement."

"The sweat lodge seems to have done the trick," Tammy said.

"I've been meaning to ask you something about the lodge ceremony," I said.

"What? Wait, I bet I know."

"Go ahead, tell me."

"You're going to ask me if I heard Mrs. LeBlanc say she pushed Serge down the steps. Am I right?"

"So, you heard it too! I was beginning to question if I was hallucinating in part because you never talked about it. I was sure you'd bring it up, I mean it's just so shocking."

"I wasn't certain. By the time I left the ceremony, I was physically and mentally exhausted. I wasn't sure Mrs. LeBlanc had actually said she'd murdered Serge," Tammy said and then looked around with concern she had spoken too loudly.

"Shhh, Buddy Bjornson is right behind you," I said softly.

"Don't worry. He's with the missus so he's removed his hearing aids. That's why she's darn near shouting at him," Tammy said confidently.

"Here's your coffee," Connie said cheerfully. She set two cups on the table. "Can I give Max a steak bone? He's like a *maître d'* greeting my customers as he is waiting outside so patiently."

"Yes, go ahead but no fat please. He and I are dieting," I said.

Connie departed with an enormous bone rolled in a paper napkin.

Speaking in a hushed tone I asked, "So you did hear her 'confession?'" I made those irritating little quote marks with my index fingers. I felt relief from the doubt I had been carrying. The feeling was immediately replaced with a new concern. "Do we have to report this? I mean, she confessed to 'redrum.'"

"Redrum?"

"Spell redrum backwards," I said.

With her finger, Tammy wrote the letters on the table — M U R D E R. "Oh, I get it. I don't know. I've been mulling this over and ..."

"Have you arrived at any conclusions?"

"I even Googled the matter. There would be considerable legal issues. One of the first would be whether Mrs. LeBlanc was under the influence of whatever it was Makwa was burning," Tammy said.

"Not to mention the stress of the ceremony on an old gal might have produced some wild dream or hallucination. It's not like a detective asked her, 'Did you 'redrum' Serge?' and she admitted doing it. It was just something she said from out in left field."

"Exactly. Then a lawyer could argue the confession was made to clergy during a religious ceremony and those communications are not admissible against her."

"So even if we brought the matter to the police, her statements couldn't be used against her?"

"According to my Google search. I've been giving this a lot of thought. What the police would have is some utterance they couldn't use to prosecute her and most likely no other evidence. Think about it … you push an elderly man down the steps, there are no witnesses, and no physical evidence," Tammy said.

"The elderly are falling all the time," I said.

"Exactly! Do you think this is the 'secret' shared by Father Gallo and Mrs. LeBlanc?" Tammy asked.

"Secret? I don't remember they shared a secret," I said.

"Yes you do. Makwa told us. You asked me a dozen times, 'What do you think their secret is?'" Tammy said.

"What did Makwa say the secret was?" I couldn't for the life of me recall this event.

"He didn't say what the secret was. In fact, Makwa didn't know the secret either. He just said they shared a secret."

"How am I supposed to know?"

"Oh, forget it then."

"Here ya go ladies, one order of the finest fish this side of the Mississippi River and one sad looking Velveeta cheese sandwich," Connie said. She slipped the two plates onto the table and asked if we needed anything else. Hearing no requests, she returned to the kitchen. Tammy and I dug into our food without talking. Connie was right, the sandwich did look pathetic and Tammy's fish so appealing. I wanted to sample a piece but didn't want to give her the satisfaction of predicting I would. Instead, I munched on the toast and sipped my coffee.

"What do we do, if anything?" Tammy asked when she'd finished her first serving of the golden brown fillets.

"Any suggestions?"

"Why don't you ask Doc, your special agent friend?"

"I already did. When I went to Detroit Lakes for the dog bite treatment this morning, I met Doc for coffee. We agreed I could ask him some questions if I kept it hypothetical with no names. So I told him the fundamentals of the story."

"What did he say?" Tammy asked.

"You may be pleased to know your analysis based on diligent Google research was much the same as this seasoned police investigator. He saw the same flaws and he added the two hypothetical clergy had best be ready to explain their every moment at the ceremony. Who sat where. Who wore what. Who said what. You know, every detail including why the hypothetical clergy were attending the hypothetical sweat lodge ceremony."

"That may be awkward to testify about," Tammy said.

"Yes, it could be very uncomfortable. I also showed him the recording at the Cenex parking lot."

"What'd he say? Was he impressed with your sleuthiness?" Tammy asked.

"Is sleuthiness even a word? He didn't comment on my investigative skills. He did say the figure in the recording could never be identified solely from watching the video."

"I think we should have a line-up," Tammy said excitedly.

"Sure, round up the ten largest people in the county and make them back into the room so we can judge which behind is on the recording." I dropped the remainder of my sandwich onto the plate. I had lost my appetite in the frustration of our inability to put an end to this matter.

"Well, speak of the devil. Mrs. Hildebrandt and Wally are coming into the café, right now," Tammy said. She was pointing directly at them with a knife in her hand. I told her to put the knife down and "be cool."

"More walleye?" Connie asked while holding a pan full of fish fresh from the fryer. They smelled so good!

"No, no thanks, Connie. They were very tasty, but I've had enough. Gotta watch the waistline, you know."

"You're so thin. You've got no waist to watch." She continued down the row of booths peddling her fish.

"Doc did say we could try to get a handwriting exemplar from our new suspect who I never named," I said.

"I've got an idea. What was the name of the farm you and I went to for the hayride with the fiddle player last year?" Tammy asked.

"I don't remember, was it Johnny Johnson or Ole Olson or Tommy Thompson? It was some silly name like that."

"Arne Arnesson, that's what it was, Arne Arnesson. He has those two Clydesdales that pull the hay wagon, remember?"

"I remember falling off the darn wagon and running to catch up. Old Arne was as deaf as a rock. I yelled and screamed for him to stop and he and those two stud horses just kept going. What do they have to do with anything?"

"Those three studs live out by the Hildebrandts don't they?"

"I suppose within a mile or so."

"Do you have any writing paper in your purse?" Tammy asked.

I dug in the recesses of the clunky old purse which was a decade past looking fashionable and had recently sprung more leaks than the Titanic. Still, I loved the old purse — she kept my life and my secrets in order. I came up with a notepad and a pen from the Lutheran Brotherhood Insurance agent. I handed both to Tammy.

"Watch this." Tammy slid out of the booth and strode over to the Hildebrandt's table. I followed not wanting to miss whatever it was Tammy had in mind.

"Good evening Mr. and Mrs. Hildebrandt. You both look fit as a fiddle and ready for the fish no doubt. Most delicious tonight," Tammy said in a perky manner.

"Evening, pastors," Wally said.

"Every time I see you two ..." Mrs. Hildebrandt began her usual "greeting."

"... 'we are together.' I know, funny how that works, isn't it? Say, I'll not bother you but a moment. You live out by the Arnesson fella with the big Clydesdales, don't you?" Tammy asked with the smoothness of a used car salesman.

"Ya, he's about a mile and a half away, why?" Mrs. Hildebrandt said suspiciously.

"I was thinking about having a hayride for the Young Christian Club. I should drive out there and look the place over and talk to Mr. Arnesson, you know get a feel for his operation. Would you mind writing out the driving instructions for me?" Tammy said and shoved the notepad and pen under Mrs. Hildebrandt's nose.

"I guess we could." She accepted the proffered bait and set it down in front of her. "You just take Highway 59 to County Road 16…"

"No," said Wally, "it's County Road 17. County Road 16 will take them to the township dump."

"If you're so smart, mister, here you write the directions," Mrs. Hildebrandt said with obvious contempt for being corrected. She had only written Highway 59 on the notepad when she threw the paper to Wally to finish.

Max was waiting with a small portion of a steak bone in his mouth when Tammy and I left Connie's feeling somewhat defeated. The cool evening air was a welcome relief from the café filled with the smell of frying fish. We strolled silently towards the Grace Lutheran parking lot where my pickup waited. I considered Tammy's revelations concerning Mrs. LeBlanc's confession. I struggled with the moral question of notifying the authorities. By the time we'd reached my truck, I decided to defer to Doc's suggestion to just "sit on it."

"I'll give you a ride to home, hop in," I said. Max jumped in first and went to the rear where he began chewing loudly on his prize. Tammy pulled herself into the passenger seat and I started the big V-8 engine. I turned on the heater and the interior light. I pulled down a paper I'd tucked in the visor earlier in the day. "Here, look at this. It's a photograph. Tell me who this looks like to you."

Tammy took the paper and examined it in the dim cab light. "Who do you think it is?" she asked.

"I don't want to influence you. Look closer. You know who it is."

"Seriously, Kathy, I don't recognize this woman. The quality of the picture isn't very good," Tammy said.

"It's Maria. It's a photo of Father Gallo's maid."

"Where did you get this?" Tammy asked.

"This morning, in Detroit Lakes, after my treatment and talking to Doc, I stopped at Walmart to pick up a few boxes of Kleenex. This flyer with the photo was posted on the public bulletin board. Look, it says, 'Have you seen this woman?' and asks the public to contact the BCA. It's the woman Doc and the other agents have been looking for."

"Brenda Maria Fairbanks is the name listed on the flyer," Tammy said.

"I know, just like Julie Patricia at the Cenex station…"

"Now you've got me confused."

"I met Julie Patricia at the Cenex. She's a shift manager who gave me the recording of the station parking lot. I confirmed her. I haven't seen her for some time and she was wearing a name tag of 'Pat.' I was confused until she explained she was using her middle name now."

"And you made light of my analysis of the Cenex parking lot photo."

"Seriously, the woman in this flyer is Aldo's Maria. He's been hiding her. I thought she was a Mexican in the country illegally. She's not Mexican, she's a Native and Aldo's been hiding her for reasons I don't have a clue."

Tammy turned on a second dome light and took out a pair of reading glasses. She studied the flyer and shook her head. "Maria has long black hair and wears glasses. This Brenda Fairbanks has short hair and doesn't have glasses and look how much longer her nose is and her lips aren't as full. I'm not so certain."

I backed the truck away from the church and drove on to Third Street. Big fluffy flakes of snow began to land softly on the windshield. I was so sure Tammy would agree with my assessment of the photograph. When she didn't, I questioned if I had jumped to the wrong conclusion. Still, Doc had accused Aldo of being obtuse at best. Maria had left the rectory and Aldo gave no explanation, and Maria's nose was every bit as long as Brenda's.

"You're sure Maria is Brenda, aren't you?" Tammy asked a block away from her car.

"I'm as certain as you are not," I said.

"Did you tell your friend, Doc?"

"No, I wanted to show you first, just to make sure I was right."

"Kathy, I wish I could see what you do but I can't."

I pulled next to her car as my smart phone signaled I had a text. I looked at the message, "The cat is waiting outside Gen Langer's room." "Oh, no!" I exclaimed.

"What happened?" Tammy asked.

I read the message, "'The cat is waiting outside Gen Langer's room.'"

"At the nursing home?" Tammy asked.

"Yes, of course."

"Do you want me to come with?" Tammy asked.

"Yes, please."

CHAPTER THIRTY

(Saturday)

A fresh blanket of fluffy snow had fallen throughout the night. Whisper loped along in the powder with the ease of an unbridled filly. She took me far out into the rolling hills and down to the lake country. I let her take the lead, not wanting to make any more decisions on this bright sunny morning. It had been a long sad night at the bedside of my friend, Gen Langer. By the time Tammy and I had reached her bedside, the tabby cat was laying curled up on Gen's chest. A stroke had destroyed the joyful countenance and we watched as life drained from her normally smiling face. Gen's niece arrived before the end and once again, I suffered from a lack of comforting words. I did my best but knew my best would never be enough. It was Tammy who comforted me with a gentle reminder Gen had moved on to a "better world" — one she had dreamed of visiting all of her life and especially those last months at the nursing home when she had a premonition her days left on earth may be few. We spoke of it often and she was at peace with her future.

Whisper slowed to a trot and then walked around Lake Number Eleven. I pulled on the reins ever so gently and she stopped by a fallen pine where earlier I had seen a mama raccoon hiding her five cubs. I got off, sat on the pine and cried for the longest time until I had no more tears. Max, as always, sat by my side, ever so close and ever so comforting. Although I was sad, I knew with Gen's arrival, heaven would be filled with her joy and the angels entertained by her jokes. I recalled she once told me how she intended to learn some new jokes when she reached her final destination.

*   *   *

When I walked into the back door of Grace Lutheran, the hall was filled with empty boxes, the boxes which held the new hymnals.

Benny stood looking forlorn in the middle of the mess. "Benny, why do you have all of these boxes piled here?"

He was nearly in tears as he forced a response. "Olive told me to take them to the dumpster."

"Then why do you have them piled up here? Do you need help? You know where the dumpster is, don't you?"

"Pastor Kathy, I took these out and Bell is a bob told me to get the hell back in the church." Now he did have tears running down his cheeks.

"Bell is a bob? Who is that?" Benny occasionally got names mixed up although I could normally guess who he was talking about. Bell is a bob had me stumped.

"The mean man who ate the devil's eggs. You called him Bell is a bob." He wiped the tears and runny nose with his shirt sleeve.

"You mean Beelzebub, the man you sat next to at the potluck, Clayton Johansson?"

"That's what I said, Bell is a bob. He is parked in his big truck next to the fire truck by the dumpster where I took the boxes."

"Fire truck? Was there a fire?" I moved back to the glass door and peered outside towards the dumpster which was hidden from view by a thick row of Norway Pines. I saw no smoke, no red flashing lights. I could see the tail of Clayton's shiny black Escalade sticking out a foot beyond the pines. I opened the door to go over and confront Clayton and then thought better of it.

"Benny, what was Beelzebub doing by the dumpster?" I put my arm around his shoulder and began to lead him down the hallway.

"Talking to the man and woman in the fire truck." Benny kicked at the last box causing it to tumble down the hall.

"What did the woman look like?"

"She's big, real big and loud when she talks real loud."

"Benny, please go out to my truck. There are two boxes in the back. Those are boxes of Kleenex. Bring them inside and put the Kleenex around the church like you always do. When Beelzebub leaves, I'll help you take all the boxes to the dumpster, okay?"

"Okay, Pastor Kathy. Can I have my morning hug now?"

"Of course." I squeezed him hard and then ruffled his curly locks triggering a long giggle from his mouth. I continued down the hall towards my office. There was a youthful bounce in my step as I considered being only an hour from watching Clayton tender his resignation.

Olive held out a ceramic mug full of thick black coffee for me as I entered the church office. "Is there anything needing my attention before the church council meeting?" I asked hoping Olive would say no.

"No, Mrs. Petersen called. I left the message on your desk – nothing important except she found Pastor Morgan on a dating website. I put the web address on the message."

"Did you look at his ad?"

"Of course I looked."

"Would you date him?"

"You know, since Charlie went to the happy hunting grounds eleven years ago, I've not given any man a second thought. I've had suitors, mind you. I simply couldn't bear the thought of having to train another husband. Charlie was a handful and it took me his lifetime to get him the way I wanted."

"The curse of being a woman. Every man we find needs so much work – so much fine tuning. A gal is exhausted from straightening them out and then, nine out of ten times, just when you get them fixed, they run off with some youngster with tight jeans and an overflowing halter top."

"Praise the lord; you've got that right, sister." Olive clapped her hands so hard Mel flew off her lap and hid under the desk.

"Getting back to Morgan, would you date him?"

"In my younger days, I'd date any of them. I got around, not slept around, but let's just say I had a lot of guys on my dance card. Yes, I'd add Morgan to the list. As a long term project, and I do mean long term, he'd need to be taken down a peg or two, you know, knocked off his high horse."

"You'd be just the gal who could do it, Olive," I said. I walked into my office. Olive had cracked the window open a few inches and the fresh air smelled so good, like when Grandma hung my bed sheets out to dry on the clothesline. I checked the time and still had half an hour before the meeting. I opened Windows Explorer and typed in the address to the dating service. I couldn't resist seeing how Morgan was marketing himself. I quickly found his site using the password Mrs. Petersen had provided. His photo popped up. As Olive said, he was worth a second look. Actually Morgan is very handsome and his photo did him justice. I skimmed his sales pitch. "Never been married, white male, in thirties, excellent physical condition, looking for same in a Christian woman. Looking for a soul mate to build a Christian media ministry. Ability to sing and being telegenic is a plus." The ad went on for several paragraphs. It occurred to me Morgan was looking for his clone albeit of the female gender.

"Checking out Morgan's search for a soul-mate are you? Say, you're available, you should answer his ad," Clayton Johansson said in an abnormally cheerful manner. He plopped himself down in the closest chair in front of my desk. He leaned back so far I thought he'd tip over. He sported a nice tan and seemed more relaxed than I had ever seen him behave. Perhaps it was a relief to resign. Maybe he was going to leave his wife, Liv, and marry Gabrielle. The vacation to Mexico might have been the tipping point in his marriage. I'd never seen him smile so broadly his teeth showed — actually it was more of a snarl like a wolf before it pounces on the fawn.

Gosh, I was really going to have a civil conversation with Clayton. "No, Clayton, I know the type Morgan is looking for and I'm really not it," I teased.

"Tammy Faye Baker, that's who Morg is looking for. He needs a Tammy so he can play out his dream of being a Jimmy Swaggart, Pat Robertson, or Jimmy Baker."

"I visited with Jimmy Baker once when he was serving his time down at the Federal Prison in Rochester. He didn't act like an inmate, more like a celebrity who was spending time with the sinners in prison."

"Fascinating, Kathy, simply fascinating," Clayton said in a patronizing tone.

"How was your trip to Minneapolis?" I asked. "Looks like you got some sun while you were down there."

"Cute, Kathy. You've been enjoying this little game haven't you?"

"Game?"

"Yeah it's a game and it's the fourth quarter, you lead and I'm pinned against my own goal line."

I glanced at the clock on the wall over Clayton's shoulder. "We should get to the council meeting. We'll be late."

"I cancelled the meeting. There will be no meeting," Clayton said.

"No meeting, why?"

"Because I just threw a 'Hail Mary' pass and scored to win the game, that's why. You've lost and there is no reason to have a meeting. I figured you and I could work out our problems without involving those boneheads on the council."

"Sometimes, no most of the time, Clayton, you baffle me. Whatever are you babbling about?"

"Let me explain it so even your retard friend could understand. By the way, I'm going to replace him with Lardass. Anyway that's another matter which you won't need to concern yourself with any longer."

"Clayton, you are ..."

"I know, such an ass, you've told me more times than a nagging wife. If you'd just shut up and listen you wouldn't be in the mess you're in. First, I know about your scheme to blackmail me or shame me or whatever you hoped to accomplish by dressing up like Gabrielle – cute, real cute. I have to admit you had me going. I was even going to resign. I have to tell you, it's over between Gabrielle and me. O V E R, he spelled out the word. You've lost whatever leverage you might have had. At worst, I may have to offer a couple of mea culpas to the council. Hell, the ways things are nowadays, I can act like Bill Clinton, John Edwards, Eliot Spitzer or a hundred other notable men and be forgiven and revered."

"Clayton, you may be forgiven but you are delusional to believe you will ever be revered," I said. My face and chest were flushed. I wasn't certain where he was headed with this conversation, however, I could see my entire plan circling in the toilet bowl. "What's the point of this conversation? You've accused me of plotting against you by leaving hints I know about your love affair with Gabrielle Durand. So what, Clayton. So what if I did?"

"Exactly, the same conclusion I came to, 'so what if' she did? There was nothing I could do about it. I reasoned I best resign … until the last hour when I was given these." Clayton reached inside his jacket and then removed and tossed several photographs, face up, on my desk. There I was, stark naked, in front of the sweat lodge. I looked at the second picture and there I was again, hugging Tammy, both of us without a stitch of clothes. There were eight photographs in all, each taken during the sweat lodge ceremony. I looked up at Clayton. He'd held a single photograph back and was staring at it. "You take a nice photo, Kathy, very nice indeed." I wanted to throw up at the thought of Clayton Johansson leering at my naked body.

I took a deep breath fearing I was about to hyperventilate or faint or both. I exhaled slowly and asked, "Who gave these to you? Who took these pictures?"

"Doesn't matter does it? I have them and I'm told there are a few more."

"You are even more disgusting than I ever believed you could be."

Clayton fanned himself with the photograph he held in his hand. "Now, I could be wrong, you may want to remain as the minister here at Grace Lutheran Church and face the music when word surfaces you and your friend Tammy were participating with the long haired Indian fellow in some pagan ceremony and all of you buck naked to boot. Oh my god, the news will fuel the gossip in Pelican Falls for the next decade. I mean, knowing the men have all seen these photos on the internet, could you still hold your head high at Connie's?"

"Clayton, you wouldn't …"

"Listen, honey, I'm just the messenger here. Remember, I was in Mexico with my lover when these were taken. I wouldn't be the one to post them on the internet although I don't doubt for a second the devil himself may be prodding some sinner with his pitchfork to do just that."

I bit my lip so hard, I could taste blood. I refused to let him make me cry. "This is criminal. You are blackmailing me. I'm going to report you to the police."

"Go ahead, like I said, I'm just the messenger here. I'm looking out for what's best for Grace Lutheran. So, go ahead, call the police. They will take the photographs as evidence of what I'm not certain. I know when they file their reports they will have to say what scandalous behavior there is in the pictures, and those reports and the photographs are open to the public."

"What do you want, Clayton, what is it you want from me?"

"The same thing you wanted from me, honey, to resign. Remember, it was you who cast the first stone," Clayton said.

As if I was hallucinating, his body took on the appearance of the devil, full of hate and anger. Not the cute little red devil with the pitchfork but the embodiment of all the evil on earth. He put the remaining photograph inside his jacket and left as quietly as he had entered.

CHAPTER THIRTY-ONE

(Saturday)

"*Whoever took these photographs must have been over there by the fountain,*" Makwa said. He stood at the sweat lodge examining the picture I'd given him, after blacking out all the important parts. "If you and Tammy would please stand right here and here, just like the photo, I'm going to walk over to the fountain and compare the angles." Makwa positioned us in front of the lodge just as, to his eye, we appeared in the picture and then stepped backwards towards the fountain comparing the photo and his staged scene as he moved.

"I truly cannot remember being so embarrassed since my bikini top fell off in the high school swimming pool," Tammy said. She'd calmed down considerably since I had initially showed her the pictures. At first she wanted to confront Clayton and then strangle Mrs. Hildebrandt who was her prime suspect as the photographer. I convinced Tammy we had to regain our composure and plan our response. I'd already resolved to resign as the pastor and slink out of town, and the sooner the better. We'd driven to the LeBlanc's Chateau de Fleur Roses and shared the entire story with Makwa. He agreed with Tammy although he added strangling Clayton in addition to Mrs. Hildebrandt. I reminded them both how wrong we'd been about accusing Holly Hollenbachen. I was still stinging from Clayton's allegation I had cast the first stone.

"Tammy, come over here, Kathy, stay where you are. I want a second opinion on this spot," Makwa yelled from maybe forty yards away. Tammy jogged to Makwa and after a couple of minutes, hailed for me to join them. "I believe this is where our suspect stood with the camera, likely with a telephoto lens and some sort of low light attachment," Makwa said holding the photograph in the air for me to compare with where I'd been standing. I needed to lose ten pounds.

Photos don't lie. Makwa had nailed the angle but a pessimistic voice inside my head shouted, "So What!"

"Makwa, tell us again what happened before we arrived for the ceremony. I feel as though I've never heard the entire story," I said. I sat on a cold marble bench to listen. Tammy joined me. Her presence felt warm and comforting.

"I had labored much of the day, no all day, putting the final touches on the lodge, preparing the sage and medicines, asking for a blessing on everything including the fire. Frankly, I'm so focused, like 'in the zone,' I don't notice the arrival of the fire trucks until I hear this man with a white fireman's helmet shouting orders to bring up the hoses. It is only then I become aware of the flashing red lights blasting through the blackness of the night. In the distance, I hear a lone siren, perhaps the police or an ambulance trying to catch up."

"What did you do?" Tammy asked the same question I was thinking.

"Do?"

"What happened next," I asked and hoped he wouldn't ask, 'Next?'

"I stood by the fire and watched as several men hauled a hose towards me, all led by the chief like Teddy Roosevelt charging up San Juan Hill. It was only when they were a few feet from me and the fire chief took note of my presence. Perhaps I'd become invisible during my pre-ceremony preparations."

Years ago, I used to laugh at such preposterous statements by Makwa. I have matured enough to consider most anything possible.

"I shouted for the men to stop as they were about to destroy my fire and the stones for the ceremony," Makwa said. He held both arms up high as he re-enacted his story. "The chief stopped dead in his tracks and looked at me as though I were some aberration or ghostly reveler who'd strayed from the Halloween party."

"I imagine he didn't expect to find you," Tammy said.

"I imagine he didn't expect to find some naked Indian standing by a fire in the gardens of the Chateau de Fleur Roses," Makwa finished Tammy's thoughts.

"You were naked?" I asked, more than a little surprised.

"I was, naked as the day I was born. Standing there facing the fire chief and all of his minions. I'd just finished washing my body and was squatting by the fire to drive the chill away when they surprised me."

"Seriously?" I asked having heard Makwa occasionally stretch the truth during his story telling.

"Seriously, and I doubt anyone was more surprised than the fire chief's wife when she brought up the rear huffing and puffing. The poor woman nearly fainted at the sight."

"Oh, I doubt she'd faint, fell over laughing perhaps," I said. "What did you do next?"

"Being a modest soul, I covered my member with a proper loin cloth, raised my hand and shouted, 'How!'"

"You are such a tease, come on now, this is serious," I pleaded.

"Actually, I was saved from further intercourse with the chief and his wife by the Widow LeBlanc who made a timely appearance at the scene. It was she who explained the circumstances of the fire and the sweat lodge to the interlopers and when the chief's wife insisted on further explanations. It was Mrs. LeBlanc who drove them away."

"They left without so much as issuing a warning for having an uncontrolled fire?" Tammy asked.

"The topic never came up. It was the chief's wife who made herself a pest and was slow to leave. She peppered me with questions about the lodge, the ceremony, the participants, and my identity. She even hinted this was some ancient pagan rite taking place on the devil's eve. She lifted her camera to take pictures, for the newspaper she said, however Sofia stepped in her way and ordered her to leave. Sofia is no wallflower. Let me tell you, she's got some balls, excuse the crass native vernacular."

"The chief's wife, Mrs. Hildebrandt, never got any photographs?" Tammy asked.

"She snapped two I can recall, however Sofia was holding her hand in front of the lens."

I stood rubbing my posterior, it having nearly frozen on the frigid bench. Tammy did likewise, even jumping a few times to get the circulation flowing again. Our lesson was over. "Makwa, let's follow the tracks away from the fountain to see where it leads," Tammy suggested.

Tammy led the way, quickly picking up two sets of human footprints in the snow. Makwa commented the trail was a few days old and how ice crystals had formed and melted and reformed on the edges of the track. We followed the trodden path away from the garden and down the hill. Where the footprints led into a large snow drift, Makwa pointed to how deep the tracks had crushed through the drift. "Whoever made these prints were heavy people, very heavy," Makwa pronounced with the certainty of a professional tracker.

"How do you know they were big?" Tammy asked.

"Us native men are endowed with such knowledge at birth," Makwa said.

"Endowed with a few other things, I've observed," Tammy said.

"Like being big BSers," I added. Our mood was lightening. As gloomy as our predicament appeared to be, Makwa had a way to calm the panicked. Our tensions melted like the snow drifts on the sunny side of the hill.

We trudged through the snow sinking, I noticed, only a fraction as much as those who laid the tracks ahead of us. "Wait, look at this," Tammy stopped and reached into one of the deep tracks pulling up a paper wrapper. "It's a Baby Ruth candy bar wrapper — one of those small bars they hand out for Halloween. I'll bet Mrs. Hildebrandt was eating this as she marched down the hill, celebrating her successful photographic safari, capturing two female pastors, *au natruale.*"

"Tammy, think about how many kids were trick and treating and throwing their candy wrappers around. The wind could have simply carried the wrapper up the hill until it landed in the track," I said.

"Wet blanket, that's what you are. Mrs. Hildebrandt is my parishioner and I just happen to know she favors the Baby Ruth over all other candy bars. By her own admission, she's addicted to the Baby Ruth bar."

Tammy was right. I was being a naysayer … a skeptic. I was feeling so guilty about this entire scheme. I did not want to point an accusatory finger at anyone, even if it was as plain as the nose on my face. I didn't want to be accused once again of casting the first stone. We lost the tracks at the bottom of the hill where the incline met the sidewalk which had been plowed. We took the long way back, down the street and up the lazy curving alleyway into the shade of the towering pines. When we arrived at the location where we'd met the fire truck, Tammy pointed to three Baby Ruth wrappers blown against the chain link fence. This time I didn't argue. I was ready to surrender to Mrs. Hildebrandt being the photographer and the note writer. The evidence, I had to admit, was stacked against her. I told Tammy of Mrs. Hildebrandt's surreptitious meeting with Clayton near the church dumpster and how Clayton had chased Benny from the area. By then, we'd reached Makwa's cottage.

"Come into my humble guest quarters where the kind and gracious Mrs. LeBlanc has put me up with room and board in return for my excellent manly company and superior knowledge of the ways of the native people," Makwa held the large oak door open for Tammy and me to enter. "Shoes, ladies, Mrs. LeBlanc insists your shoes be removed. Not to worry about cold feet as the Italian marble floors are amply heated to a toasty eighty degrees."

The cottage was anything but "humble." Makwa gave us the grand tour of the four bedroom, five bath, guest house. There seemed to be a story about every feature. The gold-plated faucets came from Spain. The wool rugs were hand woven and imported from Iran before the embargo. The dining room chandelier was flown over from France along with an artist to assemble it. Every piece of furniture, every stone, every stick of wood had a history. We settled into a four season room replete with a fireplace from Sweden and wicker furniture from Thailand.

"Does Mrs. LeBlanc realize you may never leave?" Tammy asked.

"Oh, there's a clock ticking on our relationship of which we are both well aware …"

I interrupted Makwa with the question I could no longer hold inside my head, "Did you hear Mrs. LeBlanc say she killed her husband, Serge?"

"When?" Makwa replied.

"Ever, what difference does it make when? Did you hear her confess to murdering Serge?" I raised my voice in frustration.

"It is a long story. Would you ladies like some tea? There are over twenty different blends in the pantry."

"Let's skip the tea and tell the story, long though it may be. Please just tell the story," I pleaded.

"Mr. and Mrs. LeBlanc had a complex relationship – he, Serge, the undeniable patriarch, the unquestioned superior and she, Sofia, the ruler of the household, the queen. Serge, in fact, was seldom present at the estate. He had numerous business ventures in Canada and the United States. He kept a jet at the airport which he piloted about the country. Sofia became a lonely woman, wealthy yet childless, of the highest social standing yet shunned by the community as being too uppity. She took to the bottle and then to pills. It was Aldo who helped her get into the finest rehab center and kick her habits."

"I'm sorry, Makwa, maybe we should have some tea. I see this as being a very long story," I said. "Let me go make the tea but don't continue the LeBlanc story until I return. Perhaps you two could plot how we are going to get out of this mess." I left the sunroom and found the pantry and the store of teas. I couldn't decide, didn't recognize any of the fancy printed names on the silver tins so I closed my eyes and picked three. It wasn't but maybe ten minutes and I was back with thin china cups filled with sweetened tea and some chocolate truffles I'd sniffed out in the jars lining the pantry shelves.

"Okay, resume … the lonely dowager is cured of her addictions and resumes her sad life in Pelican Falls," I said.

"She truly is a lovely person and generous to a fault. Now, moving on to your question of some confession – let's just assume a wife learns her husband is about to do serious, perhaps even fatal harm to someone. Would it be murder if the wife intervened to prevent this tragic calamity?"

"What exactly happened?" I asked.

"Exactly, we'll never know. In general, Mrs. LeBlanc gave Serge a little shove at the top of the stairway, just to get his attention concerning the matter of discussion, and unfortunately Serge lost his balance, tumbled down the substantial stairway, breaking his neck in the process."

"She told you that?" Tammy asked.

"And more, my dears, much more … and it involves your arch enemy, Clayton Johansson."

"I knew Mrs. LeBlanc muttered Clayton's name during the sweat lodge ceremony. I just knew it," I said with the pleasure of recognizing I hadn't been delusional.

"I've not heard you mention Clayton Johansson is an attorney," Makwa said.

"I didn't know he was," I said.

"I thought as much. When Clayton resided in the Twin Cities, he practiced law. He was a firm of one and specialized in tax law. Serge was one of his clients. It was a few years ago Serge was visited by special agents from the IRS who were conducting a criminal investigation concerning some foreign bank accounts owned by Serge. It would seem Serge 'forgot' to account for these on his tax returns. I will cut to the chase. Clayton, who managed these foreign accounts, took the fall for Serge. Clayton paid the fine, never went to jail, and voluntarily surrendered his license to practice law. In return and under a veil of secrecy, Serge transferred the ownership of the Skull Lake Resort to Clayton. That, ladies, is how Clayton came to settle in Pelican Falls."

"You've learned all of this in the short time you've been here?" Tammy asked.

"Sofia and I spend evenings chatting. Mostly she talks and I listen. It is as if she's had years of solitude and the stories come pouring out like water through a broken dam."

"She had Aldo to talk to," I said.

"And they did spend hours in conversation, although, as Sofia tells it, she was guarded in what she discussed. There was always the priest-parishioner relationship and it caused her to refrain from certain topics."

"Days ago, you suggested Sofia and Aldo 'shared some secret.' Was the murder of Serge the secret?" I asked.

"I don't know for certain if Aldo is aware of that incident. I've come to learn they share another secret," Makwa said. He sipped his tea, smacked his lips and continued, "When Clayton moved to Pelican Falls, he joined Serge in a business venture, sort of a silent partner. For years Serge ran several logging operations in Northern Minnesota. As the demand for paper decreased and the building industry folded, he had to close the doors or find some other product. As Sofia tells the story, it was Clayton's idea to venture into specialty timber like basswood to make window blinds. They went after tamarack for fence posts and cedar for fancy custom-built outdoor decks. Then Clayton discovered two lakes filled with pine which had been harvested and lost when the lumberjacks floated the logs across the water to the mill. Those preserved logs are milled for expensive custom furniture."

"What was so secret about all of this?" Tammy asked.

"Most of the trees they harvested and all they recovered from the lake bottoms were on the reservation – on land owned by the tribe," Makwa said.

"What's the big deal?" Tammy asked.

"The 'big deal' is that with the assistance of the official foresters and some conspiring with dishonest tribal officials, the tribe never received a payment for most of the timber," Makwa said.

"Okay, okay, I know the secret," I said like an excited school girl who knew the capital of Wyoming. "My friend Doc told me Brenda Maria Fairbanks, the woman gone missing from the White Earth Reservation, was the bookkeeper for the tribal forestry business. Doc told me Brenda went missing after there were suspicions raised about the misappropriation of money. Brenda is Father Gallo's Maria. See Tammy, I knew the picture on the 'missing person' poster was Maria, I told you so," I said with the satisfaction of putting the final piece in a thousand piece jigsaw puzzle.

"I still think it's a bad photograph," Tammy said.

"When Father Aldo learns Brenda Maria is in jeopardy ..." I said.

"Who told him that?" Tammy asked.

"Slow down. Let me finish the story. Sofia overhears a conversation between Clayton and Serge in which they conclude Brenda 'has to go,'" Makwa said.

"Sofia told Father Gallo and then he hid Brenda at the rectory," I said, certain I was correct.

"Aldo knew Brenda from his days serving on the rez. In fact, I grew up a few tepees down from Brenda. She was always so shy. I can't recall her ever speaking even when we teased her. When Sofia brought this situation to Aldo, he went to Ogema and convinced Brenda to come to the rectory to act as his housekeeper. Aldo let everyone believe Brenda was an illegal from Mexico so no one thought it strange she never left the premises – hidden in plain view."

"After Serge died, wouldn't Clayton look for Brenda? I mean if he intended her harm or felt she was a threat to him?" Tammy asked.

"I asked Sofia the same question. She believed Clayton's financial interest in the enterprise is so concealed Clayton felt safe. If the irregularities ever came to light and Clayton was implicated, he would point the finger at the dead Serge," Makwa said.

"Like Clayton took the fall for Serge, now it was Serge's turn, albeit from the grave," I said.

"Yes. When your special agent friend, Doc, showed up at Aldo's, he panicked and sent Brenda away so she wouldn't have to be put in jeopardy."

"Where did he send her?" Tammy asked.

"She's at the Chateau de Fleur Roses, in the big house with Sofia," Makwa said.

"Isn't Sofia afraid she is going to be implicated in the entire affair?" I asked. "She knows about the financial crime against the tribe, she murdered Serge, and now she's hiding a material witness."

"Sofia isn't concerned at all. You see, three months ago, the doctors gave Sofia less than a year to live," Makwa said. "Her only desire is to unburden her soul from all earthly possessions and leave this world with a cleansed spirit."

CHAPTER THIRTY-TWO

(Saturday)

Max's loud barking first alerted me someone was knocking at my door. It was after eight and darker than black outside. "Now what?" came to mind as I slid in my slippers over to the front door and turned on the porch light. I looked out through the door window and there stood Gabrielle Durand holding a small dog, a pug if I wasn't mistaken. "Now What?" screamed in my head. Adding to my confusion, Max continued to bark. After all that had happened today I hesitated to even open the door. I took a couple of deep breaths and swung the door wide open.

"Gabrielle, what a surprise! What brings you out on such a cold night and so late?" Whatever it was, I was certain I didn't really want to know.

"Pastor Kathy, this is my pug, Priscilla. Remember we talked about having our pugs play together? I thought I'd drop by and our puppies could have a play date," Gabrielle said ever so slyly.

"I'm afraid 'my pug' isn't up to playing tonight," I choked on the words.

Gabrielle stepped inside and lowered her Priscilla to the floor. "I understand, but couldn't they just meet anyway?" She unzipped her parka obviously intending to make herself at home. I wondered if Clayton was outside laughing his ass off.

"Gabrielle, I don't own a pug. My cousin Sara isn't from Biwabik and she's as alive as you and me. Saying I'm sorry doesn't begin to express how rotten I feel about lying to you. Those stories were all a scheme ..."

A smile beamed across Gabrielle's face, "... to get to Clayton. I figured out the little scheme while I was in Mexico. I asked myself, why was the preacher woman so friendly to me, then it hit me. She's just playing with Clayton's mind."

"I have no excuse. All I can do is ask for your forgiveness."

"Oh, Pastor, I just thought I'd have some fun with you, what with bringing my little Priscilla over and well, just seeing your face made it all worth the effort to come out on this snowy night," Gabrielle said.

A feeling of relief swept over my body. I relaxed a bit and rubbed the tension from my neck. Then I wondered what was it she really wanted? I try not to be given to drama, but it occurred to me Clayton had dumped Gabrielle because of me. Was she a scorned woman bent on revenge? I backed away from her. Evidently she noticed my reaction and moved closer, raising her arms as she came. "Let me give you a hug, Honey. What you did causing Clayton and me to break up was the best thing to ever happen to me."

She wrapped her arms around me. Every muscle in my body braced for an attack. I imagined her hands on my neck and tried desperately to remember those self-defense moves the handsome sheriff's deputy had shown me. All that followed was a sincere embrace, held too long, however, without malice. It had been a trying day with more twists than a slithering snake.

When Gabrielle freed me, I stepped back and invited her into the kitchen. Priscilla was already frolicking on Max's back. We moved into my small kitchen where I'd been working on my laptop. I quickly covered the photographs lying next to the computer. "Can I get you something to drink, tea, coffee, hot chocolate?"

"Don't you have anything stronger, Honey? It's been a tough day for me what with just getting back and getting used to life without Clayton." She pulled a chair away from the table and plopped down. "Come here, Priscilla, come sit on mommy's lap." The little dog abandoned Max and in a flash leaped into "mommy's lap."

"I do have a bottle of brandy although I've got nothing to mix it with," I said.

"Maybe with a few cubes of ice." She stroked the little dog's silky ears. The pug closed her eyes and began to snore louder than Grandpa watching a Viking's game on a Sunday afternoon.

I moved over to the cupboard above the sink and reached up to get the brandy. I noticed a bottle of Bailey's Irish Cream Tammy had left after a recent visit. I offered the Bailey's to Gabrielle. She declined declaring her waist was already bulging over her jeans. She looked plenty thin to me. I set the brandy down on the counter and it was then I saw all my carving knifes were within arm's length of Gabrielle. I slid them back to the splashboard and poured us each a healthy shot of brandy.

Gabrielle was smiling when I handed her the glass and sat across the table from her. "Honey, you don't need to worry about me. I'm not here to hurt you. I'm here to thank you and celebrate Clayton's defeat." She raised her glass high. "To the end of Clayton Johansson!"

I hesitated to raise a glass to what I saw as a victory by Clayton Johansson. "You aren't going to join me? I thought you'd be delighted Clayton was finally going to get his just desserts." Gabrielle said with a now empty highball glass in her hand.

"I'm sorry, Gabrielle. I met with Clayton this morning and I'm quite certain he is nowhere close to losing or reaping what he has sown. If anything, it would appear he has come out the victor," I explained.

"Have you spoken lately to Father Aldo?"

"Not today, why?"

"I thought he would have called you and told you of our meeting," Gabrielle said.

"No, not a word."

"I met with Father Aldo this morning and he is the one who suggested I talk to you."

"I must admit, I don't know what you are talking about, Gabrielle," I said.

"You know what they say, 'assume and you make an ass out of u and me,' Gabrielle said. She poured herself a glassful of brandy, took a gulp, and continued, "You know Clayton and me went to Mexico together. The first few days were pleasant enough. Then Clayton, who'd been on his computer checking emails and Facebook, began to cop a nasty attitude. See this black eye?" She pointed to her left eye which was indeed swollen and discolored even under the layers of makeup.

"He didn't?"

"He has a terrible temper. I'm not sure what set him off, but by the time we left Mexico, we were flying in separate seats, his in first class," Gabrielle said with misty eyes.

"I'm so sorry, I feel responsible …"

"Don't. We're done. It is long overdue. I regret having ever been involved with him. When we met I was on the rebound from Ron and frankly the list of eligible bachelors around here is not very long. Anyway, we are done. I visited Father Aldo, a confession which turned into a long counseling session."

"I've had my own sessions with him. He's a very good listener and a compassionate man of wisdom," I said.

"I confessed everything to him. I told him how I was living a lie and wanted to start fresh."

"So he told you to come here and talk about this?" I asked.

She reached into her large purse and pulled out an accordion folder. She laid it on the table between us. "Father Aldo said I should bring this to you." She pulled out two spiral notebooks and a stack of dog-eared documents.

"What are these?" I asked, my curiosity was becoming unbearable.

"These are what will put Clayton behind bars," Gabrielle said with certainty.

I poured myself a second glass, something I rarely do. I finished the bottle by topping off Gabrielle's glass. The suspense was killing me. What evidence could she have which would be so damning to Clayton? Gabrielle rustled through the papers and produced an accountant's ledger like they made us use in high school bookkeeping class. She slowly opened the hardcover book as if the secrets may fly out if revealed too rapidly. I waited for an explanation.

"Father Gallo said I could go to jail for this. I don't care if I have to pay the piper. I want a clean slate."

"What possibly could you have done?"

"It started out innocently enough ..."

"Gabrielle, maybe you shouldn't be telling me this."

"Let me finish! It started out with Clayton asking me to take some cash. It wasn't a whole bunch, maybe a couple of thousand," Gabrielle said. She put her long painted fingernail on the first figure in the ledger and stopped. "It was two thousand, three hundred fifty dollars, see, it is the first amount I have written in the ledger."

I looked at the ledger and saw the amount carefully written in pencil. There were many more, maybe a hundred or more after the initial entry. I let out a low whistle and Max came to my side in response. "Are all of these figures cash Clayton gave to you?"

"This is only the first page. As time went on, he gave me more and more often."

"Why?" I asked.

"Oh, he had some sad explanation at first about wanting to keep some money from his wife. Then he dropped that reason and said it had to do with some business where he was the silent partner so he didn't want to use his own bank account."

"What did you do with all of the cash?"

"I deposited it into the Curl Up and Dye business account at the State Bank of Pelican Falls."

"Wow, didn't the bank ever ask you about how much cash you were depositing?"

"Never, I was worried, but they never said a word."

"So you have all of this money sitting in your bank account?"

"Oh no, I have this other ledger showing all the withdrawals I made and gave the money back to Clayton or made payments for him."

"You paid his bills?"

"I made every payment on his fancy Cadillac Escalade and on the mink stole he bought for me."

"I have to admit, Gabrielle, I'm flabbergasted. I'm also more than a bit confused. Why did Father Gallo tell you to bring this to my doorstep? I'm out of the business of scheming against Clayton or anyone else for that matter. I've learned my lesson and asked the good Lord for forgiveness."

"Good decision, although from what Clayton told me, you did a good job of imitating me, perfume and turquoise jewelry and all. No, Father Gallo told me you had a friend, a police officer friend, who would be interested in these records."

"But Gabrielle, if I give these to my friend, you may be in big trouble. I don't know if ..."

"Father Gallo said it could be part of your penance cuz he said you're going to need a lot of mercy. He also said I might be treated better if I make this disclosure on my own before the police discover it. Maybe I could get immunity he said and maybe you could put a good word in for me with your friend."

I finished my brandy, it burned on the way down and felt so good.

CHAPTER THIRTY-THREE

(Sunday)

I *have never felt so alive*, so energized, standing in the pulpit before the congregation. I took a deep breath and began, "Today is the 24th Sunday after Pentecost. You will remember 23 Sundays earlier we celebrated Pentecost, the day the Holy Spirit came upon humankind. It is a time to celebrate the gift of grace and forgiveness. So it is fitting today that I come before you, my congregation, and ask for your grace and forgiveness. I have already taken this matter before my Savior and know in my heart I enjoy His grace. Now I come before you and lay bare my transgressions with a plea for your mercy and grace."

I had been up most of the night preparing this sermon and talking to Gabrielle who insisted I call her Gabby from now on. She even spent the night in the spare bedroom where her pug Priscilla and Max joined her on the king-size bed. Long after the three of them had retired, I stayed in the kitchen to finish my work on the computer and put to paper the sermon I'd been writing in my mind since leaving Makwa and Tammy at the Chateau de Fleur Roses guest house. It was after hearing Makwa's story of treachery and deceit by Clayton and Serge that I decided to "come clean."

"I have been a party to a dishonest series of pranks. No, pranks would imply my actions were innocent and they weren't. By now I'm certain all of you, except Mr. Olson who has been dozing since the liturgy, are asking yourselves, 'What in the world is she preaching about now?'"

A deep male bass sang out, uncharacteristically for a Lutheran, a hearty "Amen!" The congregation laughed and I suspect most believed my sermon was some attention getting technique I'd learned at one of those weekend retreats for ministers which they periodically send me to. The parishioners probably expected me to somehow tie this opener into the canned sermon which the synod had mailed earlier in the week, the one given on every 24th Sunday after Pentecost. The more cynical may have suspected it was a novel way to ask for more money in the offering plates.

"I recently participated in a ceremony, a sweat lodge ceremony, which was officiated by an old friend of mine, Dr. Joseph Auginaush, who as it happens is Ojibwe and a spiritual leader, a medicine man or *midewinini* as he would be respectfully called in his native tongue. Now, I fully expect you all may read about this ceremony in the next edition of the Pelican Times. I will tell you when I entered the sweat lodge I was wearing no clothes. I went into the handmade lodge wearing exactly and only what God gave me at birth. It was part of the ceremony and one of the demands of participation. I did so without shame and can assure you the nakedness took on no sexual overtones."

Mrs. Olson gave her husband a big elbow. This was too big to miss. I must say, I have never witnessed such rapt attention to one of my sermons and likely, given human nature, never would again enjoy such interest. A thought raced through my mind: I've preached about a man who healed the sick with a touch of his hand and raised the dead, and they fall asleep. I talk about a naked preacher and they are darn near out of the pew, straining to hear the next words.

"This private event might have gone unnoticed but for an interloper with a camera and a long lens. There I was captured on film, naked. I never knew about this *paparazzi* intruder until our own Grace Lutheran Church Council President, Clayton Johansson, hand delivered copies of those photographs to me less than twenty-four hours ago. It was clearly Clayton's duty to call me to account for pictures I fully acknowledge are unbecoming a Lutheran minister. He has suggested I resign."

Clayton Johansson sat stone faced in his customary seat in the first pew, only feet from the pulpit. His long-suffering wife, Liv, sat beside him and they held hands on his lap. As is his custom, his right foot tapped violently as though he'd been stricken with palsy. I paused my sermon and looked at Clayton. He returned my smile with a glare capable of doing great bodily harm.

"My first reaction was to type out my resignation. Upon further reflection and prayer, I reconsidered, deciding instead to take it to you, the congregation. You called me here several years ago. I serve at your pleasure and therefore I take the matter to you for a vote."

Unlike any Lutheran assembly I'd ever seen before, the pews were abuzz. The members looked to one another and then to me, certain I'd gone mad and ready to call 911 if I talked any crazier.

"I couldn't ask you to vote without a full disclosure, without viewing the evidence so diligently laid at my doorstep by Mr. Johansson. The ushers will pass envelopes down each pew. Inside every envelope is a complete set of the photographs furnished to me by Clayton. I will admit, I have taken steps to protect the identity of the other sweat lodge participants by darkening their images."

I went without sleep to make these photographs presentable to the average Lutheran. I received substantial assistance from Julie Patricia, my former confirmand who was working a quiet night shift down at the Cenex gas station. With her remote electronic intervention and the wonderment of modern communications via Facebooking, tweeting, texting, emailing, and skyping, I was able to black out Tammy's face, breasts and bathing suit area. I added a few other subtle features such as tattoos and a birthmark and pronounced the product totally unrecognizable. I left my face untouched. I did black-out the all too controversial pelvic area. I toyed with the idea of attaching a pair of boobs filched from a willing internet model, going from a B cup to a double D and shaving about ten pounds from my butt, however in the end, I opted to keep with the honest and full disclosure policy.

I glanced over to Gabby. She insisted on attending this service and seated herself in the very front row across the aisle from Clayton. She wore a big grin as she slowly chewed gum. Clearly she was enjoying the show and anticipating a huge reaction from Clayton.

"Ushers, please starting from the rear, pass out those envelopes to each pew. Parishioners, please feel free to open the envelopes and inspect the photographs. These are the pictures for which Clayton would have me resign. I must tell you, when I participated in the sweat lodge, care was taken to afford some modesty to the three females and one male. I sincerely saw the entire event as no more than one would see in a locker room."

Frankly, I did not know what to expect. Would the envelopes be opened and passed? Would the men refrain or be restrained by their wives from inspecting the photographs. Would there be laughing and guffawing? Would they light the torches and chase me out of town after a proper tarring and feathering? I scanned the pews looking for clues. I noticed Mrs. Tingstad had moved from her customary second pew seat to the rear of the church where she was seated next to the palsy boy, in fact holding his hand. Mrs. Mavis Olson and Mrs. Bertelsen were seated shoulder to shoulder in the third pew. The black family from Somalia sat next to Mrs. Tollefson who was wearing colorful African headwear.

The four ushers finished passing out the envelopes and returned to their usual pew in the rear. A painful silence fell over our congregation. No one coughed. No one rustled their bulletins or dropped hymnals on the floor. No babies even cried or fussed. I motioned for Georgina Olson to play the old hymn *How Beautiful The Sight* and waited. The envelopes were passed one by one to each member and guest. Not a one was opened. Bridgit Bjornson's husband, Buddy, tried to sneak a peek only to earn a head slap worthy of Larry slapping Moe. By the end of the hymn, the envelopes had reached the outside of the pews. It was Mrs. Bertelsen who stood first and slowly walked to the communion rail carrying the unopened envelope. She walked to the pulpit and handed me the photographs. One by one, thirty-six others followed him or her. I had not expected this reaction and tears streamed down my face. I had taken a heck of a risk, fretted to no end over my future, imagined the worst possible reactions, and in the end it came down to this; my parishioners, my friends, for all of their foibles and idiosyncrasies, stood by me.

The last I saw of Clayton Johansson was his hind end rushing out the rear of the church. His wife, Liv, stayed in her pew as did everyone else. I can not recall clearly the rest of the service. I remember baptizing the little Michelson baby, maybe the cutest little guy I ever sprinkled water on. He giggled with delight when I held him high over my head for the congregation to welcome. "I present to you our newest member, Jason Michelson!" I shouted. At the end of the service I stood to greet each congregant. I vividly recall the warm words of encouragement, the hugs, the tears, and the overwhelming feeling that the Holy Spirit had, just like the first Pentecost, entered into each of our souls.

CHAPTER THIRTY-FOUR

"*Gabrielle is going to come out of this without much pain,*" Doc pronounced when he joined me at Corner Café in Detroit Lakes. After much cajoling by Gabby, I'd brought her to meet with Doc at the Becker County Sheriff's office located in a building as cold as a mortuary.

After my doctor's appointment where she pronounced me healed of the dog bite, I whiled away my time across the street in the old Carnegie Library. Seated at the computer station, I read and answered over a hundred emails, most supportive and loving. I fielded a few dozen emails from regional media outlets asking for interviews. Evidently, a naked female preacher has mass market appeal. I knew instinctively if I pushed them off for a week, I'd be "yesterday's news," and someone, like Paris Hilton or Lindsay Lohan, would do something more outrageous. The most challenging email came from the synod. It noted several telephone messages had gone unreturned and it was most urgent I contact the Bishop. I returned a terse message saying Monday was my traditional day off and I would call on Tuesday. That will get the Bishop's undies in a bundle. I reflected on yesterday's sermon. At the same time I announced I had been photographed naked and made those pictures available, I heralded the arrival of the Holy Spirit into our lives, the most magnificent event we'd ever experience, the welcoming of the Holy Spirit into our hearts – a life changing event that would live on for eternity. Not a single email, not a single voicemail, not a single text message mentioned the Holy Spirit. What can I say? It's the human condition, nonetheless disappointing.

I made a quick stop at the candy shop. I was surprised to hear *Oh Little Town of Bethlehem* playing inside the store. The interior was festooned with Christmas wreaths, candles, and ornaments. Gets earlier every year I mumbled loud enough for the clerk to ask if she could help me. "Yes, I'd like three caramels for Tammy, two of the big truffles for Olive and a bag of juju bears for Gen." A tear fell down my cheek when it hit me that Gen would not be sharing her juju bears with me anymore. She will not be telling me those corny jokes or dispensing the wisdom that only comes with age. "Don't let the bastards get you down Katy," she called me Katy. No one else on earth called me Katy or shared juju bears with me. I missed her very much.

"Lady, are you all right?" the store clerk asked. I guess I had been standing there crying. I wiped my cheeks with my sleeve.

"I'm fine. I was just thinking about a dear friend who passed away. The juju bears are for her."

"Three dollars and fifty-three cents," the unsentimental clerk replied.

I strolled down Main Street with the uncomfortable feeling everyone was looking at me, pointing at me. I knew I was just as anonymous as always, however I could not shake the feeling. The puppies in the pet store window drew my attention. Dogs were like that, they could always ease my discomfort, even through a barrier of glass. Two Cavapoos rolled over one another on yesterday's Fargo Forum, a suitable place for old news. They paused to watch me and soon had their front paws on the window. Their pink tongues licked at the glass. It was all I could do to walk away without leaving with one in my arms.

I waved at the bald-headed barber who lounged in his chair waiting for the next customer. The bakery window was full of pastries and the wonderful aroma of fresh baked bread and cakes. It was only yesterday I vowed to begin my new life which would begin with a new diet. I've only done this a gazillion times. Sometimes the diet doesn't live past the bakery. This time I was motivated by the photographs of my naked body. There were, I had to admit after reviewing the photographic evidence, a few places that could use some slimming. I continued down the street to the Corner Café. The front entrance was littered with flyers and in between the handprinted ad and photo for the manure spreader and a lost poster for a missing Boxer, was a flyer announcing a book signing by my favorite author, a local man who after retiring as a police officer began writing crime mysteries. I checked the headlines of the three newspapers displayed in the vending machines and was relieved the headlines didn't announce, "Local Preacher Reveals All."

I found a table by the window, next to where six or seven retirees were rolling dice to determine who would pay for the dozen cups of coffee they each consumed during their two hour BS session that was coming to a close. Posted on the aged green walls were a myriad of handprinted signs declaring the various rules of the place. "No sharing the senior pie special. No sharing All You Can Eat Specials. Ornery customers will be charged double." When the chatty waitress in the pink uniform arrived, I ordered tea and one poached egg with dry wheat toast, a single slice. My eyes fixed on a plate stacked with pancakes drowning in butter and syrup set before a woman who was as skinny as a broom. Life is not fair, I noted.

Doc arrived and ordered within minutes. He said Gabby would meet me at the Community Center in an hour. I asked him if the interview was successful and he assured me all was well. I never knew how much to ask of a police officer out of concern they would be disclosing some confidential information or worse they would tell me it was none of my darn business. So for awhile we just chatted about the Vikings and other equally unimportant topics. Eventually my inquisitive nature got the best of me. Grandma often scolded me, "Curiosity kills the cat." While I valued her wisdom, I have never seen a cat struck dead by poking his nose into a mouse hole or turning a stone over to chase and torment a cricket.

"Is Clayton in trouble?" I asked.

Doc scrunched up his face and didn't answer right away. The silence was awkward. "I'm about 99% certain by this time next year, Clayton will be serving a lengthy sentence at the prison in Stillwater. So yes, in my estimation, Clayton is 'in trouble,'" Doc said and then smiled, evidently at the thought such an evil man would get his just reward.

Not able to leave it alone I asked, "Was Gabrielle of much help?"

"This goes no further?"

"I swear. I'm naturally nosey and in this case, my personal future may well depend on the outcome of your investigation so I'm even more so," I said to justify my questions.

"No further, because this is going to be tomorrow's headlines when the arrests come out. Yes, Gabrielle gave us evidence, not just information but valuable evidence we may have found eventually although it could have taken months and given Clayton time to conceal his activities."

"She seemed to know a lot when I spoke with her over the weekend," I said as bait to learn more.

"When Father Gallo produced Brenda Fairbanks, our investigators had a big piece of the crime disclosed. We learned how she discovered huge swaths of reservation lands being harvested and no payments to the tribe. This was accomplished in part by Clayton making cash bribes to tribal officials who made sure it was kept secret. Mrs. LeBlanc was also very helpful. While she had no direct involvement, she overheard some conversations shedding light on a couple of mysteries. So, all in all, our week in the northland has been most successful."

"Did Mrs. LeBlanc talk about Serge's death?" I regretted the question as soon as it slipped past my lips.

Doc cocked his head and raised his eyebrows. My ill-timed question did not escape his investigator's nose. "No, why would she. He just died in a fall down the steps." He paused and sipped his coffee making a slurping sound that lingered in the air like his next question. "Didn't he?"

I felt like the rat who had just put a paw on the baited trap. Grandma should have said, "curiosity kills the rat." "Yes, of course, he just fell." I searched Doc's stone cold blue eyes for a reaction. Nothing. My face stung from his gaze which was assessing each twitch and tick for signs of deception. I was a walking advertisement for, "She knows more!"

Doc was gracious enough to let it drop, sort of, "You know, Sara had a little wrinkle on her forehead when she was stressed. You get the wrinkle, too."

"I guess it's been a very stressful few days."

"Yeah, I'm sure it has. No sense making it anymore so, is there?"

"No, thanks," I said.

"Sara talked about you and your grandparents endlessly."

"Fond memories, I hope," I said.

"Only the best … I must admit though, after hearing some of the stories, I was surprised to learn you had become a woman of the cloth, a minister."

"It's genetic," I replied.

"Genetic?"

"Yeah, from my father. Now it's time for me to ask you, 'This goes no further right?'"

Doc laughed and nodded in agreement.

"Lake Louise Bible Camp is right down the road between Detroit Lakes and Pelican Falls. I was conceived there one steaming summer evening. My mother was attending the camp for a week. My father was a camp counselor and the son of the minister at Grace Lutheran Church. So it is genetics and I've come full circle returning to my roots at Grace Lutheran."

"No shit?"

"Are you asking a question?"

"Not a very artfully crafted one I admit, but yeah, is it true or just some clergical humor which escapes my pagan-like mind?"

"Honest to goodness, my good man. My mother was sixteen. My father was eighteen. We all made the best of it and I was raised by two of the most wonderful people on God's green earth. I hold no animosity for either of them. Frankly, they just drifted away, perhaps in shame. Things were different then, especially in a small town. I listen to my father on the radio now and then."

"Let me guess, a televangelist?"

"No, sports announcer. He does a respectable play by play and I can even discern some similar vocal patterns even though we've never met."

"Your mother?"

"Grandma said she stayed around to nurse me and when the carnival came to town the next summer, she left with a barker. I have post cards she sent for a few years and then they stopped and I've not heard a peep since the last birthday card mailed from Wyoming."

"I shouldn't have brought this up," Doc said. I think he had seen the tears well in my eyes even though I turned and brushed them away. Not much escaped the attention of an agent.

"No apology needed. I'm fine with my life. Like I said, my grandparents were the best."

"Were your father's grandparents in the picture?"

"Never met them. I imagine I would have been an enormous embarrassment to them. They are both dead, buried in the Grace Lutheran Cemetery. I put flowers on their graves and talk to them once in awhile. Some days I get an eerie feeling when it's just me in the church that I'm not alone. Perhaps it's Grandpa Olson who has returned to check up on his old congregation. My dog, Max, senses it also. He'll growl for no particular reason when he comes into the church. It's as if he sees an intruder."

We sat in silence for a few minutes, perhaps reflecting on our conversation and trying to think of a graceful exit.

"What will you do now? Are you staying in Pelican Falls?" Doc finally asked.

"I don't know. I need some time to digest what has happened and pray and mediate. I need a day alone!"

CHAPTER THIRTY-FIVE

(Wednesday)

"*It was only two weeks ago the three of us sat here and poured out our concerns.* In only two weeks, those problems have been resolved and quite favorably I might add," Father Gallo said from his cozy recliner in the rectory library. Tammy and I had joined our friend for an evening get together. Earlier in the day, we had all held events for the young people which ended at eight and gone straight to the rectory with Makwa in tow. He had graciously spoken to my youth group about the trials of reservation life. He spared no details which the youngsters ate right up. Now we settled in before the crackling logs in the fireplace and refreshed ourselves with some sort of chocolate with double caramel lattes. Father Gallo has sworn off hard liquor in preparation for his pilgrimage to Rome. Makwa doesn't imbibe and Tammy and I agreed we'd both been going to the bottle too often.

"I haven't had an opportunity to tell you all about my meeting with Mrs. Hildebrandt," Tammy began what promised to be a very long story. "Let me begin at the beginning. Yesterday your friend Doc stopped over to visit me at the church. He said he was in town doing some interviews and just wanted to check up on me, you know, with the threats and all. I gave him a list of all the evidence and he said he was impressed."

"Did you show him the list of evidence against your first suspect, Holly Hollenbachen?" I teased.

"You laugh; wait until the story is over before you mock me, sister. After I laid out my case against Mrs. Hildebrandt, Doc left without saying what if anything he was going to do about it. So today, right after Zumba and before lunch, who comes slithering into my office but Mrs. Hilda Hildebrandt her-big-Self. She throws what I later learned was all of the printed copies of the naked photographs of you and yours truly on my desk. No apology, more of a belligerent claim I'd put the cops on her. I got the impression Doc laid the law down and while Hilda was going to be compliant, she wasn't going to be contrite."

"I don't think I'd like to have Doc coming down hard on me," I said recalling his steely-eyed stare he had used on me at the Corner Café.

"No, me either. Anyway, I asked Mrs. Hildebrandt why she'd written those awful notes and do you know what she said?" Tammy asked.

"The devil made her?" Makwa ventured a guess.

"Close, it was Holly Hollenbachen and menopause behind the devious deeds."

"Sweet Jesus," Father Gallo declared. "How does Holly interact with menopause to force Hilda to stalk you?"

Tammy pointed a long accusatory finger at me. "See, my soul sister, Holly Hollenbachen was behind the plot all along. I knew I was right. Call it women's intuition, or whatever, I just knew she had something to do with it."

"Why?" I asked. "Why did she want to see you leave Pelican Falls?"

"She believes I'm a satanic worshipper who has infiltrated the church."

"Where would she ever get such an idea?" Makwa asked.

"When Holly and I were traveling together, I was carrying a leather bound notebook. It was a going away gift from a Jewish friend in San Francisco and it had the Star of David on the front and two ceremonial shofars, you know the ram's horn, on the back. Holly saw this and rather than ask me about it, she Googled the symbol but screwed it up and mistook it for the pentagram. The Star of David has six points and the pentagram five points. When Holly is doing her faulty research, she finds satanic worshipers use the pentagram with the two points up as a symbol of the Sigil of Baphomet. In fact, the church of satan has a darn trademark on this symbol. Then Holly learns the satan worshippers use the horned goat as a symbol and she jumps to the conclusion the shofar, the ram horns on my notebook, are further evidence of my true nature."

"Oh my, this is getting so bizarre, I might break my promise to eschew the brandy," Father Gallo said. Hearing "brandy," Aldo's dog came rambling in from the hallway to rest at his master's feet. As always he gruffed a hello as he passed by.

"Holly and Hilda are going to Weight Watchers together on Thursday nights. Holly shares her suspicions with Hilda who jumps on the allegations, probably her journalist instincts kicking in. Thinking back, Hilda did visit me one day at my office. Just out of the blue, she drops by and says she's thinking of doing a story on the life of a female preacher in a small town church. I sucker for the deal and answer all of her questions. I remember her being especially interested in the mementoes I have on the office bookcase. There are a few crystals, there was a yin and yang symbol a friend from my martial arts class gave me, another friend sent me a small Ganesh statue from India."

"What is a Ganesh?" I asked.

"It is a religious symbol of an elephant-headed god used by the Hindus in India. So Hilda does her investigation and concludes I am indeed a worshiper of false idols at best and a practicing Satanist at worst. She and Holly, during one of their Weight Watchers meetings, concocted this plot to drive me out of town."

"When she sneaks up on my sweat lodge and sees you and Kathy naked, she takes the photographs and knows she has the final proof of your evil intentions," Makwa said.

"And she shares the photographs with Clayton to drive me away," I said.

"Sort of a modern day witch hunt. My, you two are fortunate you weren't living a few hundred years ago in Salem," Father Gallo said.

"I explained the symbols and how Holly was mistaken to Hilda. She begrudgingly accepted my defense. She also told me she and Wally would no longer be attending my church. They would be joining Randy Peterson's church."

"Your feelings must have been soooo hurt," I sarcastically volunteered without regard for my standing as a minister.

"I wished her well and lifted the spell I'd cast upon her earlier in the day," Tammy said.

"You haven't explained the second part of Hilda's behavior, the menopause," Makwa said. He rose and moved to the fire soaking up the warmth. Feeling a tad chilly, I moved next to him and exposed my backside to the flames.

"Ah, yes, the menopause. Hilda said she has been experiencing severe hot flashes and dizzy spells, both of which are having an adverse affect on her moods and decision making abilities. She said it has gotten so bad Wally has remodeled their garage, put a heater inside, and moved in until she gets a grip on herself. That was her explanation," Tammy said.

We all shared a laugh and when we stopped, Father Gallo spoke, "I'm afraid I should offer an explanation as to my unforgivable behavior. By now, you three know my Maria is Brenda Fairbanks. I'm told she is being cared for in a safe place by the state police. I must apologize for the charade I allowed to continue. I know you believed Maria was an illegal from Mexico and I allowed you to harbor such a belief. I thank you for not calling the police to turn my 'illegal' over to the authorities."

"I may be the only one who doesn't have the story about Maria, I mean Brenda," Tammy said.

"It was a secret Mrs. LeBlanc and I shared. Sofia confided she'd learned of a plot to harm a bookkeeper at the tribal headquarters in White Earth. She described the woman who she'd seen just once and I knew it was Brenda Fairbanks. You remember Brenda, Makwa, you went to school with her."

"On those rare days, I went to school, yes, I do remember Brenda. I used to steal her lunch money and beat her brothers just for sport," Makwa said.

"That was before I 'saved' you, I might add so as to not brand you in front of Tammy as some ruffian. A while back, I met in Waubun with Brenda and explained I had information she may be harmed.

She told me she wasn't surprised and had already received some threats from a tribal official."

"Did she say why?" I asked.

"It would take too much time to explain. It had to do with a fraud she'd discovered which was cheating the tribal members out of a fortune. She knew who and what they were doing and a couple of tribal officials were taking bribes to get the matter concealed."

"So you hid her?" Tammy said.

"I did. She was content to stay here and make herself useful. She came from an abusive home anyway so she was happy to move into the maid's chamber. We agreed she could stay until we saw an opportunity for her to safely go to the authorities. You see, she'd already disclosed the matter to her own people and all that produced was a death threat. She was safe and sound with me. When your friend Doc came knocking, I was so taken back, I'm afraid I didn't make a good impression. I told Maria about Doc's visit and she was afraid. It took a few days to calm her down and convince her to meet with him."

"Doc said you were being less than candid with him. I'm glad it worked out for Brenda Maria. I should tell you Clayton sent a terse email offering his resignation. Liv called to tell me Clayton was joining Morgan's church and she'd be staying at Grace Lutheran. She also asked me for Doc's telephone number. Now this goes no further, right? Liv said she has some information the police will find very interesting," I said. "Oh yeah, and Gabrielle, I mean Gabby announced she is going to join Grace Lutheran. Sorry Father, you're losing one."

"So, you have a net gain of zero, Tammy is losing two is it? Randy is gaining two and Morgan picks up one. How about you Makwa, can I count you into my fold?" Father Gallo asked.

"You can be a sly old fox, can't you?" Makwa said.

"I can't imagine why you'd accuse me, a humble old priest of such a thing," Father Gallo replied.

"These ladies haven't heard the entire story with Mrs. LeBlanc and her future plans," Makwa said.

"I'm about worn out with more disclosures. I'm sure these ladies have no interest in what the future holds for the widow LeBlanc. How about those Vikings last Sunday?" Father Gallo said.

Speaking for both of us, Tammy said, "Big deal, they finally won one. I want to hear about Mrs. LeBlanc."

"Me too, especially because Father Gallo doesn't want the topic brought up," I added.

Makwa cleared his throat and moved back to his chair. "Mrs. LeBlanc, as you all know has few remaining months to live. She confided as much to Aldo some months back. She's been making plans for her estate and insists the Chateau de Fleur Roses is preserved and used as a gathering place where people of all races, ethnicities, and religions can come together. Aldo, am I describing the circumstances correctly?"

"Not eloquent but adequate," Father Gallo said.

"Aldo and Mrs. LeBlanc have had long conversations about this and in particular about who should manage this organization. She favored Aldo as he has extensive work in the Native, Hispanic, and African communities. Ah, but that would interfere with plans to travel to Rome so Aldo, the fox, tells Sofia, he has the perfect candidate. Aldo calls my cousin, Rudy, I mean Running Bear over in Pine Ridge and tells him Makwa is needed urgently back in Minnesota. Running Bear is instructed to tell Makwa that Kathy is in trouble, but Makwa must not speak of this to anyone including Kathy."

"Now Makwa, you are painting such a lurid picture. I admit I am guilty as you allege, however, look to my intentions. Isn't that what I taught you as a youngster?"

"You are correct, you did teach me that principle and I'll apply it in this case. You must find a way to get to Rome, it's your passion. You've a keen ability to assess others. You know Sofia will be attracted to my animal-like manliness. You know I would climb Mount Everest to rescue Kathy. You know Kathy truly does need help with Clayton. So you set the stage, put your actors on their marks and with a front row seat, you watch your theatrical production."

"Ah, the same keen mind I saw in you the first time we met when you broke into my van up on the rez. I recall how quickly you were able to put together a defense and win my heart. I'm proud of you son," Father Gallo said.

"I knew you would be Father. I'm pleased to announce I've accepted Sofia's offer. I begin immediately and with some good fortune, Sofia may live long enough to see the fruits of her labor. She's done an enormous amount of preparatory work already. Her accountants and attorneys have the infrastructure in place. The architects have the blueprints on the table. The contracts have been awarded for the remodeling. I've been impressed with her efficiency."

"I hope you hold no grudge."

"None whatsoever. Frankly, I admire your skill at these matters. Someday I hope to be so wily, so fox-like," Makwa said.

"Am I to understand that when you came strolling down my driveway two weeks ago, you were coming to rescue me?" I asked.

"How romantic!" Tammy said.

My skin blushed from my chest right up to my ears which had turned the color of ripe tomatoes.

L. D. BERGSGAARD

A COMPLETE BIOGRAPHY IS AVAILABLE ON FACE BOOK

AND ON MR. BERGSGAARD'S WEBSITES:

WWW.LDBERGSGAARD.NET

WWW.LDBERGSGAARD.COM

CPSIA information can be obtained at www.ICGtesting.com
Printed in the USA
LVOW07s2138071114

412596LV00001B/5/P

9 781457 532412